WOMAN
IN THE
WIND

WOMAN
IN THE
WIND

A JACKSON GAMBLE NOVEL

GREGORY STOUT

LEVEL
BEST BOOKS

Author Photo Credit: Carol Stout

First edition

ISBN: 978-1-68512-469-4

Cover art by Level Best Designs

This book was professionally typeset on Reedsy.
Find out more at reedsy.com

For Carol, as always, the brains of the operation.

Praise for Woman in the Wind

"Greg Stout is back with his tough, captivating, and enviably witty PI, Jackson Gamble; with language that compels the reader forward; characters so real they stand in front of you; and an intricate maze of corruption that will challenge your problem-solving abilities."—Libi Siporin, author of Murder on the Tuscan Trail mysteries

"A simple stakeout job tangles hero Jackson Gamble in a sprawling investigation. Faced with more suspects than Nashville has honky-tonks, the plot takes readers down dark, scary alleys. What turns an ordinary person into a killer? The answer won't make you sleep better."—Linda Lovely, author of the "HOA Mystery" series

Chapter One

Roydell D. Jones was the toughest five hundred dollars I ever earned. Roydell was a six-foot, four-inch redbone hailing from Lafayette, Louisiana. He had a reputation for being a mean drunk and a fondness for driving fast cars belonging to somebody else. Fat Wally Sadler, the bail bondsman, had hired me to take a drive up to Corbin, Kentucky, on a hot, sticky Friday in August to find Roydell and bring him back to Nashville in time for a Monday morning court date. If Roydell didn't show, Fat Wally stood to lose the twenty-five-thousand-dollar bail he had posted to get Roydell sprung. If he did show, Roydell stood to lose the next three to five years out of his young life for crossing a state line with a brand-new, arrest-me-red Corvette he had appropriated from a Chevy dealer's lot after closing time.

I locked my office a little after four o'clock and headed north and east, toward the Kentucky state line. I stopped for gas and a greasy, all-you-can-eat catfish dinner at a roadhouse outside Somerset before finally arriving in Corbin about nine-thirty that night. Fat Wally had given me the name and address of a woman Roydell was known to be friendly with as a place to start looking. The woman's name was Glory. The address turned out to be a peeling, four-room shotgun shack across the road from the former Louisville & Nashville Railroad yard. In the Kentucky darkness, blue and yellow CSX diesel switch engines rumbled back and forth as they shuffled loaded coal hoppers recently down from the mines in Harlan County. I rapped on Glory's sagging screen door and waited.

The romance had evidently cooled since Fat Wally had gotten his information. Glory came to the door holding an ice bag against a nasty black eye and a split lip that had taken a couple of stitches to close. In her other hand was a half-empty bottle of Southern Comfort that she waved around like a conductor's baton as she talked. However, between the lip and the liquor, she wasn't able to express herself very clearly, except to say that Roydell had left her sometime in the late afternoon.

"You find that son-of-a-bitch, you cut his balls off and send 'em back here to me in a coffee can. I'll pay you a hunnerd dollars if'n you do." I gave her my sympathies and said I'd see what I could do. Then I waved Glory goodnight and drove off into the night, no closer to my man than when I had started.

Four hours and half a dozen roadside taverns later, I turned up Roydell in a nearly deserted country and western bar out on Route 25. The Corvette, now with its fiberglass right front fender shattered and partly dragging on the ground, was parked outside along with a couple of rusty pickups and a Harley Hog with ape-hanger handlebars that must have set somebody back close to thirty K. When I went inside, I found Roydell sitting by himself in a booth in the back, with a dozen empty longneck Pabst Blue Ribbon bottles on the table and a Jerry Jeff Walker song, "Mr. Bojangles," on the jukebox to keep him company. He was very, very drunk. His eyes were half closed, so that only the whites were showing through narrow slits, and his massive body was rocking back and forth in languorous time with the music. Like an old friend sharing the burden of some deeply personal sorrow, I slid quietly into the booth across from him. As a show of goodwill, I folded my hands on the table where he could see them.

After what seemed like a suitable interval, I said in a low voice, "Fat Wally says you need to come back, Roydell. He says I got to bring you." I smiled sympathetically. "You want to have another Blue before we go, that's okay with me."

Nothing happened at first, and I thought maybe he had already passed out right there in the booth. But then, like faded cherries in a worn-out slot machine, his eyes rolled uncertainly back into focus. He looked me up and down, the way a barracuda sizes up a prospective meal. Then he grinned

2

and shook his head from side to side.

I said, with more confidence than I felt, "Look, Roydell, I'd like this to be easy for both of us. This isn't some middle-school field trip, you're out on bail. Even if you hadn't boosted that 'Vette, you broke three or four laws I could name you just by crossing the state line. As an agent of the court, I have the authority to bust you right where you sit. I don't want to do that, but I will if you make me."

He made a low, rumbling noise that could have been a laugh. Then he shrugged, took one last swallow of his Blue Ribbon, and started unsteadily toward the door. I followed, about three steps behind.

Four or five steps would have been smarter, but it was late, and I was beyond tired. We were nearly outside when Roydell dropped his shoulder and turned sharply on his heel. By the time I saw it coming, it was too late. He caught me alongside the jaw with a roundhouse right that lit up the inside of my head like a flashbulb in a broom closet. He had me by three inches and an easy fifty pounds. I hit the deck, fast and hard. My mouth filled with the brassy taste of blood, and there was a noise in my ears that sounded like an ambulance on its way to a four-car pileup.

When I got back to my feet, Roydell was waiting for me. He was holding a ten-inch kitchen knife for courage and had a look on his face that said he wasn't going to be bashful about using it. The few customers still left in the bar had prudently cleared out of their chairs and retreated to safer ground on the opposite side of the room. I had my .380 tucked into a shoulder rig beneath my jacket, but since I had no wish to turn a routine roundup of a bail skipper into a justifiable homicide, I left it where it was. Instead, I reached for a foot-long piece of galvanized pipe wrapped with heavy tape that I had stuck in my belt. I managed to get that into my hand as Roydell started for me.

He came at me pretty much the way a drunk will do, lurching full speed ahead and swiping haphazardly back and forth with the pig-sticker. The beer had slowed him down just a bit, so I didn't have any trouble getting out of the way of his lunge. As he went by, I took two quick steps to my left and whacked him hard above the wrist with the pipe. He dropped the knife and grabbed his injured arm with his good hand, howling like a wolf in a trap. I cut that short with a second rap behind his right ear.

While he was still on the floor, I cuffed his hands behind his back. Then I horsed him to his feet and waltzed him clumsily outside to the parking lot. I loaded him face down into the back seat of my car. I tied his ankles together with some mechanic's wire I had in the trunk and used another length of it to hog-tie his ankles to his wrists. I was on the road and out of town before anybody had a chance to telephone the cops. Roydell snored like a lumberjack all the way back to Nashville.

I turned Roydell over to Fat Wally in the parking lot of the West End Avenue Denny's about the time the sun was coming up. Then I went home to pour half a quart of bourbon over four molars Roydell's haymaker had loosened up and to try to get some sleep.

Monday morning, I was parked in a dentist's chair. Including his fee and a prescription for some Hydrocodone, the bill was four hundred and fifty-eight dollars and some change. That left me with a little over forty-one dollars plus gas and meal money, a wicked bruise, and a badly swollen jaw to show for my night's work.

Tuesday morning, I was back in the office. The swelling in my jaw was down, and the ringing noise in my ear was almost gone. I was hoping my next job would be simple.

Chapter Two

Something that would turn out to be anything but simple wandered into my office a little after two o'clock that same afternoon. He was late. He had called first thing in the morning to make an appointment for ten-thirty. He wouldn't give me a name, which I didn't much like, but he insisted it was urgent that he talk to me. I waited around reading the morning paper and playing solitaire games on the computer until noon, then decided that whatever he wanted mustn't have been that important after all and hiked across the street for lunch. Today it was clam chowder, the white kind, and a strawberry milkshake. I was hoping to be back to eating solid food by Friday.

My would-be client, when he did finally show up, turned out to be about fifty-five, half a head shorter than six feet, and weighed considerably north of two hundred pounds. A lot of that was rolled up around his waistline. He had yellowish-gray hair that looked as if he had gotten it cut at a barber college. The hair seemed, oddly, to match the color of his skin. His teeth and the fingers of his right hand were nicotine-stained. He wore a rumpled tan seersucker suit, a pale blue cotton broadcloth shirt, and a green-and-white striped tie that had been pulled loose at the collar. The armpits of his suit jacket were soaked through with sweat, as if he'd had to run a couple of blocks to keep from being later than he already was.

He looked me up and down, as if he'd been warned not to expect much and was still disappointed. "Are you Jackson Gamble?"

"Like it says on the door." I nodded toward the customer's chair. "You the guy who called earlier?" His handshake was like grabbing the back end of a dead fish.

He sat down heavily. "That was me. Sorry to be late. Something came up."

His watery gray eyes darted quickly around, inventorying the room. There wasn't much to look at. In addition to my desk and the chairs we were sitting in, I could number among my visible assets a telephone, a seldom-used coffee pot, an outdated computer on a rolling stand, a microwave oven, a small refrigerator, a bookcase filled with paperbacks I'd run out of shelf space to store at home, and a couple of battered green file cabinets that held all I had to show for ten years' worth of a private detecting career. Hanging on the wall above the files were a framed copy of my license and a reproduction of a calendar issued by the Pennsylvania Railroad during the 1940s and updated for the current year. I no longer remember the reason why, but every December, I get a new one in the mail, just like it.

"I love what you've done with the place," he said at last. "You decorate it yourself?"

"I try to keep the overhead down. You want some water?"

"No, thanks."

"Or maybe a drink?" I was fishing now.

He said no to that, too, but not without thinking about it for a couple of beats. "What happened to your face?"

"Bail jumper," I told him. "He was vacationing in Kentucky. He decided he wasn't quite ready to come back."

"It looks like he made a pretty good argument for staying put."

"I was able to help him come to his senses." I made an attempt to grin and ended up wincing at the pain. "In my business, the customers sometimes express their sentiments nonverbally. They don't generally write letters to the editor."

"Ah," he said, brightening. "I'll take it from that that you know who I am." He leaned back in his chair and crossed one thick leg awkwardly over the other. "How'd you recognize me?"

"What do you think? Your picture is in the newspaper every Friday. You're Albert Glass. You write that 'Glass Houses' watchdog column for the *Times*. I have to tell you, Mr. Glass, it's not the best likeness."

He seemed pleased at being recognized. "You can call me Albert. Are you a regular reader?"

"More like an occasional one. I stopped being shocked by the kinds of things you write about a long time ago."

He looked at me with a trace of irritation. "There's more to what I write than shock value. If you'd kept up with my column, you'd know that our paper has done more to expose fraud and corruption in high places than all of our competitors combined. That series we did last year on organized crime in the vending machine business resulted in no less than fourteen indictments, including a couple of high-flyers in the Department of Revenue."

But no convictions anywhere, I might have added.

"No doubt you keep your loyal readers glued to the edges of their seats," I told him. "And since you're obviously something of a known quantity, do you mind telling me why you didn't want to give your name when you called this morning?"

He shifted heavily in his chair, causing one of the legs to creak in protest. "I figured if I told you who I was, you might wonder why I needed to talk to a private investigator. I didn't want you making telephone calls all over the city asking questions before I had a chance to explain the confidential nature of what I need you to do."

"That was a reasonable assumption. Not necessarily a right one, but from your point of view, probably logical."

He reached into his inside suit pocket and took out a small notebook. He flipped it open to a page near the back.

"On the other hand, I did a little digging of my own before I called you." He was bristling with confidence now, back in his familiar métier as the city's hardest-hitting investigative reporter.

"I can't wait," I told him.

"I found out you were a cop for eight years, and according to my sources, a reasonably honest one. You wore a uniform for several years. You turned out to be a real shiny penny, made detective quicker than most, and got loaned out part-time to the district attorney's office. You partnered with a woman detective named Wanda Beaudry, who left the force shortly before you did. You were canned after three more years for unspecified reasons and went into business for yourself as a gumshoe. You're forty-six years old. You've never been married, but you have a lady friend who's employed by the Department of Children and Family Services, and you own a house in a fairly *déclassé* neighborhood which you bought fifteen years ago with an adjustable-rate mortgage. Not the best idea, as you probably already know."

He snapped the notebook shut and dropped it back into his coat pocket.

"And from the looks of this setup you've got here, I'd say you've been late more than a few times with the monthly payment."

"Let the watchful eye of a free press ever be the safeguard of our precious liberty." I raised my empty malt cup in mock-salute. "Except you got a few of the details wrong. I didn't get fired. I resigned. Although to be honest, it was a photo finish at the end."

"Is that so?" He arched his eyebrows meaningfully. "Feel like setting the record straight?"

"I couldn't care less about the record," I said. "But since you're thinking about paying me to do a job, and since you brought it up, I guess you're entitled to know who you're dealing with." I leaned back in my chair and propped my feet against the bottom drawer of my desk.

"You been in town long enough to remember a guy named Boyce Ozburn?"

"I do remember." He lit a cigarette and inhaled deeply. "About fifteen years ago, right? He was a circuit court judge who set aside a couple of jury verdicts in exchange for what turned out to be some hefty contributions to his campaign fund. The press got hold of the story and forced him into early retirement. Nobody was ever able to prove anything, but the allegations were enough to torpedo his career in the public sector."

"There's those tireless newspapers again, burning the midnight oil," I said. "Except there was a little more to it than that.

"Such as?"

"Such as, when I was working for the D.A., I got wind from one of my contacts that Ozburn could be encouraged, shall we say, to hand down directed verdicts in certain civil trials, as long as the money was right. I

8

investigated Ozburn off and on in my spare time for nearly a year. I built a pretty decent circumstantial case against him, but shortly after I took it upstairs, the D.A.'s office decided the case was too hot to handle because it was political. Ozburn was a presiding judge with twenty years on the bench. He was a shoo-in for an appointment to the appellate court. But there was an election coming up, and none of the higher-ups wanted the kind of stink an all-out investigation of a sitting judge would raise during an election year. That struck me as breaking faith with the electorate, and I said so.

"My boss at the time was a senior ADA named Roger Seacrist. He called me into his office one day and told me just exactly how the cow ate the cabbage. From where he sat, that pretty much boiled down to me keeping my mouth shut and putting a lid on the Ozburn investigation if I wanted to hold on to my detective rank. He said I had the opportunity for a great career ahead of me, but that I'd have to learn to play ball if I wanted to move up the ranks."

"Not entirely unreasonable," Albert said. "It's the way the world works."

"Without a doubt. Anyway, I thought it over for a day or two and then decided that wasn't how I wanted my life to play out, so I leaked some of what I had to a *Banner* reporter named Dick Dohrn. I didn't give him everything. I just dropped enough on his desk to get him started asking questions on his own. The story broke a few weeks before the election. The D.A.'s office caught a lot of heat, and a few people who were counting on getting reelected, including Boyce Ozburn, didn't.

"It didn't take long for Seacrist to figure out I had talked to Dohrn, but he couldn't prove it. So, instead of getting fired, I got a substandard fitness review from the chief of detectives and was ticketed for a reduction in grade back to a uniform. Before the paperwork got processed, I turned in my shield."

Glass gave me a look of cynical amusement. "And now Dohrn is an editor, working across town at the *Times*, Ozburn has made who-knows-how-many millions in the real estate business, and Roger Seacrist has gotten back into politics. And if the polls are close to right, he stands a better-than-even chance of getting elected governor in November. Besides screwing yourself out of your pension, what did you get out of it?"

"Sometimes I wonder myself. The best answer I can give you is that I did it because Ozburn was dirty. And because I was young enough and dumb enough to think that I was doing the right thing."

"And if the same thing happened today?"

"Good question. I might not be so self-righteous."

"And so now you're on your own, and you get to spend all your time saving the world from the fate it so richly deserves, is that it?" He looked around for an ashtray. I retrieved an empty Diet Coke can from my wastebasket and handed it across the desk.

"If that's what you call chasing after bail-jumpers and deadbeat ex-husbands, then I guess that's what I'm doing, yeah," I said. "But I'm told I still have a bad habit of trying to do things the way I think they ought to be done. From what I've read that you've written, and what's been written about you, you seem to be a no-bullshit kind of guy with some pretty definite ideas of your own. I just thought before you start telling me about whatever it is you came to tell me, you ought to understand how I go about my job."

He paused to give that a moment's thought. Then he nodded and let his fleshy face relax into a wide grin.

"Truth of the matter is," he said, "I'm looking for a woman."

Chapter Three

"I'll bite," I said, sitting up in my chair. "What woman? And what is she to you?"

"Her name is Darlene Munson. She's a source."

"Of what?"

"Information, what else," Albert said, as if I should have known what he was talking about. "She's been secretly feeding me leads for the past few months on a story that, between you and me, is going to stand the November election on its ear. At this point, I'm not at liberty to say too much about it, but I can tell you for a fact that it involves some big names on and off the ballot. I'm talking household names here, Gamble, and not just local yokels, either. When this story breaks, it's going to make that story we did last year on scamming video games look like grade school kids shaking nickels out of a piggy bank."

"That's pretty much all it turned out to be," I reminded him. "Maybe you didn't see. It was in all the papers."

"Funny. These guys are going down hard enough to crack the sidewalk," he said flatly. "I guarantee it."

"You mean assuming you've got this Darlene Munson available to back up your story?"

"There's Darlene, yes, and something much more." Glass lit another Camel and watched as the smoke curled lazily through a shaft of afternoon sunlight streaming through the window.

"Up until a few days ago, she had me working pretty much on bits and pieces of information she had put together from her recollection of overheard conversations. It wasn't a lot, but it was enough to get me started asking questions on my own. And the more poking around I did, the more I was convinced she was actually on to something. Unfortunately, there was no hard evidence I could use as a foundation for the story. No documents, in other words. No video and no corroborating witnesses. Putting together what I found with what she had, it might make fodder for a late-night talk show, but with nothing more solid to base it on, it was just speculation. Newspaper-wise, we'd have been lucky to get half a column on the back page of a Sunday advertising circular."

He paused for a moment, as if he had momentarily lost his train of thought, and I noticed his hand was shaking. I said, "You sure I can't offer you a drink?"

This time, he didn't think about it. "Well, okay, maybe a short one. It's been a tough day."

"I'll bet." I retrieved a fresh plastic mouthwash cup and a half-empty bottle of Jack Black from my bottom desk drawer and poured him a generous snort. In one motion, Albert grabbed the cup and tossed the contents back.

"Good stuff," he said.

"Another one?" I asked.

"Maybe for the road." I poured another shot into his cup and placed it on the corner of my desk where he could reach it.

"You were telling me about Darlene Munson," I reminded him.

"Right," he nodded. "So, about ten days ago, just when I was ready to give it up as a dead end, Darlene telephoned. She wanted to meet with me. She was excited. She said she had gotten her hands on some real evidence. She was talking names, places, dates, everything we needed to document the story, all wrapped up in a nice, neat package. She wouldn't let me have the whole thing, but she copied off a couple of pages and showed it to me when we met. It was enough to convince me that what she had was the real deal."

"Then we're talking about a written file."

"The part she showed me was a scan attached to an email. I'm guessing the rest is a spreadsheet file or maybe a ledger. And with that file, plus what I've managed to turn up on my own, you could be reading the biggest story the *Times* has ever run, right there on page one of tomorrow's final edition."

12

"The suspense is killing me," I told him. "But before you start spending your Pulitzer Prize money, I have a couple of questions."

"Such as?"

"Such as, who exactly is Darlene Munson? And how would she have gotten her hands on whatever is in this file you're talking about?"

"I'm afraid I can't tell you that."

"And that's because?"

"Because, to put it bluntly, you don't need to know. And because until we finally break the story, nothing is more important than keeping her and the information she has in her possession safely under wraps. After that, it'll be out there for everybody to see."

"How about this, then? The part of the file you saw. What's in it?"

"Names, plus dates and numbers, like I told you. All pointing to an indisputable record of political corruption. For the time being, that's all I'm going to tell you."

"Okay, political corruption. For the sake of discussion, let's assume she works in some government office, state, or county, or whatever, and this file she has is real. What's in it for her when the story gets printed?"

"Same as you, back when you were being a boy scout. She gets to see honest candidates elected to office in November. And she also has the satisfaction of knowing that she did the right thing. Other than that, I couldn't tell you. I've given up trying to guess other people's motivations. Maybe she thinks she's striking a blow for the democratic process."

I gave him a hard stare. "Come on, Albert, you know better than that."

"Meaning what?"

"Meaning you're leaving out the most obvious thing. Her motivation wouldn't have anything to do with money, would it? Like a little something upfront from your newspaper? How much are you going to have to pay her to get what you want?"

"Not one dime." He gave me a look that was somewhere between contempt and horror, like I had just committed high-order journalistic heresy. "No matter what you think, we're not a supermarket tabloid. The *Times* would never pay money for a story."

"Well, then, let me ask you this. If she's as civic-minded as you say, and if she trusts you enough to be giving you this information, why don't you both just go to the cops, or the TBI, or…what the hell? Just go ahead and run with your story? You'll still have your headline."

"I already explained that. The information she's got involves some very well-connected people, including, quite possibly, members of the law enforcement community. She's afraid that once the story is out in the open, somebody with enough muscle and enough brains to connect it back to her might figure she's too much of a liability to keep on walking around."

"Of course." Albert's bullshit, and that's what I was pretty sure at least some of it was, was starting to annoy me. I said, "So, what you're saying, then, is that the cops are rolled up in this mess, too? It's not just politicians?"

He shook his head. "I don't want to comment on that."

"Well, comment on this, then. Is what she's afraid of a real possibility?"

He answered, a little too quickly, "Anything's possible, although, in this instance, I think as long as she keeps quiet about what she's doing, I don't see how anyone will be able to connect her to the story, and that's what I've been telling her. But just so she'd feel safe, right after she called about the file, I had her temporarily move out of her apartment and check into a motel."

"What motel, or is that a secret, too?"

"No. It's the Rustic Retreat in Harding. It's one of those old-time places with tourist cabins. To be frank, it's kind of a dump, but I thought nobody trying to track her would ever think to look in a place like that. I considered having her register under an assumed name, but I figured that'd only make her more nervous than she already was."

"And who else knows she's there?"

"As far as I know, nobody except me and now you. What would be the point of her being there if it was common knowledge where she was?"

"Well, then, no flies on you. You seem to have thought of everything," I said. "Except that you still haven't told me why, if you know where she is, you now need to find her. Or is there more to this shaggy dog story than what you've told me so far?"

"Yeah, there is. You see, two days after Darlene checked in, she disappeared."

"Ah," I said, enlightenment coming at last. "Disappeared how?"

He made a small movement with his hands. "I don't know. I haven't been able to reach her, and she hasn't called me since last Friday. So, naturally, I did a little looking around at the motel on my own. I discovered that she hasn't checked out, and her things are still in the cabin, but nobody at the Rustic Retreat remembers seeing her for the past several days."

"It couldn't be she just got tired of sitting around by herself in some crappy motel, could it? Harding is a pretty small town, and unless she enjoys listening to crickets or charting constellations in the summer sky, there's not much going on out there to keep a young woman entertained. Maybe she got tired of playing Candy Crush on her phone and took off to stay with some friends. Or maybe she just went back home."

He gave me a look like a teacher might give a slow child unable to grasp a simple concept.

"Give me a little credit, will you, Gamble? She's got an apartment here in the city. After I got Darlene moved into the motel, I went back to her place. I stuck a piece of one of my business cards in the space between the door and the frame, so that it would fall on the floor if anybody went in or out. I figured that way, I'd know if somebody else had come looking for her. As of this morning, it's still right where I left it."

"And now you're out of ideas, and you want me to track her down for you, is that it?"

He rubbed his hands together distractedly. "No, that's not it at all. I know her better than you do. I'll do the tracking. The only thing I want you to do is keep an eye on her motel room until she comes back."

"And then what?"

"And then nothing. I just need you to maintain surveillance. If she comes back, call me. If she goes out again, stick close and find out if she's staying someplace else or if she's moved in with somebody. Then report back to me, and I'll take it from there. What I don't want you to do under any circumstances is make contact with her. I can't emphasize this enough. She is not to know that anyone is keeping tabs on her."

"That's all? Just hang around and watch her room in case she shows up?" If my jaw hadn't still been sore, I would have laughed out loud. "I don't think so, Albert."

"What do you mean?"

"I mean, this story has more holes in it than a chicken wire fence. Either you're being played, or I'm being sold a bill of goods."

He shook his head. "You're losing me, Gamble."

"Think about it. If Darlene Munson has really gotten her hands on some kind of political dirt that's as explosive as what you're talking about, then for sure, she has to be close to somebody who's involved in whatever it is that's going on. Otherwise, how would she have found out about it? If that's so, and if spilling the beans is going to get her into deep enough trouble that she has to fear for her life, then we're back to the original question. Why would she suddenly decide to take the story to the newspapers?"

"Maybe for the same reason you dropped a dime on Ozburn. She found out about something she didn't think was right and didn't trust the authorities to do anything about it. And maybe she reads my column and decided I was somebody she could trust."

"Right." I tapped my pencil on the edge of my desk. "Suppose that's true. Suppose whatever she's got is on the level. After this story breaks, what happens then? Assuming she's actually in danger, how are you going to protect her once her name turns up in the morning paper?"

"Simple. When I have the file, I won't need to use her name. Nobody has to know where it came from. She'll just be an anonymous source. That's why it's so important that she turn it over. Once that's done, she's in the clear. I write the story, I name the names, and I take the heat."

"Then I'll ask you again. Why hasn't she given you the file already? Have you considered the possibility that you're being set up?"

"For what? Why would anybody go to all that trouble?"

"I have no idea. I haven't met the woman. Maybe you didn't smile back when she batted her eyes at you from the other side of a cocktail lounge. Or maybe she's helping somebody else get even with you for a story you wrote last month. Maybe your friend Darlene is just a lonely woman looking for a little attention. Hell, Albert, this town is full of wannabees who wouldn't stop at anything short of a triple murder if they thought it'd get them their fifteen minutes of fame."

He shook his head doggedly. "There's a file, I'm absolutely sure. And it's genuine. The part she showed me squared perfectly with what I developed on my own." Then, irritably, he added, "You know, I'm beginning not to like your attitude here. Do you want this job or don't you?"

"I never said I didn't. I just like to have an idea what I'm getting involved in before it blows up in my face." I jotted a couple of notes on my desk pad.

"Let me get a couple things straight here. You said Darlene checked into the Rustic Retreat on Wednesday of last week. Is that right?"

"That's correct."

"So then, you made the reservation?"

"Also correct."

"And did you drive her out there, or did she drive herself?"

"She drove herself. And before you ask, she drives a red convertible, fairly new."

"And you're sure she actually checked in?"

"No question about it. I talked to her on the phone right after she got there, and then again the next afternoon."

"So that would be Thursday. Did you call her, or did she call you?"

"I called her. In her cabin. That's how I know for sure she was there."

"And after that, she went into the wind?"

"Yes. Our agreement was that she would check in every day. When she didn't, and when I tried to reach her, she was already gone."

"And you tried her cell?"

"Of course I did. She must have turned it off. Either that or the battery's dead."

Or else she is, I thought. "Is her car still there, do you know?"

"No, it's gone."

"Okay. So then, wherever she went when she left, she drove herself. What does she look like?"

"Attractive enough, if your taste runs to zaftig women who wear lots of makeup. She's about thirty, maybe five-two or three, and a little on the heavy side. She has blonde hair done up big, brown eyes, big tits and a fair complexion. She likes to wear short skirts, tight jeans, four-inch heels, and lots of jewelry like what they sell on QVC. Also, she has a butterfly tattoo on her ankle."

"Left ankle or right?"

He took another drag on his cigarette. "What the hell difference does it make? She's only got two legs."

He had me there. I said, "Do you have a photo?"

"Unfortunately, no."

"Well, unless she's gotten a complete makeover since you saw her last, she shouldn't be too hard to spot. When she checked into the motel, how much luggage did she have with her?"

"I saw one suitcase and one overnight bag. Maybe enough stuff for a week."

"More like one night, the way you've described her. Do you know whether she has a boyfriend? Could she have gotten lonely for a little companionship?"

"She never mentioned anybody." He dropped his cigarette butt in the Coke can, started to reach for another, then decided otherwise. "Look, Gamble, I don't mind sharing a little information with you, but don't you think you're asking a lot of questions for a simple stakeout job? I've already told you I don't need you to look for her. I just want you to watch the motel until she comes back."

I sighed. "Okay, Albert. I'm not saying I buy any of this, but we'll play it your way for the time being. I'll take a run out to Harding and see what I can turn up. But I'll caution you right now not to expect much. Either way, I'll report back in a couple of days, or sooner if I have something to tell you. But if nothing develops by the end of the week, I've got better things to do than sit around some bedbug nursery doing crossword puzzles. You'll have to decide after that whether you want me to pursue things further. If not, no hard feelings. But if you do, then I'm going to ask a lot more questions about what you've got cooking here, and I'm going to expect some better answers than what you've given me so far. Otherwise, you'll have to find yourself another boy, okay?"

He nodded grudgingly.

"Good. You didn't ask, but my rate is five hundred a day, plus expenses. On a job like this, I like to have a couple days in advance."

I expected an argument about that, too, but instead, he made a show out of taking out his wallet and counting off fifteen crisp hundred-dollar bills.

"Will that do?"

"Very nicely, thanks." I opened the top drawer of my desk and put the money inside. Then I took out a pad and started to write him a receipt.

"I don't need that," he said with a wave of his hand. "I trust you."

"I trust you too, Albert, but I'd still take the receipt if I were you." I finished writing and handed him the slip of paper. "I need someplace where I can reach you."

He recited a telephone number, which I wrote down.

"Now here are my ground rules, Gamble, just so we understand each other. You can call me at that number any time of the day or night, but if I don't pick up, just leave a message, and I'll get back to you. Under no circumstances do I want you coming down to the office looking for me or trying to reach me in any other way. No matter what else happens or what else you think is happening, the confidentiality of this story comes first."

"Do I take that to mean nobody at the *Times* knows you're working on this?"

"Nobody else, period, except for you and Darlene Munson, of course. That's why I don't want you doing any nosing around on your own."

"Understood."

"Also, I know your reputation as, how shall we characterize it? Someone who likes to color outside the lines, but I want your absolute assurance that you'll follow my instructions just the way I've given them to you. It may seem to you like a waste of time, but that's what I'm paying you to do. This job is important, and I can't afford to have it fucked up by somebody who can't follow directions. Are we clear on that?"

The customer is always right, I told him.

"Just make sure you don't forget it." Then he gulped down his second shot of Jack and was out the door.

Chapter Four

After Albert Glass left, I propped my feet up on my desk and glanced back over my notes on Darlene Munson, the woman he claimed he needed so urgently to find. Albert had given me a name, a general description, and a lead on her whereabouts that was almost five days old and getting colder by the minute. He had also given me a slightly cockeyed story about a newspaper investigation he was convinced would be the biggest thing since Watergate provided he could lay his hands on a file that Darlene supposedly had.

It bothered me, though, that Darlene Munson, whoever she was, hadn't just handed her information over to Albert and left it at that. That suggested that, regardless of what Albert had said about the *Times* not paying for stories, Darlene was holding out for money. Otherwise, why try to stall Albert? And if it turned out she really couldn't get money from the *Times*, then maybe she thought she could get it from somebody else—perhaps even the supposedly powerful people who were named in whatever document she was holding. If that was the case, and she was running a side hustle trying to shake them down, then she was either very foolish, or else she had gone to great lengths to be sure she would get the money and somehow make a clean getaway. That might explain why she had disappeared from the motel shortly after she'd checked in.

Regardless of what Darlene's motivations might be, the job Albert hired me to do didn't sound particularly difficult or particularly interesting, either. Just hang around a small-town motor court for a couple of days, wait for a woman with a butterfly tattoo to make an appearance, and then stay close in case she took off again. Nothing to it. An amateur birdwatcher on a slow day could handle the assignment without getting off his camp stool.

And yet, for some reason, I was having trouble getting comfortable with the idea that my part in the proceedings would be as simple as Albert had tried to make me believe. It occurred to me that maybe what Albert really wanted was for me to act as a decoy just in case somebody had already tumbled to what he and Darlene were up to. In that case, Albert probably already knew where she was. If anybody was watching, hiring me would create the impression that he thought she was still coming back to the motel soon and he needed me to wait for her. That way, whoever was following him might be thrown off the track and start following me instead. That also meant if things started to go sideways, as far as Albert was concerned, I was expendable.

I toyed briefly with the idea of putting in a call to my friend Dick Dohrn at the *Times* to get a bit of background on Albert Glass, or what he might be working on. Then I decided, for the time being, I might as well go along with the gag and see what developed. Besides, I reminded myself I had been hoping for work that would be simple. And on the off chance that Albert's story was even close to being on the level, this was about as simple a job as I would ever get paid to do.

Before leaving the office, I telephoned my lady friend, Maggie Totten, to let her know that I might be out of pocket for a day or two. I was hoping she'd be out of her office or meeting with a client, so that I could get by with just leaving a message. That way, I wouldn't have to explain what I would be doing overnight, but no luck. She picked up on the second ring.

After preliminaries, she said, "You're going where? And you're doing what?" The tone of her question made it abundantly clear what she thought about what I was telling her.

"Some old-time motel in Harding," I said. "It's a simple stakeout."

"You mean simple like that road trip up to Corbin last weekend?" Maggie could be a worrier, sometimes for good reason. We had met three years earlier when I was working on a case that involved tracking down a fourteen-year-old girl named Gabrielle Hawkins, who had gone missing from her home. Gabrielle was a student at the high school where Maggie worked as a guidance counselor. The case turned out to be much more complicated than I'd originally thought, and by the time things came to a head, Maggie had very nearly gotten killed by the little girl's abductor after he broke into her house. To save her life, I'd had to put a bullet in his head. It was an experience neither of us had gotten completely past. To my amazement, Maggie didn't blame me for what had happened. Instead, over time and with patience, we helped one another progress beyond the nightmares. And although things haven't quite gotten to the point where we've moved in together full-time, Maggie and I have unquestionably become what most people would call an item.

"Not like that at all," I told her. "This time, it's a nothing job. I might not even have to get out of the car. I'm almost ashamed to take the guy's money."

"But you did take it," she said.

We made small talk for a few more minutes, and then we said goodbye, but not before she made me promise to call her the next day, "Just to be sure." I told her no problem.

After I finished with Maggie, I checked in with the answering service to let them know I would be out of the office for a day or two. I retrieved the overnight kit I kept packed and ready in the bottom drawer of my filing cabinet. Then I locked the door to the inner office and rode the elevator down to the street and into the hazy sunshine of a muggy Tennessee summer afternoon. I walked the short block over to Commerce Street, retrieved my ancient Thunderbird from the U-Save Self-Park, and cranked the air conditioner up to full blast for the drive out to Harding.

The 'Bird was a baby-blue coupe, a survivor from the go-go days of the mid-1960s, when gas was cheap and the Beatles were topping the charts. I'd acquired it from a client who was temporarily short of funds. He had pressed the car upon me until he could make good on what he owed. That was five years ago. Since then, the client had died and the debt written off, but the car, now permanently in my service, soldiered on. Apart from its unquenchable thirst for 91-octane fuel and a worn spot in the driver's seat that I would need to do something about, I had no reason not to keep it. It was comfortable, dependable, and its four-barrel 390 V-8 ran happily, if not cheaply, on unleaded premium.

As I pulled out of the parking lot onto Seventh Avenue, I caught sight of an older Ford sedan painted a cop-car shade of blue lurch away from the curb and squeeze into traffic a few cars behind me. I didn't get a clear look at the driver, but I got the unmistakable feeling I had picked up a tail. Well, what the hell? A car like mine isn't that hard to keep in sight, and if the guy wanted to go for a ride, he was welcome to tag along.

It was after five o'clock, and going-home commuters had brought traffic on Broadway to a near-standstill, so I had to wait through several lights before I got positioned to turn left onto the I-40 entrance ramp. Finally, on a yellow, I managed to slip through. Two cars later, the Ford turned on a red, narrowly missing a collision with a pickup coming from the other direction. I had to give the guy credit. If he was following me, he was determined. Not subtle by any means, but definitely determined.

In heavy traffic, I took I-40 east, exiting at I-65 south. Once or twice, I caught sight of the Ford in my rear-view mirror, still on my six, but not close enough for me to get a clear look at the driver or the license plate. Then, somewhere past the city limits, I lost sight of him for good. Maybe he was better than I had credited him, or maybe he was just a heavy-footed commuter in a hurry to get home to the missus before she overcooked the pot roast. Ten minutes and as many miles later, I exited at Highway 96 and drove another half-mile to the Rustic Retreat Motor Court.

In the long-ago days before Interstate highways and cookie-cutter chain motels furnished by Wayfair, the Rustic Retreat was the kind of place that might have appealed to budget-minded Midwesterners making the long drive from Chicago or Indianapolis down to Miami or to Redneck Riviera resort towns like Mobile or Pensacola. Today, the Rustic Retreat's clientele would more likely be long-haul truckers, lovebirds looking for a spot for a quickie, or straight-commission salesmen traveling without expense accounts.

The Rustic Retreat consisted of a dozen compact, white asphalt-shingled cabins clustered around a circular gravel driveway. In the center of the circle was a sun-scorched flower bed that held the remnants of what had once been marigolds and pansies but was now a thriving expanse of nutsedge and spurge. Next to that was a hole in the ground with a fence around it that used to be a swimming pool. Nowadays, it appeared to serve no other function than as a mosquito hatchery, a place where leaves and other debris floated in a foot or so of coffee-colored water. At the end of the property nearest the highway was a larger building that a red sign identified as the OFFICE. Below that, a second sign added, hopefully, VACANCY.

I pulled slowly around the court and parked in the shade of a gnarled, lightning-scarred locust tree. Not that I expected to find one, but there was no late-model red ragtop anywhere in sight. I walked around to the office and peered through the dusty window. Inside, a young man with oily brown hair and acne-scarred cheeks was propped up in a swivel chair behind the counter, sipping from a can of Mountain Dew and staring intently into the flickering eye of a small black and white portable television. He wore a yellowed dress shirt with a sweat-stained collar and a skinny black necktie that went out of style about the time the gang gave up doing the Bristol Stomp down at the malt shop. The sign on the counter said his name was Hubert Bedell, and that he was the Night Manager.

The screen door banging shut behind me drew Hubert's attention away from the tube. He set his Dew on top of the television and hoisted himself reluctantly out of his chair.

"Help you, mister?"

"I'd like a room," I told him. "Something toward the back, away from the highway, if it's available." Then I added, by way of explanation, "I'm kind of a light sleeper, and I've been driving all day."

"How many nights you figure to be staying?"

"Not sure yet. Tonight, and maybe tomorrow."

"Be fifty-nine dollars plus tax for one night. Cash in advance or credit card, we don't accept no checks. If you want WiFi, that's two dollars extra." He tried without success to read upside down as I filled out the registration card. "You ever stayed here before, Mister..."

"Millar, with an 'A,'" I finished for him. "Ken Millar, Regional Sales

25

Manager with the Archer Insurance Company, out of Atlanta." I handed him a business card I'd swiped a few weeks earlier from a restaurant bulletin board. "Maybe you've seen some of our television commercials?"

"You the one with the ostrich, or the lizard?"

"It's an emu, and it's not us. We don't have a mascot."

"Okay, then I guess, no. This here set only gets a few stations, on account of we don't have no dish hookup here in the office, and the wife, she got the big TV from the house after the divorce. I'm savin' up now for a flat-screen before football starts."

"Go Titans," I said.

Hubert glanced indifferently at the card before handing it back to me. Then he turned around and eyeballed a numbered pegboard hanging on the wall behind him.

"I can put you in number eight if you want something away from the highway. We don't generally make the cabins up ahead of time unless there's a reservation, but if you can wait, I'll have the housekeeper down there in a couple minutes."

I handed over the money for one night, collected my key and receipt, and got directions to a restaurant in Harding that Hubert allowed was "tol'able." I would have liked to have stuck around to try to chat him up about Darlene Munson, but I couldn't think of a good way to broach the subject, since there wasn't a reason in the world for me to have known she was there, and he seemed fidgety and not particularly anxious to engage in a prolonged discussion on any topic. So, instead, I bade him good evening and excused myself to go check out the accommodations.

Apart from being hot enough inside to bake a ham, Cabin 8 wasn't nearly as bad as I had feared. It had a double bed, unmade, with a blanket and spread folded neatly at the foot. There was a window air conditioner, a dresser, a small desk with a chair, and a TV that was fastened to the wall with a chain heavy enough to yank stumps out of somebody's back forty. There was also a small bathroom with a vanity, a toilet, and a metal shower stall, but no tub, no towels, and no soap. I guessed those would be arriving with the sheets. The walls were paneled with something that was supposed to look like knotty pine. The curtains were flowered print, and the floor was linoleum with a small, hooked rug by the bed.

I turned the air conditioner on high and walked back outside to wait for it to do something besides make noise. Across the courtyard, I could see a cart piled high with sheets and towels. That would be housekeeping, making the afternoon rounds.

Before I got halfway across the parking lot, I had worked out a plan for what I was going to do next. I knocked softly on the door where the housekeeper was working and poked my head inside. A plump, middle-aged woman was there, dusting the top of the dresser. I put a hangdog look on my face and said, "Oh, excuse me. I was looking for somebody else."

She turned around to face me. "I'm Mattie Brown, the housekeeper. Can I do something for you?"

"I'm sorry to bother you, Mrs. Brown," I said. "I was looking for Mrs. Millar. I thought she might be staying in this cabin."

"I'm sorry, there's no Mrs. Millar staying in this cabin."

"Then possibly she's registered under her maiden name. It's Munson." I spelled it for her. "Does that ring any bells?"

She stopped dusting and folded her arms across her ample bosom. "Are you related to the lady?"

"She's my wife. I've been near out of my mind with worry. You know how it is. We had a fight, words were said. She left me. It was my fault. I realize that now, but it's been two weeks, and now I just want her to come home."

I tried to project a little frantic worry the housekeeper's way. "I came as soon as I found out where she had gone. She hasn't checked out, has she?"

"Mr. Millar—" She stopped mid-sentence, as if unable to find the words to express what she had to tell me.

"Something's wrong, isn't it?" I prompted. "Has something happened to Darlene? Has she been hurt?"

"I don't know. I don't even know whether I'm the one who ought to be telling you this, but your wife isn't here no more. She checked into this cabin last week and stayed a couple days, but then she left. I don't work weekends, so I couldn't say exactly what day, but when I got back Monday, she was gone.

27

I know she hasn't checked out, because the room's been paid two weeks ahead, and all her things are still here. But I can tell you for sure, nobody's set foot inside this here cabin besides me since last Friday afternoon.

"There's another thing you might as well know," she continued hesitantly. "I'm sorry you got to hear it like this, but while your wife was here, there was a man what was with her when she checked into her room. Then, yesterday afternoon, there was a couple of policemen that come around, asking questions about the both of them."

This time, the surprise I showed was genuine. "The police were asking about Darlene? Are you sure? Did something happen? Is she all right?"

"I don't know anything about that, but I know they was police because they showed him their badges. Plus, I heard them with my own ears. They were in the office with Chet. He's the day manager. They's talking with Chet while I was clocking in."

"Did they say what they wanted?"

"Only thing I heard was that they needed to visit with her. When Chet said she weren't here, they wanted him to let them in to look around her room. But they didn't have no warrant, so he told 'em he couldn't open up the room without checking with the owner first. Chet said it wouldn't take but a minute to call, but they told him not to bother. I didn't hear nothing else after that, because I wasn't supposed to be listening, and I was afraid they'd notice me standing by the doorway."

I said, "The first man you said visited Darlene while she was here. Did you happen to hear his name mentioned?"

"I never heard nobody say it, but I can tell you what he looked like, if you think it's somebody you might know." The description she gave wasn't quite accurate. But as I'd already guessed it would be, it was a fair enough approximation of Albert Glass, right down to the seersucker suit.

Mattie Brown continued, maternally, "I don't know what kind of trouble your wife is in, Mr. Millar, or where she is now. And I ain't one to be givin' advice, particularly when there's troublesome goin's on between married folks. But if you don't mind me sayin' so, she's a mite young for a man your age. And if she was kin to me, I'd find her and get her along home just as fast

28

as I could. She ought not to be living away off on her own like this, having strange men coming to her room the way she done."

We talked for a few more minutes as I tried, without success, to learn something more about Darlene Munson and the two "policemen" who had wanted to question her. Finally, her store of information exhausted, Mattie apologized again for being the bearer of bad news, and suggested I drive into town and talk to the police. Then she pledged me to silence, saying she didn't want to get into trouble for spreading stories around. I told her I understood and assured her she could count on me. I also promised to let her know how things turned out. She thanked me for that and said she'd keep us both in her prayers.

I left Mattie Brown to her chores and walked back across the parking lot to where I had stashed my car. It was beginning to feel a little cooler now. The sun had dropped behind the high ridges of the Cumberlands, casting the eastern slopes into deep green shadow. In the woods behind the motel, the air was alive with the insistent buzzing of locusts and the strident calls of awakening night creatures. I had a feeling tonight was going to be a long one.

Chapter Five

In the history of the Old South, Harding, Tennessee, occupies a place of no small distinction. Back in November 1864, during the dying days of the Confederacy, there was a battle fought near Harding, as Union troops under Generals Jacob D. Cox and John Allison Schofield clashed with John Bell Hood's Army of Tennessee. The conflict, which resulted in a Union victory, lasted five bloody hours, and when the smoke cleared, 2,300 Federal and more than six thousand Confederate dead were left in the field.

In the aftermath of his crushing defeat, General Hood requested, and was granted, permission to resign his command. His rank was reduced to lieutenant general. The episode left a sour taste in the mouths of many Tennesseans that lingers even today. In Hood's own case, ignominy followed him all the way to the grave, as he died of yellow fever in New Orleans in 1879, leaving behind ten orphaned and destitute children. The good people of the great state of Texas, however, have drawn the luckless general to their collective, welcoming bosom, where, for a time, two junior high schools were named after him, as well as Fort Hood, the most populous U. S. military installation in the world.

More than a century and a half later, little evidence of the epic battle remains, apart from a scattering of historical markers on nearby Winstead's Hill and along Spring Hill Pike. And except for the occasional vagrant or drunk found drowned in the sleepy Harpeth River, about the most exciting thing that happens in Harding these days is the annual Jefferson Davis Day parade.

CHAPTER FIVE

* * *

It was nearly dark when I pulled out of the Rustic Retreat parking lot and drove the rest of the way into town. I stopped on the public square for a late supper at the restaurant Hubert Bedell had recommended. As I was parking my car, I noticed a small gathering of old-timers seated on concrete benches around a Confederate Civil War monument depicting a rebel soldier standing at order arms. I wondered if perhaps they were dreaming of the day that the South would rise again.

The restaurant in question, and the only eating establishment in Harding that appeared to be open at this hour, was called "Kal's Kountry Kafe." Besides me, the only other customers in the place were an elderly man sitting at the counter nursing a cup of coffee, and a couple in a booth near the back, arguing in easily overheard, spirited whispers about something having to do with somebody's shiftless brother-in-law. In the window near the booth where I was sitting, a couple of green bottle flies were buzzing dispiritedly against the glass, apparently having exhausted their strength trying to get back outside. I wondered whether they might have the right idea, but it was late, I was hungry, and driving into town, I hadn't seen anyplace else that offered meal service.

It took a fair amount of talking before I was able to make the waitress understand that I could only eat soft food, and therefore needed to order from the breakfast menu. Finally, after lengthy consultations with the cook, we were able to settle on scrambled eggs, with grits and gravy on the side, and a Diet Coke. Afterward, with plenty of time still to kill, I dawdled over a dish of raspberry sherbet and tried to sort out the information I had obtained from Mattie Brown.

The description she had given me wasn't the best, but the man who had visited Darlene Munson in her room after she settled in was obviously Albert Glass. Between checking up on his meal ticket and trying to talk her into handing over her precious file, his appearance was to be expected. But who were the cops, if that's what they were, that wanted to talk to her? And more importantly, what reason did they have to be looking for her?

31

Albert hadn't said anything about any law enforcement being involved, so I had no way of knowing whether his omission was because he didn't want me to ask more questions than I already had, or if he was truly unaware of what was going on. Either way, I didn't like it, if only because it introduced one more variable into an equation that looked a long way from having a straightforward solution. In all likelihood, it also meant that whatever was the story he was working on, it wasn't quite as secret as he had led me, and possibly himself, to believe. I had an uneasy feeling that I was about to step off into a hole that would prove not to have a bottom.

By nine-thirty, I'd had all the thinking I could handle for one night. I bought a six-pack of beer, a bag of potato chips, and a leftover copy of the *Sports Illustrated* swimsuit edition at a drug store. Then, I swallowed my last Hydrocodone of the day and headed back to the Rustic Retreat Motor Court. Somebody had turned on the illuminated signs outside the main building. In flickering red neon letters, one now spelled out "OF ICE", the other "V CAN Y".

I pulled into the lot past the office, where Hubert Bedell was still riveted to his TV and backed into a parking space next to my own cabin. Business had picked up some while I was having dinner, and now there were six occupied cabins, each with a vehicle parked nearby. Neither the cars nor the cabins would provide much cover in case I needed to move around. But on the plus side, it looked as though everybody had already settled in for the night, so I likely wouldn't attract any attention sitting in my car instead of inside my own cabin watching television. I turned off the ignition and rolled down the windows to enjoy the night air and to keep from having to run the gas-swilling V8 engine to operate the air conditioner.

I fiddled with the Thunderbird's scratchy AM radio until I was able to find a local station broadcasting an Atlanta Braves baseball game. I turned the sound down low and popped open the first of my beers. Then I sat back to mull over the events of the day and wait for something to happen. Nothing much did. In Harding, fireflies winked sweet nothings at one another in the honeysuckle-scented darkness. Cicadas chirped, peepers peeped, and owls and nighthawks hooted and screeched as they plied their nocturnal rounds in search of evening meals. In Atlanta, a succession of Braves hitters waved ineffectually at the offerings of a rookie Pittsburgh Pirates pitcher who was tossing the game of his young career.

The beer turned out to be a mistake. On top of the painkillers that I had been swallowing for the past thirty-six hours, two tall boys in an hour proved to be a more effective soporific than a shot of ketamine. I dozed off in the bottom of the eighth inning as yet another Braves hitter was called out looking at a fastball right down the middle of the plate.

When I woke up, a three-quarter moon was high in the sky. The game was over, and there was nothing on the radio except white noise. It took me a few seconds to remember where I was and why I was there. I checked my watch: three o'clock. I had been napping nearly five hours. The air felt very still. Heavy dew had settled on the lawn, on the car, and on me. I shivered uncomfortably against the chilly dampness. It was time to head inside and sleep in a bed. And then I saw the blue Ford sedan that had followed me earlier, parked near the trees at the far end of the lot. At almost the same moment, I caught the faint glimmer of a light moving around inside cabin twelve.

I was wide awake now and kicking myself for half-assed detective work that, under different circumstances, might have gotten me killed. I turned off the radio, took my .380 out of the glove compartment, and lifted myself gingerly over the console, separating the driver's seat from the passenger seat. If it still made any difference, the object was to keep my car between me and the cabin where the flashlight was moving, at least until I could figure out what to do next. I mentally measured about twenty-five yards of exposed parking lot from where I was to where the Ford sedan was parked. Far too great a distance in bright moonlight to try a direct crossing without being spotted. That meant I'd have to take the long way around, through the trees.

I switched off the overhead courtesy light, eased the passenger side door open, and crept along the side of the car toward the front of my cabin. When I could get no closer without breaking into the clear, I held my breath, counted three, and sprinted for cover. No alarm bells went off, no watchdogs started barking, and nobody began shooting at me.

I scrambled as quietly as I could around to the back of the cabin and then across a narrow flagstone walkway to number six. There was a small CO-OP propane tank standing alongside the building. I used that to shield me as I ran from the motel grounds proper into the cedars. I paused in the shadows there, breathing shallowly through my mouth and straining my ears against the sounds of the forest, trying to pick up noises that didn't belong, especially those that might be moving my way. I was counting on the clattering of the air conditioners in the other cabins, plus the vocalizations of whatever varmints were living it up in the nearby woods to cover the sound of my footsteps crunching in the gravel parking area as I made my dash for cover. In retrospect, I should have considered that the noise from a half-dozen window air conditioners might also work to the advantage of persons other than me.

Satisfied I was still undetected, I started picking my way toward the sedan. I had taken no more than three or four steps when suddenly, to my left, there was a frantic, scuffling noise that quickly disappeared off into the bushes. I had disturbed some small animal, a rabbit perhaps, or a raccoon, and sent it scurrying for tall timber. At that moment, the heartbeat throbbing inside my ears seemed loud enough to bring a troop of Boy Scouts running all the way from Nashville. I froze where I stood, waiting for a bullet to find me. When nothing happened, I decided whoever was inside the cabin was even more of a tenderfoot than I was and probably wouldn't take notice of anything short of an air-raid siren.

I was close enough now to reach out and touch the still-warm hood of the Ford, and to see the license plate clearly. I made a mental note of the number. Then I took my gun out of my pocket, racked a round into the chamber, and thumbed the safety off. I wasn't seriously expecting to have to do much more than wave it around, but the lesson I had learned from my encounter with Roydell Jones the previous week was still fresh in my mind. And whoever was inside that cabin might very well be armed.

Still concentrating on the light inside the cabin, I stood straight up and moved out from behind the Ford. At precisely the same moment, I heard two quick footsteps and then a grunt of strenuous effort behind me. In less time than it took to realize what was happening, something hard exploded against the back of my head, and a vivid burst of color flashed behind my eyes. Then, with all the grace of a dying quail, I sailed over the edge of consciousness and landed face-down in the soft, damp grass.

Chapter Six

To paraphrase Oscar Hammerstein, there is nothing like a jail. Whether it's a big city lockup like Nashville's or a two-cell hoosegow like the one they have on the first floor of the City of Harding Public Safety Building, they're all pretty much the same. Behind the bars and the bricks and mortar, they are nothing more than warehouses of human despair. Old or new, they smell of urine and sweat, vomit and stale tobacco, cold coffee, busted lives, and plans gone wrong.

A pair of Williamson County sheriff's deputies found me unconscious, with my neck, face, and hands covered with mosquito bites, on the floor inside cabin twelve of the Rustic Retreat Motor Court. Hubert Bedell had yelled for the law right after he saw a car drive away and the cabin door standing open with all the lights on. The deputies listened to about ten words of my story before deciding that I was either drunk or crazy and that the easiest thing would be to let the Harding town cops figure out what to do with me in the morning.

Twenty minutes later, as the first glimmer of dawn appeared in the eastern sky, I was unceremoniously plopped into a cell, minus my gun, pills, wallet, shoelaces, phone, and ID. Nobody asked my name, or how I was feeling, or whether I needed a doctor, or if I wanted to make a telephone phone call. Nobody seemed to be worried about whether I lived or died. As long as I was quiet and didn't start bleeding out the ears or set fire to my mattress, everything would be just fine.

As jailhouses go, Harding's was more comfortable, if that's the right word, than the half-dozen or so in which I've been a guest, and the many more I've

36

seen. The mattress on the bunk was reasonably clean, the sink and toilet both worked and if there were any rats or roaches in residence, they were keeping well out of sight. And best of all, I had the place to myself. As it seemed I had been doing all night, and since there was nothing else to do anyway, I took off my jacket and stretched out on the bunk for a couple more hours of sleep.

About eight-thirty, a sad-faced duty officer named Taylor rattled the bars and asked me if I wanted breakfast. He didn't seem disappointed when I said I didn't. An hour or so later, he came back jingling a ring full of keys. The captain wanted to talk to me, he said.

He reached behind his back and came up with a set of handcuffs. "Let's just get you hooked up here, partner."

I clasped my hands obligingly. "Getting assaulted in this town is cause for arrest, I guess."

"No offense. We just don't want nobody to get hurt, that's all." He snapped the hardware into place and took me by the elbow. "Okay, let's go."

The captain's office was on the same floor as the lockup, but on the other side of the building. Between the two, enclosed by a low railing, was a reception area and a bullpen where a desk sergeant and a dispatcher sat. Neither of them showed the slightest interest in me. On the walls were framed renderings of the President, the governor, and an old white guy with mutton chop sideburns whom I didn't recognize. At the end of the hallway was a closed door with the name CAPTAIN J. PURVIS stenciled on it in imitation gold paint. Officer Taylor rapped twice on the glass, causing a few flecks of gold paint to shake loose and fall to the floor. Then he pushed the door open and steered me inside.

Even by small-town police department standards, Purvis's office was a tight squeeze, crowded as it was with a battered wooden desk and a bank of metal file cabinets in the corner. Two heavy wooden visitor's chairs faced the desk. The walls were painted institutional green and, except for a wall calendar and a street map of the city of Harding, absent of decoration. The room's only window provided a view of the front of the fire station next door. A few of the neighboring ashcats were up and outside, tossing a football around on the lawn.

Captain Purvis was a compact man whose age I would have put somewhere in his mid-fifties. He had a small, serious face with delicate, almost feminine features and darting eyes that probably didn't miss much. His hair was salt-and-pepper gray and receding at the temples. He wore tortoiseshell half-glasses and a crisp white uniform shirt, open at the collar, with a polished gold nameplate and a blue and gold enameled badge. He looked well-rested, well-scrubbed, and ready to whip his weight in wildcats.

When I walked in, the captain was scowling at a single sheet of typewritten paper that could only have been my arrest report. He did not seem pleased. Spread out on the desk in front of him were my belongings, including a leather wallet containing a chrome-plated badge marked SPECIAL DEPUTY. The shield had been presented to me in appreciation for a contribution I had made to the Davidson County Sheriff's Department benevolent fund a few years back when I was feeling flush. It carried about as much weight as a school crossing guard's badge, and it wouldn't fool anybody who'd ever spent more than five minutes around real cops, but once in a while, it was handy to have along. Nobody needed to send a memo for me to know that today was not going to be one of those days.

Purvis lifted his eyes from the arrest report and let them swing back and forth between me and Officer Taylor.

"Well?"

The other officer cleared his throat nervously. "Well, here he is, like you asked. You want me to take the cuffs off or leave him like he is?"

"Off. Don't know why you put them on in the first place."

"Nossir." Taylor fumbled around with his ring of keys and found the right one to unlock the cuffs. "You think I should stay around? You know, just in case?"

"In case of what? You think he's going to catch on fire?" Purvis gave him a look of weary indulgence. "I think I can handle it from here, thanks."

The captain waited until the door was closed again, then motioned me into a chair.

"Want some coffee? It isn't very good, but this time of the morning, it's

38

about all I can offer you."

"No, thanks," I said. I sat down where he had indicated and waited for him to start the conversational ball rolling.

He took off his glasses and folded them carefully into his shirt pocket. "Looks like you got yourself a little banged up last night, Mr. Gamble. Any of that happen since you arrived at our humble place of business?"

He spoke in a soft voice that held just a hint of an out-east accent. In a world filled with southern drawls, it sounded as out of place as a French horn in a jug band.

"Not here," I assured him, "and not last night. Most of what you see was done by a bail skipper a few days back. I had a hard time convincing him it was time to come home."

"But you were successful."

"It took a little doing, but yes, I was."

"I see." He leaned back in his chair and rested his head against the wall behind him. When he spoke again, his voice held just the smallest note of amusement.

"You know, I can't help but get the impression you must lead a very exciting life up there in the big city, what with chasing after bail-jumpers, runaway wives, and whatever else it is you do for a living." He paused to take a sip of his coffee. "Problem for you is, you're not in Nashville now. You're in Harding. Down here, people aren't looking for quite so much excitement. It's pretty much the reason why they moved here in the first place. You getting my drift here?"

"I think so."

"Then you've probably already figured out that our conversation will go a whole lot smoother for both of us if you can convince me that this is all just a misunderstanding of some sort and that you aren't planning to bring any of your rough-and-ready ways down here to our little piece of paradise." It wasn't really a question, so I didn't waste time trying to think of an answer.

"Let me come straight to the point, just so there's no misinterpreting where we're headed here. As you may or may not know, this is an election year. That means that half the county board is up for reelection, as well as the entire Harding city council. It also means that, once the new council is sworn in, the contract for chief of police is open for renegotiation. The old chief is retiring to Florida—God knows why anybody does that—and there's a very good possibility I'll be asked to replace him. I guess I don't have to tell you my chances of having that happen depend greatly on how well I'm able to keep the peace hereabouts."

"Right, got it," I said. "So, is this the part where you tell me this town isn't big enough for the both of us?"

"No. This is where you tell me how you came to turn up flat on your face inside a motor court cabin you weren't registered in at four-thirty this morning."

I scratched at a mosquito bite behind my ear. "That's easy. I was hired by a client to bird-dog a woman he's been trying to track down for the past several days, so far, with no luck. She's registered at the Rustic Retreat. You can verify that easily enough. I spoke to the housekeeper there, who told me the woman in question had gone out several days before and hadn't returned, but that she hadn't checked out, either. My client's instructions were to stick around and wait for her to come back. When she did, I was to keep an eye on her. If she left again, I was to follow her and let the client know her whereabouts. That's what I was doing."

"While you were still conscious, you mean." Purvis leaned forward in his chair and picked up the arrest report from his desk. "This woman we're talking about, would she be named Darlene Munson?"

"Yes, she would."

"And did your client instruct you to identify yourself as the woman's husband?"

"No, he did not. I thought it might be easier to get the information I was looking for if I took a less direct approach."

"Clever fellow." He gave me a mirthless smile. "What happened after that?"

"I imagine most of the rest of it is in the deputy's report. About three o'clock, I saw lights inside her cabin. I didn't see the car she's supposed to be driving, but I did see a car that I thought had been tailing me earlier. I went over to investigate. Before I got close enough to see what was going on, somebody came up from behind and cold-cocked me. Since I didn't get there under my own power, I assume the same person, or persons, dragged me inside. The next thing I knew, two very big men with very big shotguns were shining a flashlight in my eyes and reading me my rights."

"And that's it?"

"Pretty much it is, yeah."

Purvis picked up my gun and weighed it in his hand. "A Colt .380. I'm surprised, a man in your line of work. You know it's got no real stopping power."

"Yeah, well, it's a family heirloom," I said. "It has a lot of sentimental value."

"This is the kind of popgun we usually took away from the gangbangers at the high school back in Jersey. You ever take anybody out with it?"

"Not with that gun," I told him, skipping over what had taken place one night between me and the man who was trying to kill Maggie Totten. "Most of my business is missing persons and some occasional insurance work. When I was on the job, the only shooting I ever did was at the range, and that was with a .40 caliber Smith & Wesson."

"Uh-huh. But you did pop somebody, Mr. Gamble. I checked. Nashville P.D. said it was a righteous shoot."

"It was to save a woman's life. I really had no choice."

"How'd you feel when you did it?"

I said, "Excuse me?"

"You killed a guy. Regardless of your reasons, you took a man's life. I'm asking how you felt about it."

"Okay, in the moment. Not too good later on."

"Right. Think you could do it again?" he challenged.

"I don't know. I hope I never need to find out."

"I hope for your sake, you don't, either." He worked the action back and forth and dry-fired an imaginary round at the light fixture in the ceiling.

"I killed a man once in Ocean City. That's in New Jersey, in case you've never been. It's where I worked for close to fifteen years before I took this job, you know."

I didn't know, so I just sat and waited.

41

"Some dumbass crackhead was trying to hold up an all-night convenience store. It was in the wintertime and colder than God ever meant it to be. My partner and I took the call about two in the morning. We spotted the suspect on foot a block away, but he made us and took off running down an alley. When we pulled in after him, he took a couple of shots at us. Stupid thing to do. These guys always think they can out-shoot the cops.

"Anyway, we returned fire. It was my round that got him, center-mass, just like they teach at the academy. It was a lucky shot, really. We were just firing at his muzzle flash, and we could have just as easily killed a one-eyed cat. It was so damn cold you could see steam coming out of the wound."

"I was on the job," I said. "What I know, unless you're some kind of a psycho, it's the worst part of it. But it isn't anything personal."

He raised his eyebrows at that. "Isn't it? Do you know that when a man dies, he pisses in his pants? It's an involuntary thing. His insides just go slack, and he empties himself. A minute before, this guy is shooting at me, like he's public enemy number one. Now he's dying, and I'm down on the pavement with him, trying to keep him from bleeding out long enough for the medics to get there. But he doesn't make it, and the next thing I know, he's dead, and he's pissed all over both of us. I'd say that's about as personal as it gets, wouldn't you?" His voice sounded oddly disconnected, as if he were suddenly back in that cold New Jersey alleyway all over again.

"It's tough," I said.

"Tough, yeah. Things aren't ever the same after you kill somebody, even in the line of duty. You know from your own experience, it's not like on television. You don't just reload your weapon, get back in the car, and finish your tour. And it's not just the departmental foolishness you have to deal with after. For a cop, there's also the civilian review board and the mandatory counseling. And then comes the reassignment to desk duty until you're finally cleared of any wrongdoing and returned to duty. Sometimes there's even a lawsuit, and you know what the lawyers will say. 'He was scared, you didn't identify yourself properly, he's had psychological problems,' whatever. It's just something you don't ever want to have to go through, not ever again.

"Anyway, it wasn't long after that, I heard this job was open, so I applied.

This being a small community and all, I decided, the hell with all the big-city bullshit, rural Tennessee might be a little more subdued than New Jersey. Probably never have to shoot anybody ever again. I certainly don't want to." He gave me a hard stare.

"You see where I'm going with this?"

"In all three dimensions."

"Then, knowing what you already know, suppose you tell me why you were carrying a loaded weapon on a penny-ante missing persons stakeout?"

I said, carefully, "As a rule, I wouldn't be, and even though it's not required anymore, I do have a license to carry a concealed weapon. And as I explained to you, I saw somebody moving around inside Darlene Munson's cabin with a flashlight. I didn't figure whoever was in there was looking for a pillow fight, so I took it with me."

"You're lucky it didn't get you killed. Who do you think it was sapped you, if that's what really happened?"

"You can see for yourself that's what happened." I turned my head and lifted my hair out of the way so he could see the lump. "Unless you think I did that to myself shaving."

His eyes got hard as flints. "You want to file a complaint about not receiving medical attention while you were in protective custody here?"

"Protective custody, is that what you call it? Maybe I dreamed it, but I'm pretty sure somewhere along the line, I heard somebody reading me my rights."

"So, is that a yes or a no?"

"It's a hard no," I said. "I don't want to file anything, Captain. I'm just telling you what happened."

"Would you be willing to sign a release to that effect?"

"Whatever works for you." I was starting to get irritated. "Look, this has all been very interesting, but I'm hungry, my head hurts, and I need a few hours' sleep in my own bed. If you're going to charge me with something, then do it and let me call my lawyer. Otherwise, let's wrap this up so we can both get back to doing what we're paid to do."

"Why don't we?" He opened his desk drawer, took out a bottle of aspirin, and pushed it across his desk. "Anything stronger, we'll need to get you a doctor. But it could be this afternoon before we can get him here."

I shook a couple of tablets out of the bottle and swallowed them dry. When I pushed the bottle back, he said, "You're a real entertaining fellow, you know that? You ought to open an office in Ocean City. You'd fit right in with some of those wiseasses back there."

I threw my hands up in frustration. "I give up, Captain. What do you want from me? I've told you what happened. And I agree, it looks like there's more going on than a simple missing persons investigation, but at this point, I don't have any better idea than you do what it is."

His eyes got narrow, and his voice got suddenly hard. "The man that owns that motel sits on the city council. That means there are sure to be questions concerning this little episode. What I want from you is a story that won't make me sound like a bumbler when I tell it to him. If you don't have anything better than what I've heard so far, then we'll just escort you back to your cell and let you think about it for a while longer. Now, let's try it again. Who slugged you?"

"I don't know. Up to now, I thought it might be Nashville city cops, although I don't know why they'd be working down here without checking in with you first."

"Why cops?" he said, sitting up straight.

"The housekeeper at the Rustic Retreat told me that some other people had been asking questions about Darlene Munson, including a couple that flashed badges."

That seemed to spike his interest. "What kind of badges?"

"She didn't get a good look at them. Unless you've either been on the job or on the inside, one shield looks pretty much like another. It could have been one of them that took me out, or it could have been somebody else."

"How do you figure they knew you'd be there?"

"I don't think they knew anything," I told him. "I think they were just watching the place, same as me."

"Watching for what?"

"Darlene Munson, I guess."

44

He shook his head. "So now we're back to square one, and it doesn't sound any better this time around. How come so many people are following this woman around, anyway? And what's she done that's got the law interested?"

"I wasn't told that," I lied. "My job was just to wait for her and then report back."

"Who hired you?"

"I'm sorry, Captain, you know that's privileged."

His mouth turned down at the corners. "Are you working for an attorney?"

"No."

"Then you know you have no right to refuse to cooperate with the police."

"Cooperate in what way, Captain? I'm aware of what the law says about confidentiality. But I'm also aware, and so are you, that unless you're questioning me in regard to a specific criminal investigation, I'm not required to disclose anything about my client, or what I'm working on."

I was skating on perilously thin ice, and we both knew it. Legally, I was within my rights to refuse to answer his questions, and since I was working for a bona fide newspaper reporter, I might have been able to claim some First Amendment protections. But in a business like mine, where just being able to function often depends on the cooperation of local authorities, legal correctness isn't always the smartest line to follow. And even dealing with a small-town cop like Purvis, word has a way of getting around in a hurry.

I said, "Look, Captain, I know you've got a job to do, and I appreciate your situation. But I have a client and a reputation to protect, and I have to use my best judgment about what I can disclose. You know the business I'm in. If I spilled my guts every time some local LEO leaned on me hard, I'd be repossessing used cars inside of a month. The best I can tell you is that, as far as I now know, there isn't anything going on that's going to get you crossways with the city council. Whatever this is, I don't think it has anything to do with Harding or anyone living here."

"Your reassurances are comforting."

I spread my hands apologetically. "I'm sorry. For now, it's the best I can do."

"Right. Not that I expect you're interested, but to put it into terms a southern boy like you can understand, I think this story of yours smells like a carp that's been out in the sun too long. I also think I could get your license suspended for any of several reasons, including breaking and entering, criminal trespass, defrauding an innkeeper, impersonating a police officer, withholding evidence, and," he poked at the prescription bottle with a neatly manicured index finger, "possession of a controlled substance."

"I have a prescription for that," I said uselessly.

"But I won't. Not this time, anyway. Because, for one thing, I figure a man has got to make a living the best way he knows how. That includes you, even if I don't like it, or you, which I don't. And for another thing, if I did decide to sit on you, I have a feeling it'd only end up causing me more trouble than it's worth.

"But I'll also tell you this. You come back here to my town, you'd better have a solid gold reason, and you'd better check in with me first, so I know what you're doing. Otherwise, I'll kick your ass right into the gutter without as much as a how-de-do."

He pushed my belongings back across the desk at me. "Now get the hell out of here. I've got work to do."

Chapter Seven

I t took about an hour after Captain Purvis finished chewing on me before he finally sprung one of the Harding cops long enough to drive me to the city impound lot so I could retrieve my car. Purvis had returned all my belongings except for my ersatz badge, which he tossed into his desk drawer, as he put it, "for safe keeping." It was his way of telling me he thought I was out of line carrying it around and that I shouldn't plan on using it again. I couldn't see anything to be gained by arguing the point.

After last night's shitshow, I didn't think there was much else to be accomplished by continuing to maintain surveillance of Darlene Munson's cabin at the Rustic Retreat. So instead, I stuck my tail between my legs and headed back to the city to let Albert Glass know I had fumbled the ball and to wait for further instructions. On the way, I had a chance to think about what had happened and to try to make some sense of it all. One conclusion seemed inescapable. Whatever was in the file Darlene Munson had and Albert Glass wanted, it wasn't just their little secret anymore. Other people were obviously on their trail, meaning that whatever Darlene had spirited away from her former employer was red-hot.

It was also clear now that it hadn't been my imagination when I thought I was being tailed out to the Rustic Retreat Motor Court. And whoever had rocked me to sleep a few hours later wasn't just there trying out a new set of burglar tools. The way it now looked, Albert had been followed to my office, I had been followed to Harding, and Darlene Munson was being closely pursued, all by some people who appeared to be playing for serious stakes. The big question was, who were they, and what did Darlene have on them?

I was starting to wonder whether either Darlene or Albert knew what they had gotten themselves into. It was clear that I was only beginning to understand the situation myself. My original agreement with Albert was to play the game according to his rules. That meant keeping my head low, asking as few questions as possible, and not expecting much in the way of answers to the ones that did get asked. So far, that had gotten me a knot on my head, part of a night in jail, a hundred-dollar ransom to bail my car out of the Harding impound lot, and orders to clear out of town from a cranky police captain who had not been pleased to meet me. The case wasn't off to the best start.

I stopped by my house for a shower and a fresh shirt and to flush what was left of my Hydrocodone prescription down the toilet. Not that I wouldn't have welcomed any relief for my throbbing head, especially after last night's abortive heroics. But given the start that I had gotten off to so far, I didn't want to make matters any worse by trying to go about my job in an opioid-induced fog.

Before I took off for the office, I called Maggie to let her know I was back from Harding and that I'd call her again later. This time, luck was with me, and I got her voicemail. That saved me having to tap-dance around the questions she was sure to ask about how things had gone the night before.

I got back to the office about twelve-thirty and found another headache waiting. Somebody looking for something had been there ahead of me. From the condition in which he, or they, had left things, they must have wanted to find it pretty badly. The door to the inner office had been crudely jimmied. My desk had been forced open, the contents of my file cabinets and bookshelf spilled onto the floor, and furniture pulled away from the walls and upended. The telephone was at the bottom of a jumble of file folders strewn in the corner. I had to trace the cord from the wall jack to determine just where it was.

Surprisingly, whoever had tossed the office did not take the cash deposit Albert Glass had given me the day before. It was right where I left it, in an envelope in the top drawer of my desk. That meant this was no ordinary break-in by some crack addict looking for cash or office equipment to carry

48

down to the pawnshop to bankroll his next fix. These guys, whoever they were, were disciplined professionals, and they were looking for Albert's precious file. No doubt, his visit to my office the previous day had given them the idea that it was already in his possession and that he had left it with me for safekeeping.

I put the phone back on my desk and dialed the number Albert Glass had given me the day before. There were four rings, then a click, and I found myself listening to a voicemail recording of Albert inviting me to leave a message and have a nice day. I did, but it didn't have anything to do with having a nice day.

Against my earlier instructions, I made a second call, this time to the Nashville *Times*. It took a couple minutes to get through the switchboard to the city room, and I talked to a real person this time instead of a machine, but the result was the same. No, Mr. Glass hadn't been in the office all day and wasn't expected back today. No, they didn't know where he could be reached, or when he'd be calling in. Did I care to leave a message in his voicemail?

In frustration, I slammed the receiver down and took another look around the shambles that was my office. To hell with Albert, I thought. This was personal now. I called the building super and asked him to send somebody from maintenance to fix the door, then got my car out of the lot and drove over to the *Times* building at Eleventh and Broadway.

I found Dick Dohrn's office in the far corner of the third-floor city room. Dick had come a long way from his days at the city's other newspaper, the *Banner*, when I had tipped him off to the Ozburn story. Back then, he'd been an up-and-coming crime-beat reporter with an ear for a good story and a knack for interviewing people that seemed to make them want to tell him their lives' histories the first time they met him. Now, he was city editor for the second-largest newspaper in the city. With a little luck and little more time, he would probably make editor-in-chief, if not at the *Times*, then someplace else. He was that good.

His appearance hadn't changed much in the year or so since I'd last seen him. He was the same age as me, and a little heavier than before, but still in good shape. He was tall, balding, and dressed in his customary off-the-rack slacks that never seemed to fit quite right. He wore wire-rimmed glasses and a white, short-sleeved dress shirt with no tie. And, as always, there was a mint-flavored toothpick sticking out of the corner of his mouth, a habit he'd acquired after he gave up smoking.

He smiled when I rapped on his open door and shook my hand as he steered me into a chair. It was only then that he noticed the slightly lopsided appearance of my face.

"Good Lord, Jackson, what happened to you? You look like a truck ran over you."

"That would be your editorial opinion?"

"I'm serious," he said. "What'd you do, run headlong into some cheating husband's fist?"

"I don't do that kind of work anymore, Dick."

"Well, whatever you are doing seems not to agree with you. Maybe what you need is another line of work altogether."

"No. What I need is a long vacation. Someplace where I can lounge on a beach and have native women feed me rum and tropical fruit and have their way with me every night."

"Tell me where that place is, and I'll go with you," he laughed. "Hell, if you write a good enough review, I might even be able to get you a job as travel editor."

"Don't think it wouldn't be tempting. Right now, though, I need some information if you're willing."

"About what? Or is it who?"

"It's who. A guy who works here."

The welcoming grin dropped from his face, and he was immediately on his guard.

"What guy? And what for?"

"What guy is Albert Glass. What for," I said, skimping on the truth a little, "is his name came up in connection with something I'm working on."

"Are you going to tell me about it?"

"Not unless I absolutely have to." Then, by way of additional non-elaboration, I added, "I don't want to say any more than necessary, but I think this might be serious. You know I wouldn't be asking about your people if it weren't."

"Why do I get the feeling I'm being jerked around here?"

"It goes with the big chair," I suggested. "And because you are, a little. I need you to trust me on this, Dick."

"Uh-huh. Well then, to answer your question, Albert is a damn good reporter, but a massive pain in the backside to have on the payroll. There isn't a newspaper in the Midsouth that wouldn't trade its circulation list to have Albert on its staff, but that doesn't make him any less of an asshole."

"Is that another way of saying he reports to you?"

"Nominally, he does, but that's just so he has a box on the organization chart. Albert has a little different arrangement from the rest of the staff. He worked it out with our publisher after he broke a story that helped boost the *Times* circulation a few years ago. We're in a competitive market, and at the time, Albert was putting out must-read copy. Management felt a separate deal was necessary to keep him happy. I guess they wanted to make sure he wouldn't jump to another publication."

"So, he's on his own, is what you're saying? Is he a regular employee, or does he have a contract?"

"He's on a contract, but I've never seen it. At that, though, it would be hard to come up with a contract to describe what he actually does."

"Which is what?"

"Investigative reporting, mostly. That means he doesn't have a definite assignment as such, except to keep his eyes open for the kinds of questionable goings-on that happen all the time, but that make good copy. You know, this councilman's brother-in-law gets a city contract that wasn't the lowest bid, or that slumlord with hooks into the city inspector's office gets a pass on a building code violation. Poor kids die in the inevitable fire or porch collapse, there's an investigation, and then it turns out nobody did anything wrong. That type of thing. One day a week, he writes commentary on local and regional events, but not like what you'd find in the *Wall Street Journal*. It's more home-cooking than it is national or international. Like that thing we had a year or so ago, a couple of state representatives get kicked out of the house chamber for being too noisy protesting some resolution or other. That kind of thing. In Albert's case, the biggest drawback, at least as far as he's concerned, is that he hasn't gotten a syndication deal yet. His column just runs in the *Times*."

"Does that pay much?"

"I'd say fairly well. Not as much as a syndicated columnist makes, but he's got more freedom than anybody else on the staff. Plus, he's pretty much exempt from any kind of editorial oversight. In general, unless it's outright libelous, except for copy-edits, we print whatever he comes up with. He works on what he wants, when he wants, without any say-so from me, or without my necessarily even knowing what it is. I guess the guys upstairs knew what they were doing when they okayed all this, but it plays hell with trying to put out a newspaper when you don't know from one day to the next what he might come up with."

I thought about that for a moment. "Is Albert on the level?"

"If by that you're asking, is he honest about what he writes, I'd say yes, absolutely. There's never been a problem with any of his stories coming back to bite us."

"You mean up to now."

"I didn't mean that the way it sounded. It's just that ever since he broke that vending machine story last year, he's been looking for organized crime under every rock. If a story doesn't have a mob angle, Albert's not interested in it."

I had another thought. "I'm hesitant to ask this, Dick, but is he a drunk?"

"Why do you ask?" Dick said. But he didn't seem surprised by the question.

I shrugged. "He looks like a drunk. He sweats like a drunk. He shakes like a drunk. He's got a complexion like a fish's belly, and when I offered him something stronger than a bottle of water, it only took two tries to convince him."

There was a pause. "Yeah, well, he goes on and off the wagon with some regularity, but I've never known it to affect his work. He's what you'd call a high-functioning alcoholic." He paused to gather his thoughts.

"Look, it's no secret newspaper circulation is down all over the country. We're getting our asses kicked by the Internet, cable news, and talk radio, which means advertising revenue is down as well. Thanks to sites like Facebook, Craigslist and eBay we don't even print classified ads anymore. In fact, as far as that goes, if we didn't have an on-line edition, we'd probably be circling the drain right now. People these days want to get their information, such as it is, in real-time, without having to buy a paper or get ink on their hands. A guy like Albert helps us retain readers. So, even if he's a little hard to handle, we have to put up with him."

"Okay, so he's A-list. Do you know whether he's got anything cooking right now?"

"I know that he did, but I couldn't tell you if he still does or not."

"If I asked what it was, would you tell me?"

"I might," he said pointedly, "if I knew what this was about. Otherwise, I'd want to think about it first."

I considered that and decided he was right. Friends are friends, but what Dick was asking for now was the same trust I was asking him to place in me.

I said, "Okay, but this is between you and me, and for now, this needs to be as far as it goes. Albert showed up in my office yesterday afternoon. He said he was working on a big story, but that he had misplaced his star informant, a young woman named Darlene Munson. I don't suppose the name means anything to you?"

He shook his head. "Never heard of her."

"No, I thought not. This Darlene, whoever the hell she is, is the key to what he's working on. But because of the nature of the story, she was afraid her life might be in danger. To make her feel safer, Albert moved her out of town and into a motel, but she seems to have disappeared shortly after she checked in."

"Wait a minute," he sat up straight in his chair. "Disappeared how?"

"Unclear. I don't know if she just got bored and moved herself elsewhere, or if somebody got to her. Albert acted like he didn't know, either. He gave me a fifteen hundred dollar advance to run a stakeout at the motel in case she came back."

I thought he might say something snarky about Albert advancing me the fifteen hundred, but instead he said, "And did you?"

"I started to, last night. I found out some people besides Albert were looking for Darlene. Early this morning, they showed up to search her room. I got a little bit careless, and one of them sapped me and left me for the sheriff to find. I just got out of jail a couple hours ago."

"Now, that sounds like you," he said. "For a minute there, I thought we were talking about somebody who knew what he was doing." So, he got his dig in after all.

"Funny. Then, when I got back to town, I found that those same guys, or somebody a whole lot like them, had visited my office and tossed it while I was in the lockup. Either they checked my ID while I was out cold, or else one of them followed Albert right up to my office door yesterday afternoon. In either case, I think they knew I would be on ice for a while, so they were able to take their time looking."

"Did they take anything?"

"Far as I could tell, all they did was make a mess. When I saw how my office had been left, I tried to call Albert, but all I got was his voicemail. Then I called here and was told nobody had seen him all day. That brought me down to talk to you. Which, by the way, is something Albert explicitly told me not to do."

"Again, that sounds like you."

Dick spit his toothpick into the wastebasket, extracted a fresh one from a carton he kept on his desk, and stuck it into his mouth. "And you don't have any idea who these people are?"

"Not a clue. Could be cops, TBI, Feds, private security, the Outfit. Who knows? The car I saw was a plain-wrapper Ford sedan, so it could have been just about anybody." That reminded me that I needed to make a telephone call to a guy I knew at the DMV to have the Ford's license plate run.

"Any thoughts on what they were looking for?"

"Some. Albert told me Darlene had some kind of a file that he needed for his story to stand up. Based on the little bit he told me, I assumed he meant financial records of some kind, but for all I know, it could be love letters from the governor to his girlfriend. Whatever it is, I think that's what they were looking for."

"Why would they think you had it?"

"I don't think they know who has it. I think they're just making sure they don't overlook any possibilities. That's why they tossed my office. Look, Dick, I may be getting my head out over my skis a little bit here, but I think your man might be working on something that stands a good chance of getting him or Darlene Munson into some serious trouble. Maybe even killed. I think he knew that when he hired me. Hell, it might very well be the reason why he hired me. Either way, now, I need to know what's going on."

Dick said, "When you talked to Albert yesterday, did he give you any details about what this story he's working on is all about?"

"Not specifically, no. He said it had something to do with the November election and that when the story broke, a lot of big names were going to go running for cover."

"That's all?"

"He more or less implied that Darlene Munson had a strong connection to somebody that was involved. Somebody with enough at stake to be willing to have her eliminated to keep the story quiet."

"And he didn't say who?"

"No names. He just said he'd been working on it for several weeks."

Dick banged his fist on his desk so hard that his computer mouse jumped up into the air.

"I don't like this, Jackson. I don't like it one bit. If even half of what you're telling me is true, one of my reporters could be responsible for somebody getting killed, and that's if he doesn't wind up dead himself. Beyond that, the reputation of this newspaper could be seriously compromised. You tell me. How the hell am I supposed to react to that?"

"Unless you think it'll help you to attract more readers to have dead bodies start piling up around the masthead, you might want to give me some idea of what he was working on."

There was an uncomfortable silence. "The fact is, I'm not sure what he's doing right now. A couple months ago, he was working on something having to do with Charles Lambert. But now? I just don't know. As Albert's editor, I should, but I don't. That's what I mean about organization."

"Back up," I said. "Are we talking the same Charles Lambert who owns Black Strap Music? The country-western recording house over on Music Row?"

"Right person, wrong verb tense," he corrected me. "Lambert tried to drive a brand-new BMW through a bridge abutment about three months ago. From the photos I saw, with what they had left they could have buried Charlie and his Beemer in the same coffin."

"They don't build them like they used to."

"Guess not. Anyway, after the accident, Albert got interested in Lambert, but then he dropped it after a few weeks. I assumed he couldn't find a way to turn an automobile accident into a mob hit."

"Then we're sure it was an accident?"

"Oh, there was no question about it. Lambert was on his way home from a meeting. It was late at night and raining. He hit a slick spot and spun his car into the freeway overpass at Dickerson Road. According to the medical examiner's report, he was killed instantly."

"Hang on. Dickerson Road is north of the city. Did anybody think to ask what kind of meeting Lambert was attending that time of night in that part of town?"

He shrugged. "There wasn't any reason to. Lambert was finance chairman for an organization called the Hermitage Group. Carver Dickinson, the publisher here at the *Times*, is also a member, along with your old boss Roger Seacrist and a bunch of other movers and shakers. The Group was meeting that night at Dickinson's house in Goodlettsville."

"The Hermitage Group." It took a second while I searched my memory for a frame of reference. "Aren't they some kind of a feel-good fundraising organization? Kind of like a Lions Club for guys with too much time and money on their hands?"

"Yes and no. They do some good work, but that's only part of it. Dickinson's been promoting their accomplishments in the *Times* for the past several years."

"I wonder why I haven't heard more about it."

Dick laughed out loud. "For the same reason, they haven't heard about you. You're not a player. You don't have enough money or connections to be of any interest to them. What these guys really do is work behind the scenes to promote the city as a place to locate new businesses or to stage special events. They function like a chamber of commerce, except that individually and collectively, they've got serious political and financial clout. I know they've been able to lure several corporations to relocate their home offices here. A few years ago, they gave a pile of money to some schools in poor neighborhoods so they could set up computer labs and fund after-school programs. It got them a lot of good press at the time. Right now, they're hard at work making sure Roger Seacrist will be the next governor, and they may very well succeed. He's starting to move up in the polls. There're still a few months to go before the election, and anything can still happen. But by and large, these guys have had a pretty good track record."

"So, they're political. That doesn't sound like the sort of crowd a guy like Lambert would be running with."

Dick sighed. "Why do I have to explain these things to you? Everything these days is political. Along with the insurance people and the bankers, the music business carries most of the water in this city. As Hermitage Group members go, Charlie was just more of a celebrity than the others."

"Was all this written up?"

"Of course, it was written up," he said irritably. "Don't you take the newspaper?"

"Not since my parakeet died," I said. "But I'd like to take a look at what you've got if it's possible. Can you get somebody in the morgue to dig it out for me?"

"Sure, but what for? Do you think Albert is still interested in Charlie Lambert?"

"I don't know what to think, except that it sounds like it was the last thing we know he was working on. Maybe Albert stumbled over something while he was investigating Lambert that started him nosing around into something else. Until we have a chance to ask him, it's worth at least a look."

"Okay. But if you turn anything up, keep me posted." He reached for his telephone. "I'll set it up right now. Do you want to see everything that's been written up, or just the stuff Albert worked on personally?"

"Albert paid me for three days in advance," I told him. "You might as well let me have all you've got."

Chapter Eight

I n newspaper parlance, the morgue is the name every newspaper uses
to describe its archived materials going back, in some cities, as far as
the 1700s. It is, in a very real sense, the life story of the newspaper. In
the pre-digital era, newspaper morgues would have been crammed floor-
to-ceiling with file cabinets, card files, storage boxes filled with articles,
sports stories, obituaries, photos and photo negatives, feature articles, and
artifacts from the newspaper's earliest years. In more recent times, many of
these records have been scanned, first onto microfiche files and then, later,
digitized for easier reference. That made digging into the life of Charlie
Lambert much easier for me, because all the *Times* had turned out to be quite
a lot, indeed.

By the time I reached the basement of the *Times* building, the morgue
attendant had logged me into a database linked to five years' worth of
articles referencing the name Charles Lambert. A great deal of what they had
archived was fluff, coverage of the kinds of activities de rigueur among the
rich and famous, including corporate titans, athletes, entertainers, society
snobs, televangelists, high-flying politicians, and music industry moguls.
As if I needed one, it was a reminder all over again why the only parts of
the newspaper I ever bothered to read were the sports, the comics, and the
editorials.

I found photos of Lambert and his wife, mugging it up in stylish evening
attire at black tie fund-raising events, Lambert and his pals teeing off at
celebrity pro-am golf outings, and Lambert acting as guest emcee at a benefit
performance of the Grand Ole Opry. That stuff I was able to get through

quickly, and except for occasional odds and ends, without learning anything very useful. But there was a considerable amount of more substantive information as well, and by the end of the afternoon I had been able to piece together a fairly complete narrative on the life and untimely death of Charles Lambert. I organized my notes into three distinct, partially overlapping piles: Lambert's personal history, business page information on his Black Strap Music Company, and background data on the Hermitage Group.

Charles Lambert was fifty-seven years old when he died. The date was April 17 of this year. The time was approximately two-thirty in the morning. Confirming Dick Dohrn's recollection, Lambert had been attending a meeting of the Hermitage Group, which had been held at the Goodlettsville home of *Times* publisher and Group vice-chairman Carver Dickinson. It was an unseasonably chilly night and there was a light rain-sleet mixture falling, making for slippery road conditions. Lambert lost control of his BMW 735 on I-65 South as he was approaching the Dickerson Road overpass and slammed head-on into the concrete abutment. He was killed instantly.

There was no mention in the sanitized *Times* account of Lambert being alcohol or drug-impaired, nor was there any suggestion of foul play. The only family left behind was his wife, Audra, and a married sister living in Columbia, South Carolina. After a closed casket service, Lambert was interred on April 22 in a private mausoleum at Mount Olivet Cemetery. The photo accompanying the obituary showed a jowly, dark-haired man who looked a good ten years older than his actual age. His face was one that might have been thought handsome once, but that now seemed vaguely dissolute, as if his path to success had not always followed smooth pavement.

Like many men who accomplish great things in their lifetimes, Charles Lambert's ride to wealth and fame included an impressive lineup of stunning victories combined with a handful of soul-crushing setbacks. A Spartanburg, South Carolina, disc jockey and amateur songwriter, Lambert dabbled around the fringes of the music business as a backwoods impresario, organizing tent revivals and booking Gospel music revues into rural auditoriums, fairgrounds, and high school football stadiums. More than once, he went broke promoting "Country Caravan" bus tours that headlined second-string performers and recording industry has-beens. The tours, it was reported, often failed to generate enough advance ticket sales to buy fuel for the bus. Other times, he was the target of lawsuits to recover the rental cost of the auditorium or even the pole tent on the outskirts of town. More than once, gate receipts from various venues were seized by city or county law enforcement to pay off rental costs or state income and local entertainment taxes.

Lambert's big break came when a song he wrote called "City Boy, Country Man" was recorded by a previously unknown yodeler named Johnny Grimes. The song originally figured to be a throwaway, the "B" side of a warmed-over Hank song that the record label hoped would be Grimes's first big single. Instead, as it sometimes happens, "City Boy, Country Man" ended up getting most of the air play and became a surprise hit that ultimately propelled Grimes to the number-seven spot for the year on the C&W charts. Grimes proved to be a one-hit wonder who disappeared back into the county fair circuit shortly thereafter, but Lambert's reputation was on its way to being made. He immersed himself first in songwriting, and when royalty money started rolling in, added producing to his resume, cranking out hits for a succession of big-name country entertainers. One article I read even described him, somewhat breathlessly, as country music's answer to such pop-rock songwriting icons as Neil Diamond, Jim Webb, Carole King, and the Brothers Gibb.

Eventually, Lambert moved his company, Black Strap Music, named for a type of dark, somewhat bitter-tasting molasses, from Spartanburg to Nashville's Music Row. Five years later, he built a two-story office complex-cum-recording studio right across the street from the RCA Tower. It was an impressive monument to his life's work, and it proved to be Charlie's high-water mark before the bubble burst.

According to *Times* financial reporter Jared Foley, Black Strap first began experiencing serious money problems about ten years earlier. And despite what was described as Herculean efforts on the part of the company, including its artists and its publicists, the slide accelerated thereafter. Before long, the situation had reached a crisis point. The writer attributed the slump to changing musical tastes among younger C&W audiences, who were abandoning *en masse* the twangy, Jimmy Rodgers-inspired, traditional country songs that had been Black Strap's mainstay, for the more synthesized, quasi-pop, "Nashville Sound" arrangements popularized by performers like Vince Gill, Jackson Browne, Poco, and the early-1970s version of the Eagles.

There were also rumblings of dubious outside investment schemes that pancaked off the end of the runway and an intimation that, after more than twenty years in the business, Charlie Lambert had simply lost some of his mojo. Accordingly, six months before his death, he completed a deal that transferred majority ownership of Black Strap to another entertainment company called Talent Management Associates. Charlie remained on board as president of the new company, but his position was more titular than it was fact.

Curiously, at about the same time stories began surfacing regarding Black Strap's money problems, Charles Lambert was named finance chairman of the Hermitage Group. It was thought, the article stated, that the appointment was made as a means of cashing in on Lambert's perceived star power and to put a popular and widely recognized face on the organization. The Hermitage Group had been formed several years earlier, near the end of the second Bush Administration. The stated goal was to promote business and investment opportunities in and around Nashville. As Dick Dohrn had said, the Group's efforts had proved fairly successful, enticing a number of corporations to locate their principal offices in the downtown area and sparking a construction boom that continues right up to the present day. Among their most recent undertakings, the Hermitage Group was working on a bid to host a future Summer Olympics as well as the next Republican National Convention and to perhaps lure a major league baseball team to the area. Another feel-good story had them donating money to several schools in poorer neighborhoods to equip computer labs and help fund after-school programs for underprivileged kids.

Included in one of the articles I read was a paragraph explaining that the Hermitage Group had taken its name from The Hermitage, the former home of President Andrew Jackson, located just east of the city. In fact, I had visited the Hermitage on a couple of occasions. Once a cotton plantation, the Hermitage these days is a museum that sees more than a quarter million tourists annually. The grounds include the Jackson residence itself, as well as the graves of Old Hickory and his wife Rachel, and some sixty-one slaves who had previously been buried in unmarked plots. An accompanying photo showed Lambert mugging it up with other Group high rollers, including *Times* publisher Carver Dickinson, Davidson County District Attorney Roger Seacrist, and a couple of brothers named Hayes who owned a string of automobile dealerships in Nashville, Knoxville, and Chattanooga. A follow-up piece revealed that Roger Seacrist was organizing a campaign to run in the upcoming gubernatorial election and that, if he declared, the Hermitage Group, as well as the *Nashville Times,* were expected to back his candidacy. In an attached sidebar was a short biography of Seacrist and a couple of paragraphs about a "wide-ranging investigation" he had recently launched into organized crime activities in the Davidson County area. No specifics were included, and if the investigation had turned up any results to date, the article didn't mention them.

Chapter Nine

I logged out of the computer, pocketed my notes, and checked my watch. Six o'clock. I had been at it better than two and a half hours and had gathered a fairly substantial amount of information about the late Charles Lambert. Whether there was anything hidden between the lines that would help me find Darlene Munson, or whether there was even any connection between Lambert's life and death and Darlene's disappearance remained to be discovered. But for the moment, at least, I had a direction in which to work.

I leaned back in my chair and rubbed my eyes. It had been a long twenty-eight hours since Albert Glass had walked into my office and sent me chasing after my own tail down to the Rustic Retreat Motor Court and back again, with an intermediate stopover at the Harding city lockup. Tomorrow morning, I decided, would be soon enough to start sorting out my new leads. At the present moment, what I wanted most was a decent meal, a bottle of beer, a hug and a kiss from Maggie, and a good night's sleep in a bed that wasn't bolted to the floor of a jail cell. I flipped off the lights and started down the hall toward the elevator. Halfway there, an intense-looking man I vaguely remembered seeing in the city room earlier flagged me down.

"Jackson Gamble?"

I said I was.

"My name is Dave Quail, spelled like the bird, not with a 'y', like 'potatoe-with-an-E' from Indiana. I'm a staff writer here at the *Times*. Dick Dohrn said I might find you still down here."

He held out his left hand for me to shake. His right was missing. There was a steel orthopedic hook in its place. He caught me looking, grinned, and rapped hollowly on his right calf with the hook.

"The leg's gone, too, below the knee. Dozen or so years back, I was in the reserves, serving with NATO forces assigned to help the Polish military look for unexploded ordnance left over from the end of the Cold War. I wouldn't have believed after all this time that there was any of that shit left, but there was. I strayed a couple meters off the marked path and stepped on a live, anti-personnel mine in an area that was supposed to be secure. The doctors tell me there's some more stuff wrong inside that'll kill me, most likely sooner than later, but these are the only things that really stick out."

"Bad luck," I said. I shook his hand, feeling acutely self-conscious and not knowing exactly why. He must have read the expression on my face because he threw his head back and laughed good-naturedly. When he did, I could see that his neck and part of the right side of his face were spiderwebbed with faded surgical scars.

"Not as bad as it could have been," he said. "If that thing hadn't been degrading underground for two decades, it would have blown me to ounces. As it was, I was still six months in recovery and rehab. Before the accident, I was a session musician, working with some of the recording companies here in town. When I got hurt, a feature writer here at the *Times* picked up my story, and the paper ran with it. I couldn't play keyboards at a professional level anymore, but that same writer took an interest in my situation. He helped me get the job I have now, which is as associate music and entertainment editor for the paper. These days, I get front-row seats comped for any concert I want to attend, plus advance copies of every new recording made here in town. What could be better?"

Not getting blown halfway to Kingdom come in an old Soviet minefield, I could have said, but I let it pass.

"You said something about Dick Dohrn sending you to look for me?"

"He didn't send me. After you left, I just asked him where I could find you. Do you have a few minutes to talk?"

"Sure," I said. "Why not?"

He looked cautiously around, as if somebody might be listening from around the corner. "Not here."

"Okay, but then you're going to have to buy me a beer."

"Got just the place. Come on." Quail led me down the corridor, then up a flight of stairs to an exit door that opened onto the *Times* parking lot. As we walked, I took the opportunity to look him over a little more closely.

Quail was in his early forties. He was solidly built, neither short nor tall, and had a pinkish complexion and thinning blond hair. He wore soft denim jeans, a black polo shirt, and a tan linen sports coat. Both the jeans and the coat looked about two sizes too large, as if he'd either been sick or had gone on a serious diet since he'd bought them. He moved with a limp, but it was so slight that if I hadn't been aware of his injuries and been looking for it, I might not have noticed.

We cut diagonally across the parking lot and out the main gate, then around the corner to a bar called Zenger's. It was a newspaperman's hangout that took its name from the eighteenth-century *New York Weekly Journal* publisher John Peter Zenger. Way back in 1735, Zenger was charged, tried, and acquitted of a charge of seditious libel for printing articles critical of New York's colonial governor and, in the process, became a symbol of the idea of freedom of the press. His namesake watering hole was small, dark, and, at five o'clock in the afternoon, starting to fill up with newspaper people.

I glanced around and saw the walls were hung with matted and framed historic front pages from various newspapers. Headlines in 72-point type screamed the news of the lead stories of days gone by, including TITANIC SINKS, KENNEDY DEAD, GLENN IN ORBIT, MEN WALK ON MOON, JAPS DECLARE WAR, NIXON RESIGNS, TRUMP IMPEACHED, and famously, PLOT TO STEAL PRESLEY'S BODY. Mixed in among the headlines were photos of politicians, athletes, musicians, and celebrities, some autographed, some not, who had also made the front pages. I looked in vain for a photo of Charles Lambert and wondered whether his untimely death might eventually earn him an honored place on the wall of fame.

As we edged toward an available high-top table, I caught bits of conversations about everything, from the weather to the upcoming election to Vanderbilt's chances of getting invited to a bowl game this season. After we got settled, with a pitcher of beer and a bowl of pretzels between us, Dave Quail came to the point.

"I guess you're wondering why I wanted to talk to you."

"I am," I agreed, "but since you're paying for the beer, we can sit here for as long as you want, or until I get drunk enough to fall off my stool."

"Then I won't keep you in suspense. I understand you're looking for Albert Glass. I want to help you find him."

"Is that what Dick told you?"

"Oh, Christ, no. He didn't tell me anything." He took a drink of his beer. "When it comes to keeping his mouth shut, Dick could give a stuffed owl a run for its money."

"Then what gave you the idea I'm looking for Albert?"

"Four things." He used his prosthesis to tick them off one by one on the fingers of his good hand.

"First, nobody in the office has seen Albert or talked to him since last Friday. Now, that in itself is a little odd, since he usually comes in at least a couple of times a week to pick up his mail and telephone messages. Second, you show up at the city room for a hot and heavy session with Dohrn during the busiest time of the day. Maybe that doesn't mean anything by itself, but right after you left, Dick asks me sort of offhanded-like whether I've talked to Albert in the past day or so. That makes me start to wonder whether there's a connection. So then, fourth, I get your name from the receptionist, make a couple telephone calls, and find out you're a PI. Now I ask you, if you were me, what would you make of all that?"

"I don't know," I said, impressed with his detective skills. "Maybe nothing. Why would Dohrn ask you about Albert? Is he a friend of yours?"

"That might be putting it a bit too strongly," he said. "I'm not sure Albert is a friend of anybody, but he is the guy who wrote about me after the accident in the minefield. He came to visit me a few times when I was in the VA hospital in Memphis, and later when I was going through rehab. Maybe that makes me a little closer to him than anybody else on the staff. I guess Dick figured if anyone would know where Albert was, it'd be me."

"But you don't."

"No, and that's why I wanted to talk to you. See, like him or not, and he can be impossible to work with sometimes, Albert is a damn good reporter. I learned a lot of what I know about the newspaper business from him. If he's in some kind of a jam right now, and I can help him, I want to do it. I feel like I owe him that much."

"And you think that because he hasn't been around for a few days, he's in trouble? I had the impression it isn't all that unusual for a reporter working a beat like Albert's to be out of the office quite a bit of the time."

Quail shook his head. "It isn't, but there's more to it than just that. In the last few weeks, the quality of his work has been slipping. He's become less thorough than he should be, and except for his Friday column, his output has dropped to practically zero. It's almost as if he's lost interest in what he's doing."

"Could it be he just fell into a bottle, and now he's having trouble climbing back out again?"

Quail raised an eyebrow. "You know about that?"

I said, "It's not that hard to spot if you know what you're looking at."

"So then, you've met him?"

"Just once, a couple of days ago. He looked like a corpse searching for an open grave."

"Well, he seemed okay the last time I saw him. You have to get used to him."

"Could be he's just coasting for a while," I offered. "Or maybe he hasn't turned up anything lately that he thinks is worth reporting."

"I don't think so. Look, Nashville isn't Washington or New York City, but it's too big a city for Albert not to be able to find anything worth writing about. For him to be acting the way he has been lately, there has to be something seriously wrong."

I took a bite of pretzel. "Such as what, do you think?"

"Such as, I don't know. That's why I'm talking to you."

"Okay, let's start at the beginning. What is he working on right now?"

"I couldn't tell you that either. I'm not sure anybody ever knows unless it's Dick Dohrn."

"What about the Charles Lambert story?" I threw out. "Any chance Albert could still be working on that?"

"Lambert?" He seemed genuinely surprised at the reference. "I can't imagine why he would be. I mean, that story played out months ago. It was just a famous guy getting killed in a car crash. Is that what you were looking for in the morgue?"

I let his question pass. "Did you help Albert with the Lambert story?"

"Well, yeah, a little bit, but it wasn't anything important. As I said, my main job at the *Times* is writing about music and entertainment. Albert figured since the record industry was a place where I had connections, I might be able to gather some insights into Lambert and Black Strap Music. I worked up some biographical material and got a couple of quotes from some folks I know who're in the business, but that was all there was to it. You probably read some of what I came up with while you were in the morgue, but it was all just background. No byline. I doubt whether I spent more than half a day on the project, total."

Across the room, a cheer went up, and when I turned to look, I saw that two tables had gotten an impromptu basketball game going, flipping beer bottle caps into a planter hanging from the ceiling.

"How about this, then? When you were helping Albert, did you run across anything having to do with an organization called the Hermitage Group?"

"Nothing about the Group itself, except that Lambert was a member."

"Then you've heard of it."

"Of course, I've heard of it. Who hasn't? You'd have to be deaf, blind, and comatose not to have run across something about them either in the papers or television."

Some days, I thought, that was a pretty fair description of my level of civic involvement. "Okay, here's something else. Did Albert ever mention a woman named Darlene Munson? Have you ever heard that name before?"

He shook his head. "No, never heard of her. Look, Gamble, what the hell's going on here? Who are you working for?"

I couldn't see any harm in telling him. "Albert Glass."

His face registered genuine astonishment. "You're shitting me."

69

"I'm afraid not." I poured each of us another glass of beer. "Albert was in my office yesterday afternoon. He paid me three days in advance to do a job for him. But along the way, I ran into some problems that are starting to look like they might be serious, and now nobody seems to be able to find Albert."

"And you figure this trouble is connected to Charlie Lambert?"

"Not necessarily, but right now, I don't have anything else to go on. Lambert is the last high-profile story anybody can remember Albert working on. Also, Lambert had a lot of irons in the fire before he died, including selling his business and being involved with the Hermitage Group. Which, incidentally, has thrown its weight behind Roger Seacrist for governor. Any of that could have the potential to interest a reporter like Albert. That's why I wanted to see what the *Times* had in its records. I think it's at least a possibility he never stopped working on the Lambert story at all. I think Albert somehow figured out a possible connection between the Group, the governor's race, and Darlene Munson's disappearance. He just stayed with his original story and followed it off in a different direction without saying anything about it."

"I guess that could be," Quail said. "Sometimes, when you start working on a story, you don't know where it's going to take you. In this case, the easiest way to find out is to see what Albert has in his records."

"Albert keeps written records?"

"Every reporter keeps some kind of record. What did you think, we all had eidetic memories? Some of us use a voice recorder. Albert is old school. He keeps handwritten notebooks."

I had to admit I hadn't given it much thought one way or the other. "Do you have access to Albert's notebooks?"

He gave me a wicked grin. "He keeps them locked in a file cabinet at the *Times*. Five minutes and a couple of bent paper clips are all the access I need."

"You're going to break into his office?"

"No-o-o-o," he said slowly, "not into his office. You can't lock a cubicle. His file cabinet, on the other hand, might take a minute or so, but I can get into that, no problem. That is, unless you have a better idea?"

I didn't and said so. Quail checked his watch and drained the last of his beer.

"Listen, tell you what. I've got to get going right now, but if you hear from Albert before tomorrow morning, give me a call at the office. Otherwise, I'll start nosing around his files and see what I can find. Then let's plan on meeting back here about this time tomorrow. We can compare notes and then you can tell me what you really think is going on."

"Maybe I will."

We exchanged phone numbers, and then he disappeared out the door. I sat by myself for a few more minutes, finishing my beer and thinking about my new acquaintance. He was a good man, I decided. One worth trusting. He was decisive and inquisitive and had a strong sense of loyalty to a man who had helped him get started in the newspaper business. Also, he had managed to maintain an infectious good humor in the face of fearsome injuries that might have left a lesser man embittered for life.

When I got back to my car, I tried calling Albert's telephone number one more time. Albert still wasn't picking up, but his voicemail, obliging as ever, invited me to leave a message. I hung up before it had a chance to wish me a good day.

Chapter Ten

Instead of heading straight home, I stopped to have dinner with Maggie at her townhouse and then, as things turned out, ended up staying the night. Unfortunately, after knocking back a few more Stella's than I should have, I started telling her about my day. Never a good idea. Especially when I got around to describing what had happened in Harding the night before, including the part where I had spent half of it sitting in my car and the other half in the city lockup after first getting knocked on the head.

She wasn't impressed by my dedication to the job. Instead, she said, "What you're telling me is that this woman, this...what did you say was her name?"

"Darlene Munson."

"Darlene, right. What you're telling me is that you're not the only one looking for her?"

"It looks that way, yes."

"And whoever else is looking is willing to play rough." There was a pause while she took a sip of her drink, in this instance, vodka and cranberry juice. "And they could have killed you if they had wanted to. Does that sound about right?"

I had to admit, it did. And I waited for what I was sure she was going to say next.

She looked at me hard.

"Look, when I signed on with you, I knew what you did for a living, and I knew sometimes there were risks involved. But this sounds like more than that. This sounds like whatever is going on between this reporter and this woman he's got you looking for, somebody is going to wind up getting hurt.

72

I mean, for all you know, she could already be dead, right? And if she is, then what?"

"Then I stop looking, and it becomes a police problem." It sounded glib, I knew, and I instantly regretted not coming up with a better response. I waited for her to say something else, and when she didn't, I said, "Is this where you say you're not happy about what I do for a living and that you wish I'd find another line of work?"

"No." She put her hand gently to my face. "This is where I remind you of a promise that we made to one another way back in the beginning. Do you remember what it was?"

I did. Not long after we met, when Maggie first told me she was starting to have feelings for me, she could tell I wasn't sure about how to put into words a similar commitment. So, rather than make it a do-or-die proposition, she reminded me of an old Dusty Springfield song that had a line that went, "You don't have to say you love me, just be close at hand."

"I'm trusting you to stay close at hand," she said. "That means you have to stay alive and, in a perfect world, out of jail. Do you still think you can do that?"

"No matter what," I said.

"Then don't go getting yourself killed."

That night, we stayed up late to watch an old movie called *Sunset Boulevard*, which starred Gloria Swanson and William Holden. The story had to do with a washed-up, silent movie-era actress named Norma Desmond, who invites Joe Gillis, a struggling scriptwriter, into her decaying Sunset Boulevard mansion to help her resuscitate a turkey of a screenplay she had written in hopes of resurrecting her career. We nearly made it to the climactic—and-everybody's-seen-it-a-million-times—final scene before we both fell asleep on the couch.

"Mr. DeMille, I'm ready for my closeup."

When I opened my eyes several hours later, it was full daylight outside, and Maggie was in the kitchen frying pork sausage. Sometime during the night, she had awakened to retrieve a blanket from the upstairs bedroom and throw it over me. I awoke feeling rested, well-cared for, and except for some minor residual soreness in my jaw and a tender spot on the back of my head, nearly good as new.

While Maggie finished cooking breakfast, I went upstairs to shower, shave, and change into clean clothes.

Since Maggie and I have gotten seriously involved, we have each moved a number of personal items into one another's residences for what have become increasingly frequent sleepovers. In my case, that meant socks, underwear, a couple shirts, and some toiletries. Of course, that was virtually nothing compared to the mountain of makeup, undergarments, feminine products, blouses, skirts, slacks, and shoes she kept at my place. I was good for one night, maybe two at her place. Maggie could have stayed at my house for a month and never worn the same thing twice.

Over breakfast—an English muffin spread with peanut butter, pork sausage on the side, and a Diet Coke for me, and oatmeal, sausage, orange juice, and strawberry yogurt for Maggie—we shared the morning newspaper and got caught up on the local news. In no particular order, repair work on Interstate 40 would be commencing shortly, and commuters were encouraged to find alternate routes to work downtown. Because of the ongoing hot spell, fishing in area lakes was slow. Of special note, a Planned Parenthood clinic that was known to be providing abortion services for poor women was firebombed during the night. Included in that story was a statement by District Attorney Roger Seacrist that his office "…would prosecute to the fullest the person or persons involved, regardless of the fact that public sympathies seemed generally to lie with the perpetrators." He went on to say that the organized crime investigation undertaken by his office late last spring was nearly complete and that there would be an announcement of the findings within the next few days.

That last bit of political puffery reminded me that I still had work of my own to do, so after Maggie and I cleared the table and she went upstairs to get dressed, I turned my attention back to the notes I'd made on Charles Lambert the previous afternoon. I still wasn't sure what I was looking for, except that I had to think that whatever had gotten Albert curious about Lambert in the first place almost certainly must have been something with the potential to make page one of the newspapers. If what I had learned about Albert from Dick Dohrn and Dave Quail was even close to correct, nothing else would have interested him enough to pick up the thread.

Reviewing what I had learned so far, Charles Lambert, former songwriter and country music impresario, was killed in early spring in an automobile accident. Some months earlier he had sold his recording business to a third party called Talent Management Associates, or TMA, a company about which I knew absolutely nothing. At about the same time, Lambert was named finance chairman of the Hermitage Group, an organization of high-rolling do-gooders and civic boosters. Carver Dickinson, the publisher of the Nashville *Times,* was a member of the Group. So was Roger Seacrist, Davidson County District Attorney. The *Times* was supporting Roger Seacrist's run for governor in the fall. Albert Glass, who had opened an investigation into the life and death of Charles Lambert, was an employee of the Nashville *Times*. Albert believed that a woman named Darlene Munson was in possession of a file of some sort that would tie all the facts known so far into a neat bundle that would make big news. However, Darlene had gone missing, and so Albert hired me to bird-dog her. For reasons not yet known, it also appeared that one or more agencies of law enforcement were looking for her and had taken an interest in me in the process. And now, Albert Glass was nowhere to be found.

That begged a couple of questions. What exactly was TMA? What did it do, and who owned it? Did Carver Dickinson or the Heritage Group have any connection, directly or indirectly, to Darlene Munson? And most importantly, what was I not seeing?

By the third time through, I was spinning my wheels. Lines and words were running together into a hopeless tangle of nonsense prose. More and more, the only thing my mind seemed able to grasp was that two people were going to get hurt because of something that was staring me right in the face, if only I could make it out. Frustrated, I reached for my phone and dialed Dick Dohrn's number at the *Times*. He picked up on the second ring.

"What's the word from Albert?" he asked, without preliminaries. "Have you been able to get hold of him?"

"Not so far. I was hoping you'd have something for me."

"Not a thing. I tried reaching him myself three times last night and again this morning." He took a breath and let it out. "I'll tell you something, Jackson. The way things stand now, I'm thinking seriously of bringing in the police."

"To what end?" I took a swallow of Diet Coke.

"To help us locate Albert. If nothing else, they could put a trace on his phone. At least then we'd know if he's okay."

I said, "You could do that, but I'm not sure we've gotten to that point just yet. And even if he stays missing a while longer, what are you going to tell the cops? Albert's only been out of pocket for a couple of days. Given his line of work, in their book, that's hardly cause for alarm. Besides, he is still my client, and I probably owe it to him to make sure he doesn't find himself tripping over a bunch of clumsy cops right in the middle of whatever he's working on."

"Then what do you suggest?"

"Let me go on doing what I'm doing. A guy like Albert is much too high-profile to stay lost indefinitely. Right now, my bet would be that he went someplace to have a drink or two, got rolled up onto the beach in a tsunami of Old Crow, and turned off his phone so he could sleep it off without anybody bothering him."

Dick didn't say anything to that, but I could tell he wasn't entirely sold on the idea.

"You find what you were looking for in the morgue?"

"Better to say I got a lot of information. When I figure out whether it's what I'm looking for, I'll let you know."

"Do you think Albert's disappearance is related to the Lambert story?"

"At this point, I don't know what else there is to think. Look, Lambert was a busy guy, and he hung around with a lot of well-connected individuals. Unless something we haven't thought about pops up, what else have we got to go on?"

There was a short silence at his end. "Did Dave Quail talk to you last night before you left?"

"So, then you did send him looking for me."

"He sent himself," Dick said, a little defensively. "I just told him where to find you. But even if I had, what of it? I lost a lot of sleep thinking over what we talked about yesterday, and it's got me thinking Albert really has gotten mixed up in something serious. And if he has, then so have you, and so has this young woman you're both looking for. If you'll let him, Dave Quail can help you."

"And help the *Times* too, if there turns out to be a story in all this, is that it?"

"I'm going to pretend I didn't hear that," he said. "Albert Glass is an employee of this newspaper. You're my friend. Dave Quail is both. What's the harm in me not wanting any of you to get hurt?"

I realized my comment was just a bit out of line. "You're right, Dick, I'm sorry. No harm at all. And I appreciate the thought. I really do. I just wish you'd give me a little more time to work this out on my own before you send for reinforcements, that's all."

He gave me a long sigh. "It surely seems to be taking me a long time to pay you back for the Ozburn story. All right, twenty-four hours, and that's it. But for Christ's sake, keep me posted, will you?"

I promised I would and hung up.

Before I kissed Maggie goodbye and went on my way, I made one more call to ask a favor of a deputy coroner I knew named Claude Briscoe. I knew it would probably be a waste of time, but it bothered me a little that the publisher of the Nashville *Times*, Carver Dickinson, was as closely involved with the Hermitage Group as he was. I had no particular reason to be suspicious, but if there was something being glossed over in the *Times* account of Charles Lambert's auto accident, who better to sanitize the story than Dickinson? And who stood to be more of a nuisance in making sure the story got a second look than Albert Glass? I figured a quick check of Lambert's death certificate would help resolve at least that question once and for all. As I expected it would, it cost me twenty dollars, but Claude agreed to see what he could find out and call me back.

Chapter Eleven

It wasn't nearly as exciting as Christmas morning, but the repairs the super had made to my office door were enough to warm the cockles of my ex-cop's heart. I had to give the guy credit. He hadn't skimped on materials. I had a brand-new steel door, a heavy steel frame, and a no-shit deadbolt lock. The next scumbag that wanted to break in would have to bring his own wrecking ball, or at least a good-sized sledgehammer and a couple of sandwiches.

I worked into the early afternoon cleaning up the wreckage of my office and checking in at regular intervals with Albert Glass's voicemail. For all the response my calls got me, I might as well have used the time trying to get in touch with Santa Claus, or maybe my congressman. Either Albert hadn't bothered to respond to his messages in nearly two days, or else he had and wouldn't—or couldn't—answer them.

Just to be sure I wasn't overlooking the obvious, I tried an old telephone book and then called directory assistance, to see whether Albert was listed under another number. He wasn't. And since I hadn't heard anything more from Dave Quail or Dick Dohrn, I felt safe assuming Albert hadn't showed up back at the office, either.

I was starting to think Dick might have been right. Maybe it was time to bring in the cops and let them take over the whole mess. But somehow, I wasn't convinced the situation was right for that just yet, if for no other reason than, what was there to tell them? That an investigative reporter who didn't keep regular office hours and who was also a known alcoholic had slipped his tether for a couple of days? Would that be enough to get a warrant for telephone surveillance, or to enter his residence to search for—what, his dead body? Maybe my wanting more time to work things out was simply a defensive reflex, a need to salve my injured ego, not only for having botched my original assignment, but also for managing to misplace my own client in the process.

While I sat brooding over what to do next, the telephone rang. It was Claude Briscoe from the coroner's office, calling back with the information I had asked for. I could tell from Claude's tone of voice that he didn't think what he had for me was worth a double sawbuck, but I also knew he'd expect to be paid just the same. In this business, the merchandise comes with no guarantee of quality.

According to Claude, Charles Lambert had been transported by ambulance to County Hospital at four forty-five on the morning of April 17. He was pronounced dead on arrival at County. He had suffered massive head injuries, as well as multiple lacerations of the face, neck, and upper body. His sternum had been crushed, and his spine snapped near the second, third, and fifth vertebrae. The cause of death was attributed to cerebral trauma, but that was mostly because there is only so much space for cause on a death certificate. He could just as easily have bled to death from the fragments of windshield that slashed his throat or been killed by the impact of the steering wheel as it caved in his chest and stopped his heart in mid-beat. Although the airbag had deployed, it had apparently done so when the car clipped a mile-marker sign near the overpass. By the time the Beemer hit the bridge, the bag had already deflated, providing no cushion against the much more violent impact of the overpass.

On a hunch, I asked, "Any chance this could have been a suicide?"

"How do you mean?"

"I was thinking maybe death by BMW. I read where Lambert sold his business a few months before he was killed. Could he have been in some kind of financial trouble, or maybe he was despondent over having to sell the signature accomplishment of his lifetime? I don't imagine that's an easy thing to do."

"Depends on how much he sold it for. For all any of us knows, it made him rich. Anyway, you'd have to talk to the cops about that. All that showed up here was a guy mashed up in a car wreck. What he might have been thinking about at the time is anybody's guess."

"Okay," I said. "Was there anything else?"

"I was on vacation that week, so I didn't do the actual postmortem. I'm just looking at the paperwork filled out at the time. It says here there were significant amounts of alcohol and cocaine in his system. He was a big man, so it was a borderline call, but there was enough of either one to make him at least partially impaired. Put them both together, though, plus the road conditions and the lateness of the hour, and I'd have to say, it's not too surprising what happened after that. The highway patrolman who filled out the accident report estimated that Lambert had struck the bridge at better than ninety miles an hour. The most logical guess is that our man fell asleep behind the wheel and woke up in the company of the angels. Formal identification of the body was made later that morning by somebody named Audra Lambert. I don't know, I guess that's the guy's wife."

There was one new and interesting wrinkle to Claude's report, however. Since the accident, copies of Lambert's death certificate had been requested by four different parties, including the Metro police on April 19th, the National Life and Casualty Insurance Company on May 9th, Albert Glass of the *Nashville Times* on May 22nd, and Christopher Priest, an assistant prosecutor from the Davidson County District Attorney's office, on July 8th. That last request was only a little more than two weeks old. Claude said if I wanted a paper copy for myself, it would cost another ten dollars. I thanked him just the same and promised to drop the twenty I owed him in the mail.

Death certificates are part of the public record, so they're pretty much available to anyone who asks. Looking over the list of requests for Lambert's death certificate, I could explain all but the last one fairly easily. The police would have needed a copy to close out their investigation, as would the insurance company to process the claim for death benefits. The third week in May was about the time Albert was working on his story, so he probably would have asked for one in the course of developing background data. But why was the D.A. so interested nearly three months after the fact? And more to the point, was there a connection between that request and the two cops that had been nosing around the Rustic Retreat Motor Court asking questions about Darlene Munson? Finally, it now appeared to be established fact that Charley Lambert was driving under the influence of both alcohol and cocaine, yet the newspaper accounts of his death failed to mention it. I could only assume that was because disclosing his condition would reflect poorly on the deceased as well as the Hermitage Group.

Answers are where you find them, so I got back on the telephone and called the one person connected with the case I hadn't spoken with yet, Mrs. Audra Lambert. It took some considerable effort to talk my way past an aggressively officious houseman and then a few minutes more of waiting on hold until the lady herself came to the phone. When I finally got her on the line, I told her who I was and, in a general way, explained I was working on an investigation in which her late husband's name had come up. No problems, I assured her, just a few details that needed clearing up. She sounded less than enthusiastic but agreed to let me have a few minutes if I could come right over. I said I'd be there in half an hour.

* * *

The address Audra Lambert gave me was in Hendersonville, a community on the city's north side. The house itself was a three-story French Provincial that might have been a little smaller than Ryman Auditorium. The lot was somewhere around three acres, with a hundred or so feet of frontage and two boat docks on Old Hickory Lake. The property was protected by a six-foot powder-coated steel fence that ran the length of the property on three sides. If you were accustomed to spending your afternoons floating on the lake while hobnobbing with music industry royalty, or maybe sharing an evening with a few dot-com masters of the universe, the place might not have seemed like anything very special. Otherwise, you'd probably find yourself straightening your tie and wishing you'd worn your good suit before you got halfway up the driveway.

I pulled into the circular driveway past twin sentinel gateposts, where a small FOR SALE sign hung discreetly and parked in the turning circle behind a blood-red Porsche Panamera whose license read "4-AUDRA." I wondered, idly, if machines could talk, what would Stuttgart's jazzy set of designer wheels have to say to my geriatric, two-ton Motown monster.

I pressed the doorbell and waited as an answering chime echoed softly inside the house, playing the first eight notes from "What a Friend We Have in Jesus." After a moment, the front door was opened by a guy who looked as if he might have been chiseled from a block of granite. He was close to my height and weight, but that was about as far as the similarities went. He was twenty years younger and an easy ten inches broader across a chest that looked hard enough that you could crack walnuts against it. He wore New Balance sneakers and a light blue warm-up suit with a matching headband. His forehead was dappled with fine droplets of sweat, the way the hood of a car beads in the rain after a fresh application of wax. A stub of a toothpick protruded from one corner of his mouth. A raging case of acne and a receding hairline strongly suggested his impressive physical development had been helped along with regular injections of HGH.

He stood in the doorway looking me over as if I'd misread my invitation and had shown up for a black-tie dinner wearing cargo shorts and an aloha shirt.

"Help you?"

"Jackson Gamble to see Audra Lambert." I recognized his voice from the telephone and showed him my ID. "I called earlier," I added helpfully. "She's expecting me."

He glanced indifferently at the ID and nodded. "You were supposed to be here twenty minutes ago."

"Traffic on the Interstate," I said. "It's a bitch this time of day."

He nodded. "Wait here. I'll see if Mrs. Lambert is still available." Then he stepped back inside and shut the door in my face. I stood on the porch and sweated in the mid-day heat.

Out on the lawn, a couple of red squirrels were chasing one another up and down the trunk of a big oak tree, chattering back and forth in high-pitched, excited tones. As I stood watching, one of them noticed me and interrupted the game long enough to sit up on his haunches and scold me in squirrel talk for having the bad manners to stare. I tried explaining that I meant no offense, just force of occupational habit. He let me know in no uncertain terms he wasn't buying it.

In only slightly less time than it must have taken Noah to construct the Ark, the front door opened again, and Sweatsuit motioned me inside with a jerk of his thumb. I followed him down a long, paneled entry hall to a set of double doors at the opposite end of the house. Sweatsuit, with what by then I was beginning to understand was his customary charm, stood to one side and indicated that I was to go in. As I started to step past him, he stopped me with a hand placed firmly against my chest.

I said, "Do we have a problem?"

"Not yet."

"Then what?"

"Just a friendly word of warning," he said, not sounding very friendly at all. "I don't know who you are or what your game is, but lately, Mrs. Lambert has had no end of operators coming around wanting interviews or selling investment schemes, trying to get their hands on her money. If you've got any ideas about that kind of thing, I'd advise you to just leave right now the way you came in."

"No money," I said. "No interviews and nothing to sell. Just a couple of questions, and I'll be on my way."

He shifted his toothpick from one side of his mouth to the other. "Make sure questions are all it is. And another thing." There was a pause, I guessed, for effect. "When she tells you it's time to go, you're gone."

His routine was getting perilously close to its sell-by date. "What happens if I stop on the way out to tie my shoelace? Are you going to turn me over your knee and spank me?"

The muscles in his jaw tightened, but he kept his voice under control. "You don't want to fuck around with me, friend. I could break you into half a dozen pieces before the first one hit the floor."

"You could be right. And I'm not your friend. But unless you think the lady of the house would appreciate having us smash up the furniture while we find out, you'd better take your hand off me right now. Also, if I were you, I'd throttle back a little on whatever it is you're juicing with. That stuff will take years off the back end of your life."

"Like you care." He glared at me, and I thought for a second he might actually make a move. Then the moment passed, and he let his arm drop harmlessly to his side.

"There'll be another time," he said.

"There usually is," I agreed and left him standing in the doorway.

Chapter Twelve

No other way to say it, Audra Lambert was a fine-looking woman. No, that's not right. Not even close. She was much more than that. She was drop-dead gorgeous. The photos I'd seen in the newspaper didn't come within two zip codes of the genuine article.

I guessed her to be a little north of forty, but not far enough that the breezes had started to turn cold. She was wearing a white linen skirt, a yellow and white striped blouse, and a delicate gold necklace that held a single diamond. Her eyes were a rich hazel. Her hair was honey blonde. She wore it combed straight back from her forehead and gathered into a short ponytail, the way a swimmer or a tennis player would. She had high, aristocratic cheekbones, flawless skin, and smooth, suntanned legs that seemed to stretch into the middle of next week.

At twenty-five, she would have had a figure that only the luckiest of men would ever get nearer to than an airbrushed centerfold in a slick-paper men's magazine. Now, fifteen or so years later, give or take, she had a slightly softer, fuller shape that fit her as comfortably as Ben Franklin fits a hundred-dollar bill.

She was talking on the telephone, sitting with her legs crossed on a small settee in front of a set of French doors. Beyond the doors was a swimming pool, a manicured lawn, and a carefully cultivated garden that was a riot of red, yellow, and orange flowers. Pansies, I guessed, although, for all I know about flowers, they could just as easily have been Venus flytraps. Beyond the lawn was Old Hickory Lake, with the sunlight dancing atop the waves. A power boat that easily cost somewhere in the mid-six figures was tied to one of the two docks. A pontoon party boat was moored to the other.

On the opposite side of the room, in an elaborate gold-leaf frame, hung a portrait of General Nathan Bedford Forrest. The old Klan founder and Grand Wizard was depicted riding a dappled charger, smartly arrayed in the gray-and-gold dress uniform of a Confederate cavalry commander. He was waving a saber over his head and scowling at the world as if he was ready to jump-start the War of Northern Aggression, as it is still called by some, all over again. From the severe expression the artist had painted on his face, it looked as if part of his duties in the afterlife included passing review on Audra Lambert's gentlemen callers. I didn't even want to guess what he must have thought about me, although seeing the portrait made me wonder for the hundredth time what was behind this part of the country's fascination with him, as the old slaver seemed to be represented everywhere. There is a Nathan Bedford Forrest State Park on Kentucky Lake, and until recently, a bust in the state capitol building as well as a bizarre statue, since removed, of Forrest mounted on a horse located alongside Interstate 65 south of downtown that some wag had doused with a bucket of pink paint.

When Audra Lambert saw me come into the room, she said, "I'll have to call you back," and put the phone down on the table next to her.

"Mister Gamble." She extended her hand for me to shake.

"Mrs. Lambert," I said, taking it. "I appreciate you seeing me. I hope I'm not intruding?"

"Not at all." She motioned me toward a satin-covered armchair. I showed her my license. She looked at it carefully before handing it back.

"You know, when you called, I didn't have the slightest idea what to expect. I'm afraid the only experience I've had with private investigators is on television."

"And?"

"You'd do nicely, I think." Then she added, "You must get asked this all the time, but I'm curious how someone gets into your line of work in the first place."

I shrugged. "It's a pretty common story, really. Most of the operatives I know are either ex-cops or former FBI agents. They put in their time and retire. After a few years, they get bored with fishing or playing golf every day and start looking for something else to keep themselves busy. Besides P.I. work or security, there isn't too much else we're qualified to do."

"Is that what you did?"

"Well, I was a cop, if that's what you're asking, but I didn't retire. I was, what shall we say, encouraged to seek employment elsewhere."

"You mean you got fired." She threw me a look of mock horror. "Is this something I should know about before I start answering any of your questions?"

"It was politics mostly and not very exciting. In this state, you can't get a license if you've got a criminal record."

"Even so, you must have a very interesting life."

"If you're talking about what I do for a living, it's not nearly as exciting as what you might think. Mostly, what private investigators do is run errands for attorneys. The rest of the time, they investigate inventory shrinkages, chase after bail skippers, runaway spouses, and missing children. Other times, they're chasing insurance scammers and ex-husbands who don't keep up their child support payments."

"Then I'm afraid you've come all the way out here for nothing, Mr. Gamble. I have no children, and my husband hasn't run off with another woman. He was killed in an automobile accident several months ago."

"I know that Mrs. Lambert and I'm sorry for your loss. That's not what I wanted to see you about. I specialize in missing persons investigations, not domestic work."

"I see." She picked up a tall glass from the table next to her and sipped the contents. As she did, I found myself noticing a generous expanse of thigh showing through the slit in her skirt. She caught me looking and shifted on the couch to cover it up again. From the other side of the room, Nathan Bedford Forrest fairly bristled in disapproval.

I cleared an imaginary obstruction in my throat. "Look, Mrs. Lambert, I don't want to take up any more of your time than I have to, so why don't I just ask what I came to ask you, and then I'll be on my way."

"Have something to drink first." She poured me a glass of something dark from a frosted pitcher, then reached for a bottle of clear liquid. "It's just iced tea with a little splash of vodka. If you want something stronger, I'll have to get it."

"Iced tea is fine. I'll pass on the vodka," I waited while she poured before taking the offered glass.

"Mrs. Lambert, the reason I wanted to speak with you is that I've been retained by a client to help locate a certain young woman who's gone missing. I'm sure you'll understand when I say that I'm not in a position to tell you very much about it, but in the course of my investigation, your husband's name has come up."

"Come up in what way?"

I tried to think of a way to phrase it delicately, then decided there wasn't one. "The client who hired me works for one of the newspapers here in town. After your husband was—after he died, this individual was working on a story about him. A retrospective about his life and his music, as I understand it. Now, I don't know if there is any connection between your husband and the woman I was hired to find, but right now, I'm chasing down whatever leads I can find."

"So, let me see if I understand this. You think that because this person, this reporter you mentioned, was writing a story about my husband and then later hired you to look for a missing woman, that they must somehow have been acquainted with one another, is that right?"

"I'm suggesting there might be," I said, realizing as I said it how thin even that must have sounded.

"I see." There was a pause. "Does your young woman have a name, Mr. Gamble?"

"Yes. Her name is Darlene Munson."

Time seemed to hold its breath as Audra Lambert drummed her fingernails against the side of her glass.

"It would seem that perhaps you coming to see me may not be a waste of time after all," she said at last. "The woman you're looking for was my late husband's secretary, or should I say his personal assistant. My husband was screwing her every chance he got."

Chapter Thirteen

And there it was. I don't know which surprised me more, the clarity of the picture now that the puzzle was coming together, or the evident ease with which I had managed to put my hands on the missing piece. Albert Glass. Darlene Munson. Charley Lambert. And maybe even the Hermitage Group. All were connected. And the file, whatever was in it, was the glue that held it all together.

Audra Lambert took a sip from her glass and looked at me speculatively over the rim.

"Now that we've aired out that little bit of dirty laundry, I expect you're going to tell me why you're looking for Darlene. What's she done to attract all this attention?"

"In a minute. Let me get one or two other things straight first. How long did she work for your husband at Black Strap?"

"Do you mean in a professional capacity, or otherwise?"

"Let's stay with professionally for now."

"In that case, the best I can remember, she was there about two years."

"And after your husband sold Black Strap, did she continue working for the company?"

"Yes, she did. Whether she's still employed there, I wouldn't know."

"Then it's possible she's moved on." I made a mental note to find out. "Have you been in contact with her at all since the change of ownership?"

"No," she said coldly. "I can't think of anything we would have to discuss." She paused, as if to gather her thoughts. "Mister Gamble, if you've learned anything at all about my late husband, then you must know that he—what's the term? He lived large. Big cars, big house, big parties, big-name talent. And none of that should be too surprising, considering where he started out and what all he finally accomplished."

"Nothing to be ashamed of," I said. "He threw a long shadow."

"Yes, he did. And that was all fine as long as the money kept coming in. But when it stopped—and it did stop, and rather abruptly at that—his interest shifted to politics and, unfortunately, to other women. So, as you might imagine, keeping track of my husband's extramarital affairs has never been at the top of my list of things to do. And even if it were, there were so many, I would hardly know where to start."

"Personal assistants or mistresses?" I said and regretted it instantly. She gave me a look that could have etched my name into a gravestone.

"I'm sorry, Mrs. Lambert, I don't mean to open any old wounds. I'm just trying to gather information. As your husband's assistant, would Darlene have had access to his personal correspondence, or to the company's financial records?"

"Correspondence, yes, obviously. I don't know about financial statements. Black Strap was a privately held company, so financial information was not widely available. Why is that important?"

"Because to get back to your original question, there's a strong possibility that Darlene's disappearance may be related to documents that have something to do with Black Strap. A file of some sort is what I've been told. Whatever it contains is supposedly sensitive enough to provide a motive for somebody to silence her." When she didn't say anything to that, I said, "That means somebody might want to kill her."

"And?"

"And I think there's a likelihood that either she stole it from your husband, or else he gave it to her for safekeeping."

"Do you know any of this for a fact, or are you just guessing?"

"Call it an educated guess," I said. "I've been doing this for a long time."

"Well, then, maybe you also have some idea of what this mysterious file might contain?"

"Not for sure. For all I know, it could be the formula to turn lead into gold. It's just that based on what I've been able to turn up so far, nothing else makes sense."

She frowned a little at that. "Well, as you say, you've been doing this a long time. But I wonder, and please don't be offended, Mr. Gamble. But if Darlene really is in danger, shouldn't the police be working on this instead of you?"

"Unless she turns up pretty soon, they will be. Right now, as you've pointed out, there's very little hard evidence to support anything I've told you. If something turns up to suggest she's met with foul play, then the police will obviously have to be brought in."

"Something like a dead body, for instance?"

"That would definitely get their attention, yes. I'd hate to think things will go that far."

A look of irritation flitted across her face. "You still haven't explained what any of this has to do with my husband."

"It's like I told you," I said. "My client is a newspaper reporter. He's working on a story that he says is very big."

She took a last swallow of her drink. "Aren't they all?"

"Point taken. In this case, however, the credibility of his story depends upon the file we talked about. I don't know what it's about, but my client believes it's enough to ruin the reputations of a lot of people once he prints the story."

"And now you're trying to find the file?"

"No, that's not it at all. I don't care about the file, or the story, if there even turns out to be one. My interest is in finding Darlene Munson. I'm also trying to find my client. All of a sudden, nobody seems to be able to get in touch with him, either."

She gave me the smallest of smiles. "Excuse me for saying so, but it seems like you're doing a better job losing people than you are finding them."

I didn't know what to say to that, so I kept my mouth shut and waited.

"Let me be clear." She compressed her lips into a tight line. "My husband ran a record company, Mr. Gamble. That's it. Full stop. He wrote and recorded music. For you to suggest that he was mixed up in some kind of criminal conspiracy with his former secretary is, to say the least, farfetched. It's also slanderous and possibly defamation of character as well. If you persist in spreading such stories, I will have my attorney take steps to stop you. And if some newspaperman has got an idea that he's going to print a story that maligns my husband or his reputation, I will sue the hell out of both him and the paper he works for."

It was my turn to show a little irritation. "I'm not spreading stories of any kind, Mrs. Lambert. That's not how I make my living. I'm talking to you because I'm trying to find a young woman who's gone missing and who has in her possession something belonging to your late husband. It could be nothing at all, or it could be compromising photos, or love letters, or something that might damage your late husband's legacy. That's not something I want to see happen, but I do have a client who's paid me to do a job."

"So then, am I right in saying what you want is money?" Her eyes got narrow, and her voice went up several decibels. "Because if that's why you came here, you should know there's practically no money left. There's a mortgage on the house, and most of the proceeds from the sale of the business went to settle various debts my husband ran up when he was trying to raise cash to save the business."

A movement of some kind caught her eye, and she shifted in her seat to look toward the entrance to the room. I turned to see what it was and saw her house man standing in the doorway, his muscles tensed, looking like a big, blue panther, ready to pounce.

"I heard voices raised." He gave me a venomous look. "Is everything all right, Mrs. Lambert? Would you like me to ask the gentleman to leave?" He took two steps into the room.

"No, we're fine. Thank you for checking."

"Are you sure?"

"Yes. Everything's fine." The big man glared at me for a moment longer, then turned and left the room. But he didn't look one bit happy.

I took a deep breath. "Let me take another run at this before we get into a fight neither of us is looking for. I didn't come here to frighten you, or to threaten you in any way. And I'm not suggesting your husband did anything illegal, or even that anything illegal was taking place. As far as that goes, I really don't care. I don't want to slander your husband's name, and I'm certainly not trying to shake you down. If it turns out he was involved in something he shouldn't have been, I'll do the best I can to keep you both out of it. But none of that changes the fact that Darlene Munson's life may be in danger. Finding her before she gets hurt is my only interest."

She started to say something, but I held up my hand to stop her.

"Also...I'm not looking for any money from you, and if my questions have given you that impression, I'm sorry. You can call your lawyer if you want, or you can get that big idiot that was here just now to throw me out. But regardless of any of that, until this gets straightened out, I'm going to go right on doing the job I was hired to do."

She gave me a look I couldn't quite read, and I thought for a moment she was about to ask me to leave. Then the fire seemed to go out of her eyes, and she let her face relax into a small smile. "Apology accepted if that's what it was. But since you brought it up, I wouldn't recommend letting Elvis hear you making fun of him. He's very sensitive about his image."

"Elvis? That guy in the sweat suit that matches his baby blue eyes? His name is Elvis?"

"Elvis Preston, that's right. I don't know if his parents were music lovers, or if they just had a sense of humor. But it does make him sound as though he ought to be in the movies or something, doesn't it?"

"Or something," I agreed.

She said, with a hint of amusement, "Don't tell me you two had some kind of a disagreement."

"He seemed to want to convince me he's tough. I've met tougher."

"I suppose it's my fault for not keeping after him about his manners. It's just that since Charles died, I've had so many people trying to sell something, or get me to invest my money in one get-rich-quick scheme or another. Sometimes Elvis can be very helpful when they get a little too persistent."

I grinned at that. "Funny, but I would have said you're a woman who can take perfectly good care of herself. Where did you find him, anyway?"

"Well, I didn't go looking for a bodyguard on Craigslist, if that's what you're asking. He was recommended by a friend who employed him as a personal trainer. After my husband died, I didn't feel comfortable being in the house all by myself. I hired Elvis as sort of a house sitter. He makes me feel safer than an alarm system, and he's quieter than a watchdog. Also, he cooks and keeps the house clean."

"And those are just a few of his talents, I'm guessing."

"Now your dirty mind is showing. As a matter of fact, I think Elvis has a special friend, if you know what I mean. He's certainly never shown the slightest interest in me."

I smiled at her. "Somehow, I find that hard to believe."

"Is that a compliment?"

"I guess it is if you want it to be, yes."

"I don't know, maybe I do at that. People look at this house, and they think about the lifestyle my husband and I enjoyed, and they assume I must still be wealthy—and lonely. As a result, most of the people I've met in the last three months seem to either be looking for sex or money, or both."

"And I've given you the impression those things don't interest me."

"No. But at least you had the good manners to blush when you were staring at my legs before. It made me think you might be a little different from the others."

At first, I thought she might be making a joke. But there was a note in her voice that said maybe she wasn't. I couldn't have said the precise moment when, but in a roundabout way, Audra Lambert and I had arrived at a point where our conversation seemed to be taking a slow but unmistakable turn in a different direction. Where that might lead was anybody's guess, but all the same, I could hear a small alarm bell starting to ring in the back of my head.

I said carefully, "Mrs. Lambert, I have to ask you this. You said people are coming around asking for money. Are any of them trying to blackmail you?"

"No, they are not. Where would you get an idea like that?"

"Go back to the beginning. You are a recently widowed woman with a late husband who was an important man in the music industry. After that, he was involved, however briefly, in statewide politics. Both those roles involve a lot of high-flying deal-making, maybe even the kinds of things the public is better off not knowing. Forget about Darlene Munson for a moment. What I'm talking about now is this file that seems to have disappeared along with her. It doesn't take a great deal of imagination to ask whether you'd be willing to pay to keep it under wraps."

"That assumes that I have knowledge of whatever it is you think these people are trying to keep hidden. But as far as I know, there are no secrets to keep. I've already told you, my husband wrote and produced music. So far, the only thing I've heard from you is a story about a missing woman and a newspaper reporter whose name you haven't yet told me."

"The reporter's name is Albert Glass," I said, watching for a reaction and getting none. "Have you ever met him, or did your husband ever mention his name?"

"Albert Glass?" She wrinkled her brow, as if trying to shake the name loose from her memory. "Well, no, I don't know him, but I did meet him. I spoke with him after the accident. He came to the house to ask me some questions."

"Do you remember when that was?"

"Not exactly, no. I think it was about two months after the accident."

"That would make it around the end of June. Does that sound right?"

"Maybe a little earlier than that. Does it really matter?"

"Probably not. I'm just trying to get a timeline straight in my head. What kind of questions did he ask?"

"He wanted information about Charles. Where was he from, how long we were married, things like that. He said he was working on a feature story about my husband and his music."

"Is that all he wanted to know?"

"As best I can recall, that was it."

"By any chance, did he suggest that your husband's death might not have been an accident?"

She looked up sharply. "What?"

"I'm sorry. I know this must be upsetting. I'm just wondering if it's possible your husband may have decided to take his own life for some reason."

"That's ridiculous. Charles's life was not perfect, but he had no reason to kill himself."

"What about money problems? It seems to have been common knowledge, at least in the music industry, that Black Strap was facing bankruptcy. For a lot of people, the thought of losing something they spent their entire life building up might be too much to live with."

She paused for a moment, collecting her thoughts. "Tastes in music change, as I'm sure you must know. In Charles's case, he wasn't able to adjust. Younger audiences were looking for a different sound, and sales of music distributed on the Black Strap label fell off. We burned through most of our savings and then took a mortgage on the house to try to save the business. After that, Charles invested in a couple of questionable deals that didn't pan out to try to make some money, and when that didn't work, he tried gambling as a last resort. Eventually, there was no choice except to sell the business."

I tried to sound sympathetic. "That must have been very difficult for him."

"At first, he was heartbroken to see his life's work wither and nearly die. I know I was. But then, he seemed to get past it, and I thought maybe he was ready to start over with something else."

"Like a new label, for instance?"

"That was one possibility. Maybe something retro. You know, go back to the roots of country music. We talked about it. I was even looking forward to it myself. I thought it might be fun to make a new beginning, just the two of us, like we did in the beginning. The way our marriage was falling apart, we needed a new direction. But then there was the accident, and that was the end of that."

I considered that. "And when you spoke with Albert Glass, none of this came up?"

"No. As I said, he told me he was gathering information for a feature article on my husband's musical legacy."

"And that was the only time you spoke with him?"

"That's correct."

96

"How about another reporter, a man named Dave Quail? Do you remember talking to him?"

"No. And before you ask, I've never spoken to anyone on *Sixty Minutes* or *Face the Nation*, either. Is there anyone else you'd like to know about?"

"I think that just about covers it."

"Good. Then let's talk about something else."

"All right, let's try this. Were you active in your husband's business? For instance, when you took a second on the house, or when the business was sold, did you have to sign off on any of the paperwork?"

"Well, the house was in both our names, but not the business." She paused to brush an errant strand of hair away from her face. "We had an understanding. I kept out of his day-to-day affairs, and he kept out of mine. As part of the bargain, I got to live my life the way you see here, and he had an attentive wife to accompany him to whatever was his business or social function of the week."

"Did these functions include meetings of the Hermitage Group?"

"Definitely not. The Hermitage Group is a private club for men like Charles who have big bank accounts and bigger ambitions. It was strictly off-limits to anyone not directly involved. Why, I don't know. I don't think they ever did anything really important besides talk big and occasionally get their pictures into the newspapers."

"Well, it looks like they're pretty close to getting one of their members elected governor this November."

"Oh, yes, Roger Seacrist. How could I have forgotten that grubby little man? Before that, it was a political convention, or a major league baseball team. I got tired of hearing about it. With Charles, there was always something larger than life, waiting right around the next corner."

"Big men dream big dreams," I said.

"Now, you sound like Charles. Every man has a dream, he'd say. Some are just bigger than others. You know, I think the two of you might have had a lot in common."

Given the direction my life had taken, I couldn't imagine what it might have been, but kept my opinion to myself.

Audra poured herself another drink and sank back in her seat. Outside, a breeze rattled the leaves in the big magnolia tree behind the house. Off in the distance, through the open window, I could hear the drone of an outboard motor somewhere out on the lake.

"Charles and I had a dream once, you know."

I didn't know but nodded just the same.

"When we first met, I was seventeen years old and singing in a gospel choir in Rock Hill, South Carolina. I was wearing a white robe and my first pair of high-heeled shoes. Charles had a revival show in town for a couple of weekends. I could sing a little, so I was one of the local girls chosen to be in the choir.

"By the time the revival moved on, I had fallen hopelessly in love with Charles. It was a teenaged-girl thing, of course. A crush, I suppose you'd call it. I'd been out with a few boys, but next to Charles, they all just seemed, I don't know, like little boys. I wrote Charles a letter, telling him how I felt. I don't know what I expected him to do. I thought he might write me back, or maybe send me a picture with an autograph, but instead, he came back to Rock Hill and asked me to marry him. Can you imagine?

"Well, of course, I did, and even though he was almost fifteen years older than me, I never felt like it was a mistake. Charles was kind and gentle, and in those days, he shared his life with me. Then, the music was all there was. The only thing he ever talked about was raising enough money to have a company of his own, so he could write songs and make records the way he thought they ought to be made."

"He actually succeeded," I said. "Not very many men do."

"Yes, he did. We traveled around for years with those tent shows until the money was there for him to try his hand at composing full-time. Finally, he wrote his big hit, and we were off to Nashville. It was after we came here that he started to change. Maybe it was just the faster pace of things, I don't know. Or it might have been that the money got bigger. But it wasn't long before no amount of success was enough for Charles. If he wrote a hit, he needed a bigger hit to follow it up with. If a record went gold, it was a disappointment unless it went platinum, too."

"That's the way business operates," I said, just to be saying something. "If you stand still, before long, you'll find yourself going backward."

She seemed not to hear me. "Then it all came undone, the composing, the recording studio, everything that had been at the center of his life, including me. He started seeing other women. Then, when the business faltered, he began doing reckless things with our money. Not long after, he died in the automobile accident, and I was left with virtually nothing. And that's where you find me today. This house belongs to someone else now. By the end of the month, I'll be moved out." She sighed.

"Mister Gamble, Charles and I were married for almost twenty-five years. We went through years of struggle, and then success, and then, at the end, complete failure, which is what I'm left with now. You may not think much of me for saying this, but doesn't it seem to you that after all we went through, there would be at least something left for me besides memories?"

"You're talking about money?"

"Of course, I'm talking about money." There was anger in her voice now. "Do you think after all these years, I'm looking forward to moving into some low-rent studio apartment and scouring the want ads every day so I can find some kind of a job that will let me pay my bills?"

"I don't know you, Mrs. Lambert. I didn't know your husband, and I have no idea what your life with him was like." I shook my head. "It's not my job to judge you, or to try to make sense out of how things have turned out for you. I'm sorry. I wish I had something more to offer."

There wasn't much to talk about after that. Audra sat quietly with her thoughts, drumming her fingers against her glass. I stared out the window and tried to think of a graceful way to make my exit.

My visit was at an end. I had come looking for leads about a missing woman and stayed to learn far more than I wanted about another life that had turned as sour as old buttermilk. As I rose to go, Audra said, "I was thinking I'd like to live someplace warm and near the water. I've heard Key West is nice. What do you think?"

"I've never been there. But if you're asking my opinion, I don't know any place in the world that's far enough from here for you to get away from the feelings you have right now. You're going to need time to do that. Not distance."

She gave me a sad smile. "You're a nice guy, Gamble. I don't run into too many men like you. Tell me something. Is there somebody in your life?"

"There is."

"And is it serious?"

"It is, yes. She used to be a high school guidance counselor. Now, she's got a doctorate and works as a crisis counselor. Years ago, I dragged her into a case I was working on. We got involved with some very bad people. One of them tried to kill her, and I had to shoot him to save her life. It's a connection we have, and it runs deep. You don't just walk away from something like that."

"I understand." Then she added, "I've still got a few days before I have to start packing. Will I be seeing you again?"

"It's possible, if something else comes up."

She held out her hand to me. "Then let's hope something else will."

Chapter Fourteen

I t was early evening when I got back to Zenger's, the newspaperman's watering hole, where I had talked with Dave Quail the previous afternoon. He was already there, waiting for me. I found him seated at a high table for two, with his pretzels and his pitcher of beer. An empty glass sat on a cardboard coaster in front of the chair across from where he was perched. He poured what was left in the pitcher into the empty glass when he saw me approaching, then touched his finger to his lips, indicating he didn't want me to say anything. On the jukebox, some band or other that I didn't recognize was playing a cover version of the Atlanta Rhythm Section's own cover of the Classics IV hit song, "Spooky."

"You notice that keyboard solo partway through the instrumental bridge?" Quail said after the song ended.

I hadn't paid much attention, but I nodded anyway.

"That was me. When the Classics recorded that song in '68, they didn't have that part, but when ARS covered it in '79 they added it. Another band tried to release it one more time, about twenty-five years later. It barely broke into the Top 100, but I was the session keyboardist on that cut. They keep it in the jukebox here because they know it's me playing. That, and they know I spin it most times when I come in, so it makes a little money for the house." He looked at me with real sadness in his eyes. Around the room, a few patrons, regulars in the know, I guessed, nodded Dave's way and hoisted their drink glasses.

He acknowledged their gesture with a wave. "I was damn good. Could you tell?"

"To be honest…" I started, but I didn't know what else to say. It didn't matter. He was off in a place of his own and wasn't listening anyway.

"You know, I played session with some big names when they came to town to record. Toured with them, too. I traveled with Kenny Rogers once. I was on the road with Toto and Leonard Cohen. Paul Davis and Robbie Dupree, too. They were all great people. Great musicians, too. I don't know much about sports, but being on the stage with artists like that, feeling the crowd really getting into the music and hearing the applause, there's nothing like it. It's got to be the next best thing to being called up to the major leagues, even if it is just for a ten-week trip on a shitty tour bus. And then after the show, and you're back at the hotel, you've got that lanyard and the plastic ID around your neck, and you say to people, 'I'm with the band,' and, my God, the women, and the free drinks…it all just kept coming." There was real sadness in his voice when he added, "I miss that."

"You should write a book," I said.

"I'm working on it. I'm thinking about calling it *The Outskirts of Celebrity*. You know, kind of a knockoff of the thing Cameron Crowe did when he was writing for *Rolling Stone* and hanging with the Allman Brothers in 1973. Except, the groups I traveled with, they weren't much into tearing out hotel walls."

I sat quietly and let him relive the happy moments while the waitress brought another pitcher and two clean glasses.

"When we were on stage, partway through the show, whoever was the headliner would stop and introduce the members of the band. They always did that. They'd say, 'And on keyboards, from Dyersburg, Tennessee, Mr. David Quail.' And then the spot would hit me briefly, and there would be some applause, and I'd play a short riff. It was only a moment, and then it would be over, and they'd move on to the drummer, or the bass player, or whoever was next. But for those few seconds, I was alone in the spotlight, and it was like I was a headliner in my own right."

I said, "We can spin it again if you want. I wouldn't mind hearing it another time."

"Once is enough," he said, shaking his head as if to clear out the old memories. "And we've got things to talk about."

"Does that mean you found Albert's notes?"

"See for yourself." He reached into a battered briefcase under the table and pulled out three spiral-bound stenographer's pads. He passed them across the table to me. "Any of that mean anything to you?"

I looked inside the first one. The pages were filled with nonsense scribbling that looked like a combination of shorthand, Sanskrit, and the doodling of a ten-year-old who'd missed his morning Ritalin. Here and there, I could make out a reference to a name, a date, or a place, but that was about it. The rest were just pencil marks on a page.

Once, while I was on the job, I took a community college course in shorthand, thinking that it might come in handy taking witness statements. That had been several years ago, however, and my facility had since degraded to the point that about the only thing I could read anymore was the stuff that goes, "If u cn rd ths, u cn gt a gd jb n b a sctry." Even so, Albert's notes looked nothing like anything I'd ever seen before. I admitted as much to Dave Quail.

"That's what I figured." He took the notebooks from me and placed them back in his briefcase. "Even if you found these laying right out in the open, you wouldn't have been able to work out what you were looking at. That's why I also figure it's time for you to give me a little better idea of what's going on."

I didn't need him to write me a headline. "And if I don't, you don't give me the English translation of Albert's hieroglyphics, is that it?"

He nodded and gave me a wicked grin. "Well, you are a detective. You could always try to figure them out on your own."

I thought it over for the better part of five seconds before concluding that I had little choice except to bring him at least partway into the picture. Given the pace at which this case seemed to be progressing, I couldn't afford the luxury of passing up new information, no matter my reluctance to give up information of my own.

I said, "Okay, here it is. But if any of this ends up in the newspaper, or if anybody comes knocking at my door asking questions because they talked to you, we're done. Understood?"

"Hundred percent."

It took about an hour and most of another pitcher of beer to bring Dave Quail up to speed on the events of the past two days. I told him about Darlene Munson and her mysterious file and about how Albert Glass had hired me to run a stakeout on her motel room. I explained how I had spent the night before last in the Harding municipal jail and how, later, I had returned to my office to find it torn completely apart. Finally, I related my belief that Darlene's disappearance, and probably Albert's absence as well, were both connected with Charles Lambert's financial problems, the sale of his business, and quite possibly the Hermitage Group as well.

"I think you're on to something, but I'm not quite sure what," Quail said after I had finished. "Not yet, anyway. It's pretty clear from Albert's notes that he's still working on the Lambert story. Problem is, I can't find a reason why. I mean, the last entry in his notebook is from around the middle of June, and up to that point, there's nothing there that we don't already know. At the same time, there isn't anything written down to indicate where he's going with it. That means he's either carrying around in his head what he's found out since, or else he's started a new book, and he's keeping it someplace else. Why he would do that, I don't know, except to protect something very sensitive."

"Or else he doesn't have anything more," I ventured. "Maybe that's why he needed to hire me."

"That could be, I guess. I had a little trouble deciphering part of this, so there might be something more in these books than what I've been able to find out."

"I'm not following you."

"Well, every reporter has his own style of shorthand. It's something you develop as you go along. In Albert's case, I can read some of it, but the rest is as much a puzzle to me as it was to you."

"Tell me what you can read," I said.

He took out a small notebook of his own and turned to a page in the middle. "A lot of this duplicates what you already know, so I won't waste your time with that. But I did find something odd about the sale of Lambert's business. First, though, let me run a name past you. You ever hear of a guy named Robert Edward Cherry, AKA Red Cherry?"

I had. "He was connected to an organized crime outfit out of Biloxi called the Mississippi Mafia."

"That's the one."

I remembered hearing about the Mississippi Mafia back when I was on the job. It was a loose collection of criminals operating all over the Gulf Coast, specializing in prostitution, loan sharking, gambling, drug dealing, contract killings, and bribery of public officials, to name a few. The last two were particularly significant because they kept the higher-ups pretty well insulated from local and state law enforcement. The few times the big boys got pinched, either their cases were dismissed for lack of evidence, or if they ended up going to trial, key witnesses always seemed to go missing about the time they were scheduled to testify. Supposedly, the organization began to unravel after Mississippi legalized casino gambling, which put a big dent in what had been the Mafia's primary source of revenue. And then Hurricane Katrina wiped out what little remained. However, because back then, their operations stayed well to the south of Nashville, they didn't hit our local radar.

"Last I heard, Cherry was in prison."

He shook his head. "Old news. He's out. And he was more than connected to the Mississippi outfit; he was running it. He hit a bit of a speed bump back in the middle 'aughts when he was convicted of ordering a hit on some assistant district attorney in New Orleans who'd been sniffing around one of Cherry's operations and got a little too close. Red got a twenty-to-life jolt at Angola, but after eighteen months, his attorneys got the verdict overturned on some technicality or other, and he was granted a new trial. Unfortunately, the key prosecution witness was unavailable to testify the second time around."

I said, "Unavailable how?"

"Unavailable, as in killed in a railroad grade crossing accident somewhere out west. What was left of the victim was rolled up so tightly in his crushed vehicle that it took four hours with a cutting torch to extricate the body. As you might imagine, all charges ended up being dropped for lack of evidence. After Katrina tore up the Gulf Coast in oh-five, Cherry packed up and moved to Nashville, where he is living—and working—today."

"And he fits into all this how?"

"In a minute," Quail said, "First, here's another name for you. According to documents dating from the time of the sale, majority interest in Black Strap Music Corporation was transferred from Charlie Lambert to Talent Management Associates, or TMA for short. You said you ran across that outfit when you were doing your own digging."

"I remember."

"Okay, but how about this? The deal was handled by an attorney named James Austin Gannaway. Does that name mean anything to you?"

"Not a thing."

"Well then, let me see if I can put these two names together for you. Gannaway is a private practice attorney who specializes in business acquisitions. No problem there, but the odd thing is, when the sale of Black Strap to TMA was finalized, our Mr. Gannaway turns out to have been the attorney of record for both parties. Now, there's no mention of how much the deal went down for, but it had to have been fairly substantial. That normally means extensive negotiations, and yet here we have one guy brokering both ends of the sale."

"Maybe they were just in a hurry."

"We're not talking about splitting up a bar tab here, Gamble. Prudent business people don't lay rubber speeding through millions of dollars. Anyway, there's more. Talent Management is a name that rang a bell, so I did a little checking."

"And?"

"Well, you wouldn't know it from their website, which, not surprisingly, looks strictly on the up-and-up as an agency representing musicians and vocalists. And, in fact, that is pretty much what they do. However, as I expected, TMA turned out to have about half a dozen layers of ownership. I spent most of the day down at the courthouse doing a record search and making telephone calls to a guy I know at the Department of Revenue. You know, just to find out whether there was anything fishy about the taxes. And I'm still not sure I could actually make a case that anything was done illegally. That's how tangled up their corporate structure is. But when you finally get to the bottom of the paper pile, you find just one name. And whose name do you think that is?"

He lifted his eyebrows meaningfully, like a schoolteacher trying to coax a correct answer out of a pathetically dull student.

"Robert Edward Cherry," I said.

"That's the one," Quail answered with a triumphant smile. "So, all of a sudden, we're talking organized crime with a capital 'O'. After the Biloxi crew split up, the big players scattered all across the Southeast. Red Cherry landed here and is back in business doing loan sharking, union racketeering, credit card fraud, and gambling that we're sure of. Now, it appears he's gotten into the entertainment business."

"Okay," I said. "Now we have a connection between Red Cherry and Charlie Lambert, but by itself, it doesn't get us anywhere. I mean, Albert could write that story without needing some secret file Darlene Munson supposedly has. Selling a business, even to a guy like Cherry, is perfectly legal. So, unless there's more to it, I don't see what's got Albert so excited, and I certainly don't see anybody going to jail."

"Do you suppose Red is using a little Gulf Coast muscle to squeeze the record companies to get better contracts for the artists TMA represents? That would mean his agency commissions would be commensurately higher."

I let that idea roll around in my head for a moment. And then I had an inspiration.

"I don't think that's what this is about. What you're talking about might intimidate some of the smaller independents, but the major labels employ battalions of lawyers, and they have connections in both the state and the Federal government. They're also major players in the Nashville economy, and they aren't likely to buckle under to a bunch of country-fried con men. I think it's something much more complicated than that. I think it's the reason

Albert Glass is so interested in getting his hands on this file that Darlene Munson supposedly has."

"Are you going to tell me what, or do I have to guess?"

I took a sip of my beer. "It's like this. Earlier today, I met Charlie Lambert's wife, Audra. It didn't go particularly well, and I won't bore you with the details. But among other things she told me that before he lost the business when Black Strap started losing money by the double handful, Charlie Lambert took a second on his house and then made some speculative investments that went south. After that, he tried to make it back by gambling, either at a casino or the racetrack, or rolling dice in some back room. It doesn't really matter where, but whatever it was he tried to do, he came up snake eyes."

"Okay."

"Now, I'm supposing here, but it kind of makes sense that if he was truly desperate to save the business, he'd try tapping into whatever money he could get his hands on."

Quail sat up straight in his chair. "Wait a minute. You're talking about skimming some of the money held by the Hermitage Group. Lambert was finance chairman, so he would have had access to their accounts."

"Right, but among other things, that money was earmarked to finance Roger Seacrist's campaign for governor, so it wasn't as if nobody would notice it had gone missing. That money would have to be replaced before the campaign season got into full swing and Seacrist started running a full schedule of radio and television ads. That would be right around Labor Day. So, Black Strap Music was stabilized, at least in the short term, but then there was a big hole in the Hermitage Group's campaign fund account. Now, where could Lambert go to get enough money to keep alive this shell game he was playing?"

Quail's face brightened when he realized what I was driving at. "He went to Cherry."

"It makes sense," I said. "He was probably hoping for a loan. It's for damn sure no bank would lend him any money once they got a look at his financials."

108

"And, on the off-chance he could find a bank to bail him out, it would take time, and it would create a paper trail."

"That's right. But even if he gets the money from Cherry, he would've had to come up with something to collateralize the loan. Given his precarious financial situation, that had to be Black Strap. It's the only thing he still owned that would have had any asset value. So, he gets a quick fix, and the Hermitage Group gets its money back. And with a little creative accounting, maybe nobody connects the dots, at least not right away. But that left Charlie in hock to Red Cherry. And with the business continuing to struggle, the money was still flowing out faster than it was coming in. Red wasn't about to let that go on indefinitely. He had to do something. With a guy as visible as Charlie Lambert, you can't send around a couple leg-breakers to make him cough up the money, but Cherry doesn't need to do that. He's got a much better alternative, staring him right in the face."

Quail said, "Of course. He takes control of Black Strap Music."

"That's what I think. Then, as part of the deal, Cherry buys out whatever equity Lambert still holds in the company, and Lambert has no choice except to sell. Probably at a fire-sale price, but either way, it doesn't matter. The contract gets written up, and Cherry, through Talent Management Associates, owns the business outright. How many lawyers do you need to draw up papers for a transaction like that? In effect, you're selling the business to yourself."

"But wait a second," said Quail. "What interest would Red Cherry have in buying a failing record company?"

"I don't know yet. TMA appears to be a legitimate operation. Maybe the plan is to steer a few more marketable artists toward the Black Strap label. Maybe it's a way to launder money. Or maybe Red just likes country music. With these guys it's impossible to know."

"So then, Albert hasn't lost his touch after all," Quail said in a reverent voice. "And the file Darlene Munson has must be the proof that what we've been talking about is close to the way things actually happened. Lambert was keeping a separate account book so he could keep track of how the money was coming and going. Gamble, do you realize what we're looking

109

at here?"

"If we don't handle this right, I'd say a couple of shallow graves out in the woods somewhere. Was there anything in Albert's notes about the Hermitage Group?"

"Nothing that ties any of the individual members into any of this, so it's at least possible that nobody besides Lambert and Cherry—and I guess Gannaway—knows anything about this shell game they were running."

"It's more than that," I said. "How would it look in the middle of a campaign if it became public knowledge that part of the money being used to finance Seacrist's run for the governor's mansion came from Red Cherry's organization? Worse yet, what if others inside the Hermitage Group were already aware of what was taking place? Either way, if this story gets out, it'll trigger a RICO investigation that'll bring Seacrist's entire campaign crashing down on top of him. And that's not to mention the damage something like that would do to the reputations of the rest of the upstanding citizens who make up the Hermitage Group."

"Any one of whom might now have good reason to see to it that both Albert and Darlene are silenced," Quail said. "You realize if this is all even close to being true, we're not sitting on dynamite, we're sitting on a fucking nuclear meltdown. So, what do we do now?"

I took a swallow of my beer. "Unless you've got a better idea, I'd say we have to keep looking for Albert and Darlene. And we do it quietly. If what we're thinking is right, neither of them is likely to stay alive for long if they're Page One headlines in tomorrow's *Times*."

Quail nodded in agreement, but I sensed it was less than wholehearted. I had a feeling he smelled a story. I was counting on him being smart enough to wait until everybody involved was out of danger before he tried to print it.

I said, "What I'd like you to do is take Albert's notebooks home with you. Go through them as many times as you need to, but make sure there isn't something else in them that you might have overlooked. Also, you might see what you can find on that attorney, Gannaway. I'm especially interested in knowing if he's done any other work for Red Cherry."

"Anything else?"

"Yeah, two things. When I was doing my research in the morgue yesterday afternoon, I ran across an article about an organized crime investigation that's being conducted by Seacrist's office. I'd like to know if anything besides campaign bullshit has ever come out of that."

"What's the other thing?"

"See if you can find out whether Lambert's wife's signature is on any of the documents connected to the sale of the record company."

"Why does that matter? You think she has a part in all this?"

"No. I don't know. Just curious, I guess."

"All right," he said. "That takes care of me, then. What are you going to do?"

"I thought I'd drive over and scout out Darlene Munson's apartment. Albert's story about putting a piece of his business card in her front door jamb was a little too pat to swallow without taking a look for myself."

"Want me to tag along?"

I shook my head. "If even part of what we've been kicking around is right, Albert's gotten himself into some deep shit. No offense, but I'd feel better if you kept out of sight for the time being. Besides, you've got enough to do to keep you busy."

Dave finished the last of his beer, we shook hands, and he went on his way.

Thinking back through our discussion, I was feeling confident that our plan of attack would at least keep Dave Quail from getting hurt in the event things got out of hand and bodies started dropping. But then I remembered what he had said about how much he enjoyed being in the spotlight, and I started to get worried.

Chapter Fifteen

I waited around Zenger's for another hour or so, nibbling pretzels and nursing green bottles of Stella. The general idea was to wait until it got dark enough to improve the odds of success with the burglary I had planned. But I knew if I didn't get some real food into my stomach soon, I would end up drunker than a homesick sailor on a forty-eight-hour shore leave and just as likely to get myself into trouble.

I thought about phoning Maggie to see if she'd be interested in meeting me someplace for supper and then decided that might not be such a good idea. I knew if we got together, it wouldn't take long before she'd get around to asking me what I had planned for the rest of the evening. That meant I'd either have to lie to her, or else admit that I was going to commit a felony by breaking into the apartment of a woman I'd never met. Worse yet, she'd want to come along. None of those choices seemed likely to lead to a good outcome. Instead, I turned my phone off and made my way over to the bar. I decided that Thursday was close enough to Friday to try eating solid food and ordered a hamburger steak and pan-fried potatoes with onions. My jaw was still a little tender, and I had to do most of my chewing on the right side. But after five days of soup, eggs, pudding, and ice cream, it was worth the discomfort.

After I finished eating, I asked for a club soda with a lime wedge and then spent another hour chatting with a young woman named Rhonda, who was working behind the bar. There was an ESPN game on the television mounted on the wall, and, like me, she was a baseball fan, so we passed the time talking game strategy while she had me taste small samples of tropical-

112

themed drinks that she claimed to have concocted on her own. Mostly, they were overwrought blends of fruit juices, rum, and West Indian liqueurs that were sugary enough to make your teeth sing falsetto. Making an effort to be diplomatic, though, I didn't tell her that. I just kept smiling and said they tasted fine. One she seemed especially anxious for me to try, she called a Nashville Skyline. I took a sip and nearly spit it out on the bar, it was so saccharine.

"It's good," I lied. "But I guess you know the name's not original."

"It's not?"

"No. Bob Dylan used it as an album title back in 1968."

She looked at me as if she were measuring me for a saber-toothed tiger skin robe and a club to go kill it with. "Who thinks about 1968?"

"You should. Besides two assassinations, the Tet Offensive, and Richard Nixon getting elected president, that was the year Denny McLain won thirty-one games for the Tigers and Mickey Lolich beat the Cardinals three times in the World Series."

"But how would I know that? I wasn't even born yet."

So there.

Before I sank irretrievably into the generation gap that was widening by the minute, I said good night to my new friend and turned my attention back to the work I still had in front of me. A quick phone search confirmed there were just thirteen Munsons living in greater Nashville and only one who had the first initial "D." The address shown for that one was on Twenty-First Avenue, a few blocks south of the Vanderbilt University campus.

Darlene's building was a six-flat built sometime between the two World Wars. Among other things, that meant no elevator, just a central staircase that must have presented a real obstacle for third-floor tenants with a double armful of groceries. There was a single outside entrance that led to a lobby that was neither locked nor well-lit. A glance at the mailboxes showed her apartment was number five, which put it on the top floor. The individual apartment doors I saw as I climbed the stairs looked as if they'd been there since the Crash of '29. Unless Darlene had one hell of a deadbolt, the lock pick set I had stuck in my jacket pocket would be more than enough to get me inside.

As it turned out, I could have left the lock picks at home. When I reached the third-floor landing, I found Darlene's door standing partly ajar. The surrounding frame was split apart, as if someone had kicked the door open rather than using a key or a set of picks. Through the opening, a puddle of bright light spilled into the corridor. The business card that Albert said he had stuck in the doorway was nowhere in sight. That meant whoever was inside now either had already picked it up, or else it was gone when he got there.

I had told Captain Purvis back in Harding the truth when I'd said I wasn't in the habit of carrying a gun unless the situation called for it. But tonight, I had the Colt along and that's what I reached for instead of the lock pick. When I'd taken it out of the glove compartment and dropped it in my pocket, I wasn't expecting any serious trouble, I was just tired of getting beaten up, cold-cocked, and smart-mouthed by bail-skippers, motel-room creepers, and ill-mannered houseboys with hat-sized intellects. Now, it looked as if the precaution had been with good reason.

I moved in close to the wall where I figured I'd be less likely to give my presence away by stepping on a creaky floorboard, and eased down the outer corridor until I was directly outside Darlene's doorway. Through the opening, I could see a shadow moving slowly around the front room. A man's voice was softly mumbling, something I couldn't make out. I couldn't tell whether he was talking to himself or if there was someone else in the room with him.

I clicked the Colt's safety off, counted three, and kicked the door hard with my right foot. Crouching low and using the classic two-handed grip popularized by every cop show character from Lenny Briscoe to Will Trent, I drew a bead on the spot between the shoulder blades of the startled intruder.

"Hold it right there!" I barked in my best cop-show voice.

"Son of a bitch!" said Albert Glass as he spun around and leveled a revolver of his own at my chest.

Chapter Sixteen

"Okay, Albert," I said after all the hardware was put away and everybody's heart rate was more or less back to normal. "How about if we take it from the top? Where's Darlene Munson?"

"If I knew that, I wouldn't be here," he answered peevishly.

"Then what are you doing here? And where have you been? I've been trying to reach you for the last two days."

"As to your second question, I've been researching my story. I wasn't taking any phone calls because I didn't want any distractions. As to the first, that's a question I should be asking you." He reached into his shirt pocket for a cigarette. When he lit it, I saw his hand was shaking badly.

"I thought we had an agreement you were going to stay out in Harding and keep an eye on the Rustic Retreat."

"You had the agreement," I told him. "I just try not to argue with a paying customer until I have a better idea of what's going on. Besides, if you haven't already figured it out, Darlene's cover is blown sky-high. For that matter, yours is, too. So, I'll ask you again. What are you doing here?"

He sat down heavily on the couch and squinted at me, as if he was having trouble making me out from six feet away. When he did, his coat fell open, and I could see his shirt was soaked through with perspiration. He had the general appearance of a man minutes away from a massive coronary.

"I wanted to find out if she'd come back. I was worried something might have happened to her."

"And you thought, what? She'd be pleasantly surprised and reassured by having you break down her door waving a gun around?"

"My card was gone. I knocked. I thought I heard a noise. When nobody answered, I figured maybe she was in trouble and forced my way in. Turned out, nobody was here."

"Of course, nobody was here. I told you. Her cover is blown. I'm betting by now she's either dead or halfway to parts unknown."

He wrinkled his brow. "What are you talking about?"

I said, "The day you hired me, somebody followed you to my office. Maybe you didn't notice, or maybe you did and figured you'd shake the tail by having them hook onto me instead. Either way, when I left an hour later to drive out to Harding, somebody did follow me, although I wasn't sure about that until later. That night, at the Rustic Retreat, I found a couple guys tossing Darlene's room."

"Wait a minute, what guys?"

"Well, there's the question. They didn't introduce themselves. Probably it was the guy who was tailing you, and he picked up some reinforcements along the way. When I tried to get a closer look at what was going on, one of them sapped me. I got my ass hauled into the city jail and spent the rest of the morning explaining myself to a Harding police captain."

Albert's face fell like an overdone soufflé. "You brought the police into this?"

"I didn't bring anybody into anything, but I had to come up with a story that made at least a little bit of sense, or I'd still be in the lockup. I told them I was working a stakeout. That was true, and it was also perfectly legal. I didn't give up your name or what the job was about.

"Look, Albert, the point is, if Darlene is still alive, she's in a very bad spot right now. And story or no story, we have an obligation to help her."

"A fine fucking detective you turned out to be."

"Oh, I don't know about that," I said, fighting a rising urge to flatten his nose. "I was good enough to find out about Charlie Lambert's money problems. I was also good enough to tie a ribbon around him and Red Cherry, and then connect them both back to Darlene Munson and this story you say you're working on. Were you planning to tell me about any of that, by the way, or was I just the brain-dead gumshoe you had nailed to the roof as your lightning rod?"

"You were the gumshoe I hired to do a simple job. You fucked it up."

I could feel the back of my neck getting hot. "I was doing the job, but it turned out there was a lot more to it than what you led me to believe, wasn't there? So far, I've been blackjacked, busted, and burgled, all in the course of doing this job for you. And that's fine, up to a point. It's what I get paid to do. But now we're talking about organized crime, and potentially the next governor of the state of Tennessee, plus a possible connection between the two. That means any side I come down on figures to be big trouble for me and maybe for you, too. If Darlene Munson's mysterious file proves Charlie Lambert funneled dirty money into Roger Seacrist's campaign fund, and that's the story you're working on, fine. We can run with that and keep the innocent bystanders' names out of it. But if I'm going to protect you, I need straight answers starting now, or else you're on your own."

He took a deep drag on his cigarette. "I was just thinking the same thing."

"Your call," I told him. "I'm through playing guessing games with you. If Darlene or anybody else connected with this ends up dead, and the cops decide they want to talk to me about it, I will throw you right under the crosstown bus. I have no problem keeping your precious story under wraps, and I'll do my best to make sure it stays there. But covering up a murder is a whole different deal, and that's not something I'm prepared to do."

"You can't do that," he hissed. "It would ruin everything."

"Can't do what? Can't turn over evidence in a murder investigation? Sure, I can, and I for damn sure will if anything happens to Darlene Munson. You haven't been straight with me since the first moment you walked through my door. So, go ahead and tell me some other bullshit story and see if it changes anything, because as it is, it's a blessing for Darlene that you haven't been able to find her. You say she trusts you. But the way I see it, she'd be better off handing over that file to Red Cherry. At least then, she might make a little money."

And that's when I knew for sure. It was so simple I couldn't imagine why I didn't see it sooner, except that I thought maybe, just maybe, the story Albert Glass had told me was on the level.

"Darlene didn't come to you because she was a concerned citizen with a story that she wanted you to tell your adoring public. This has really been about the money all along. Tell me, Albert, how much did she want? Ten thousand? Fifty?"

He thought for a moment before answering, as if he were trying to decide whether to double down on the lie or just come clean. Then he seemed to make up his mind, and I thought his expression melted a little. "It was more like a hundred," he said. "But I told her I didn't have it. I needed some time to get it together. I was hiding her out at that fleabag motel to keep her safe until I could get it together."

"And how were you going to do that? You couldn't get money to pay for a story from the *Times*. Dick Dohrn would never go for something like that. Carver Dickinson is a member of the Hermitage Group. You think he would give you money so you could write a story that would embarrass his organization?"

"I don't need them. I have resources."

"I'm sure you do. But before you could tap into whatever you've got lined up, she skipped out, leaving you with no witness and no evidence. And ever since, you've been running around ass over elbows, trying to find out where she went. My part was just to hold down the fort in case she came back to pick up her belongings and maybe to draw off whoever was tailing you. Does that sound about right?"

He shrugged. "It's your story. Go ahead and tell it."

"In that case, it gets better, because I have a feeling that once she found out you were willing to pay a hundred grand, she got the idea that maybe somebody else might be willing to pay more. She didn't just come to you. She's shopping the deal. She thinks she's going to sell that little black book to whoever comes up with the most cash. What do you think, Albert? Who else is bidding on this McGuffin? Did she try to put the bite on Audra Lambert?" And then another thought hit me.

"Please tell me she isn't trying to sell the file to Red Cherry. If she is, she's dead for sure."

I looked around at the Walmart furniture and the Home Shopping Network wall hangings that decorated Darlene Munson's living room. I tried to imagine how far a hundred thousand dollars would go toward upgrading her standard of living. Not nearly far enough, I decided, to compensate for the risk she was running.

I shook my head sadly. "You thought you were going to buy yourself a Pulitzer, Albert, and now you've got nothing. There's got to be a word for you, but I'm not sure what it'd be. Sucker sounds about right."

Albert's eyes narrowed. "Well, I've got a word for you, too, Gamble, and that word is unemployed. Whatever happens from here on, you're out of the picture."

"Fine with me," I told him. "I'll send you a statement and a refund on the rest of your deposit."

"Keep the money," he snapped. "You never know when you might need it. Just remember. I've told you more than I should have, because under the circumstances, I thought it was the fair thing to do. Well, okay, done is done, and now you're on your own, same as me. But let me warn you. Darlene or no Darlene, my first priority is still to make sure this story gets printed. If you screw it up by sticking your nose where it doesn't belong, you won't need to worry about Red Cherry or anybody else. Because if you do, so help me, I'll kill you myself."

Chapter Seventeen

After I left Darlene Munson's apartment, I sat in my car for a few minutes, trying to figure out what it was about my conversation with Albert that had left such a sour taste in my mouth. I'd gotten fired, of course, but that was neither unusual nor unexpected. Mine is a business that specializes in exhuming and reburying unpleasant truths in approximately equal measure. And no matter what story a client tells you when they hire you, neither gratitude, nor continued employment is ever a likely outcome of the agreement.

At first, I thought the problem was nothing more than a complete lapse of integrity. In spite of what I'd told Albert when we first met, I did read his column now and then. And even though some of what he wrote was gee-whiz coverage of big-city political fluff, once in a while, it was solid stuff that brought tangible results. That was why it disappointed me to learn he was trying to raise money to pay for Darlene Munson's story. Not that I had any way of judging whether it was worth what she was asking, but somehow it seemed to me it would have had more value, to say nothing of credibility, if he'd dug it up on his own.

There was also the larger question of what he was doing in Darlene's apartment in the first place? If his story about his card stuck in the doorway was true, then somebody had gotten into the apartment ahead of him. And if that was also true, then what was he hoping to find by tossing her place? If Darlene had a file in her possession that she thought was worth at least a hundred thousand dollars, she certainly would have had more sense than to do something as obvious as hiding it under her mattress. Or maybe he thought Darlene had returned home for a fresh change of clothes, or because she just got tired of waiting around in a tourist cabin in Harding. Hell, what did I know? Maybe he expected to find her sitting on the couch with a bowl of popcorn, watching "Dancing with the Stars." But since he didn't, that meant he still didn't know where she was, or where the file was, or even where to start looking. And for that matter, neither did I.

Beyond that, Albert had mentioned having resources he could tap in order to raise the money Darlene was demanding. I supposed it was possible he had a 401K he could raid, or maybe he had a rich uncle someplace, but otherwise, where would he get the money? The *Times* certainly wouldn't give it to him, if for no other reason than that Carver Dickinson was vice-chairman of the Hermitage Group, and he wouldn't have had any interest in seeing Albert's story in print under any circumstances.

Finally, there were the two cops Mattie Brown had told me about, as well as the two guys who were ransacking Darlene's room at the Rustic Retreat. By now, I had pretty well concluded that they were the same guys who had tossed my office later that morning and that they were probably working for the district attorney's office. As far as I could see, nobody else involved in the case would have had any reason to be in either place. Maybe Red Cherry would have wanted the file to make sure his name didn't come up in any election law violation investigation, but his people didn't run around with police credentials. And anyway, his business dealings with Charley Lambert were perfectly legal. What Lambert did with the money after the sale of Black Strap was completed was none of Cherry's concern. On the other hand, the D.A.'s office would definitely have wanted to keep Albert's story out of the media spotlight, particularly in light of Roger Seacrist's candidacy for governor, and that's where I was putting my money.

In the end there wasn't any getting around it. The only way I could make it all add up was to acknowledge that it didn't. That meant Albert was still feeding me a line, and I didn't have the first idea what the truth actually was.

As I drove away, I caught a glimpse of my erstwhile client silhouetted in the light shining through Darlene's third-floor window, still nosing around. That gave me a hunch, and since I had nothing better to do, I decided to indulge my curiosity. Besides, I rationalized that Albert had paid me three days in advance. That meant I still owed him almost sixteen hours of my time, and whether he wanted them or not, he was going to get them.

I drove three blocks south to Edgehill Avenue. I made a right turn there, then another right on Seventeenth. Two more blocks, another couple of turns, and I was back where I had started, only parked in a different spot and facing a different direction. I cut the engine and the headlights and slouched down in the seat. Then I waited.

I didn't have to wait long. Ten minutes into my vigil, Albert Glass walked out of Darlene's apartment building. He paused in the doorway to light a cigarette. Then he crossed the street and climbed into a battered, ten-year-old Camry. He pulled away from the curb and drove north on Sixteenth Avenue. I let him get half a block ahead, then started my own car and fell in behind. There was no traffic to cover me, so I left my headlights off and hoped we wouldn't pass any cops before we got to a main drag.

Albert got stopped by a red light at Division, forcing me to bail out into the curb lane. After the light changed, he turned left, then right, and exited onto Interstate 65. There was traffic now, so I was able to turn on my lights and let a few other cars get between us.

I hung a short distance behind as Albert headed north on the Interstate before exiting and continuing north on Gallatin Road. It was somewhere past Center Point that I figured out where Albert had to be going. He made a right onto Rockland and then continued another short distance before turning into a quiet little cul-de-sac called Fox Park Circle. Halfway down the block, he turned past a pair of large stone gateposts into a driveway that wound toward a large house situated on the shore of Old Hickory Lake. I didn't need to follow any further. I'd been to that house before. I didn't have to see to know that the other car parked there was a blood-red Porsche or that its license plate read "4-AUDRA."

That left me with nothing else to do except go home and go to bed.

Chapter Eighteen

I spent my first day of being kicked off the case hanging around the office. I wanted to stay close to the phone in hopes I'd hear from Albert. For no particular reason, I had it in the back of my mind he might call to say all was forgiven and that he needed my help after all. In the meantime, I fired up my computer and went online to the website for Talent Management Associates. Not surprisingly, what I found was a very professional-looking layout that listed the multiple services offered by TMA. Those included representation for established and aspiring musicians, videographers, composers, and songwriters. There were more than a dozen agents listed, each with contact information and a particular area of concentration, such as country music, rock, and hip-hop, and session musicians. There was also a listing of the various artists represented by TMA, many of which I recognized. To all appearances, very comprehensive and very up-and-up. On the other hand, I didn't see as much as a mention of Black Strap Music. Turned out there was a separate website for that.

When I looked them up, it turned out the link was actually to a new company called Black Strap Entertainment. Not surprisingly, it featured other links to the artists they currently had under contract, as well as an archives link that took me to a separate area that featured a number of "late-great" acts that had long since taken their final bows and were now performing behind the pearly gates. There was no information regarding the company's current management team.

Just for fun, I dialed the telephone number shown under "Contact," and found myself speaking with a real person. When I asked to be connected with Darlene Munson, the young woman on the other end informed me that there was no such individual working there. I thanked her and asked her to connect me with someone in their HR department, where I got the same answer.

"She was a former employee at Black Strap Music prior to them being acquired by TMA," I explained.

"I'm sorry," said the voice on the other end, who identified himself as Jason. "None of the former Black Strap employees elected to stay on after the merger. I'm afraid I can't tell you anything more than that."

I thanked Jason and hung up. So. Darlene might still be employed, but not at TMA. So that was that. I wondered, then, how she was paying her rent, and it occurred to me that the hundred grand she was trying to shake loose from Albert Glass might be exactly the thing she thought might turn her life back around.

At eleven-thirty, I broke for lunch. I walked a couple of blocks from my office to a fast-food joint on Union Street, and since it was Friday, ordered a fish sandwich with fries. I finished it off with a deep-fried cherry pie and a carton of chocolate milk. Then I bought a newspaper and a Diet Coke and walked back to the office to babysit the telephone. It never rang once.

At three o'clock, I got a visit from a prospective client. Her name was Mrs. Delilah Liggett, and after twenty minutes of beating around the bush, she finally got around to telling me she wanted me to find her daughter for her.

Mrs. Liggett was an East Tennessee woman, hollow-eyed, high cheek-boned, and aged in appearance far beyond the fifty or so years she'd actually spent walking the earth. She wore a cotton print dress and low-heeled black shoes and carried a scuffed white patent leather handbag. Mrs. Liggett informed me that she was a widow. Her husband, Jacob, had been killed in a coal train derailment near Bluefield, West Virginia, twenty years earlier.

Mrs. Liggett's story was that her daughter, Amelia Anne, had disappeared while walking home from school and that she hadn't been seen or heard from since.

"How old is she?" I asked.

"She was thirteen years old when last I saw her leave for school."

I made a few notes on my yellow pad, then asked her how long ago that had been.

"Twenty years this next October," she told me in a softly sorrowful voice.

My first reaction was to ask how come it had taken so long to notice the kid had gone missing. My second was to send her packing, thinking that if I wasn't dealing with a head case, any child missing twenty years was now a grown woman with no apparent intention of returning home any time soon. But there was something in Mrs. Liggett's slightly off-kilter manner of speaking that made me want to dig a little deeper, so I asked her a few more questions and agreed to do a little checking around and get back to her. That seemed to be all she wanted to hear, and when I didn't ask her for any money, she thanked me for my time and left.

Just to satisfy my curiosity, I telephoned Metro Central Division and asked for a missing persons cop I knew there named Carl Sutton. Carl and I exchanged rough pleasantries for a few minutes, and then I asked him whether he remembered ever running across the names Delilah or Amelia Anne Liggett in his file of open investigations.

He chuckled, not unkindly, at the reference. "I was wondering when she'd finally get around to you."

""Okay, Carl, what's the joke?""

"No joke, Jackson. Amelia Anne Liggett was raped, stabbed, and strangled almost twenty years ago. It was a messy job, and it pretty much pushed poor old Delilah around the bend."

"Anybody ever find out who did it?"

"Oh, yes, absolutely. It only took a few days. A known rape-o confessed the same day homicide picked him up for questioning. No question, he did it. It was his third offense, so there was also no doubt about his sentence. He's still sitting on death row at Riverbend Max, waiting for his appeals to dry up."

"You've lost me, Carl."

"The old lady is nuts, Jackson. She can't get it through her head that the kid's really gone. She's been coming down here at least once every couple of months for all this time, asking us to find her daughter."

"What do you tell her?"

"Same thing you'll probably end up telling her. That we're still working on it, and we'll be in touch as soon as we have something to tell her."

And on that note, my Friday, and my week, ended. Nobody else came by the office. No one called, or texted, or e-mailed me. Nobody sent me an Edible Bouquet. Nobody trashed the office, or let the air out of my tires, or threatened to kill me. I read the newspaper until it was time to go home. Albert Glass's column wasn't there. A note where it normally appeared said Albert was on special assignment and would return the following week. I called Maggie to ask whether she'd like to go out for a meal and then a late movie on television, but no luck there, either. She'd made a date with some of her gal pals to head down to Lower Broad and do a little bar hopping.

"Sarah said she wanted to try one of those bicycle bars. She said they look like fun." There was a pause. "I could come by after, but I can't promise I'll have my A-game."

I knew enough to let that pass. "Do I know Sarah?"

"Sarah Bergman, I don't think so. She was married to a guy who used to teach at Broadview College. He went missing a few years ago, and she still hasn't gotten over it. We thought a night out might do her some good."

"Wait a minute," I said. "Missing how?"

"Nobody knows. He went to work one day and never came home. The police looked for him for months and never found anything. He just seems to have disappeared."

"Well, have fun and give her my best," I said. "My opinion, he probably ran off with some co-ed who dumped him after the money ran out, and now, he's too ashamed to show his face in these parts ever again."

She made a clucking sound. "You're so understanding. You should think about going into marriage counseling."

* * *

The weekend passed uneventfully. I didn't hear from Maggie on Saturday morning, so I assumed she and her BFFs had had a late night, and she was sleeping in, perhaps nursing a hangover from whatever she'd been knocking back while pedaling the mobile cocktail bar around Lower Broadway. Since it appeared I would be on my own for the rest of the day, I got busy and mowed the lawn, pulled some weeds, washed the car, and generally made out like your average middle-class suburban homeowner. I wasted the afternoon thinking about painting the second bedroom, but then decided moving the furniture was too much work and that it would be better to wait until the weather cooled off. Later, I watched a baseball game on TBS. The Cincinnati Reds whipped the Phillies in a laugher, 12-5.

On Sunday morning, I went fishing with Klein, my across-the-street neighbor. The weatherman had promised falling pressure and possibly rain for early in the afternoon, so we were optimistic about our chances. But the hoped-for clouds never materialized. Instead, it turned out to be a dazzlingly hot, clear day, and except for a single ten-minute stretch when we got into a school of white bass on a feeding free-for-all, there wasn't much doing. We gave it up about three o'clock. I told Klein he could keep the fish.

Sunday night, with still no word from Maggie, I nursed a couple of cold beers and took in a late-show rerun of *Body Heat*, which is surely the most erotically charged film to come out of mainstream Hollywood in the late twentieth century. Audra Lambert hadn't said I reminded her of William Hurt, or even Richard Crenna, but as I let my thoughts drift back to Thursday afternoon, I decided she would have made a stunning Kathleen Turner. About the time Ned Racine was staring at the four walls of a jail cell coming to the realization of how completely Matty Walker had fucked him over, I flashed on a mental image of Albert Glass's Camry parked in Audra Lambert's driveway. And I wondered, was it possible that one of them was setting the other up for some kind of a sucker play?

Halfway through a commercial selling a set of kitchen knives you could use to cut through a steel bolt—with a free extra set thrown in, just pay separate shipping and handling—the telephone rang. It was Dick Dohrn, from the *Times*. He sounded as tired and subdued as I ever remembered hearing him.

Dick didn't waste time with pleasantries. "Can you come by the office first thing in the morning?"

I said, "What time is it?"

"Now? It's twelve-thirty. Don't tell me I got you out of bed."

"No. Still up. What are you calling first thing?"

"Zero-seven hundred. Earlier if you can make it."

I yawned out loud into the mouthpiece. "Let me check my appointment book."

"I'm serious, Jackson."

"Okay, you're serious. I'll be there at seven. What's the problem?"

He said cryptically, "There have been some developments. Dickinson wants to talk to you."

He didn't come out and say so, but I got the message anyway. Albert and Darlene were very much on somebody's front burner.

Chapter Nineteen

I'd never met a newspaper publisher before, so I didn't know what to expect from Carver Dickinson. Dick Dohrn wasn't much help filling me in, either. When I pulled into the *Times* parking lot at seven o'clock Monday morning, Dick was already there waiting, leaning on the fender of a dark blue Tesla Plaid I wouldn't have guessed he could afford. He looked like he'd spent the night in a rag bag. His clothes were rumpled, and there were pouches under his eyes big enough to hold a chicken salad sandwich. He greeted me with a tired wave and led me inside through the employee's entrance.

On the elevator up to Dickinson's eleventh-floor office, Dick dropped the news on me. "Albert quit."

"Quit what, smoking, drinking, or breathing?"

"His job," he said, as if I should have known.

"When?"

"Friday morning. He walked into the office and handed me his resignation."

"Well, at least you know he's still alive."

He gave me a look of weary patience.

"Okay, seriously," I said. "Did he give you any idea why?"

"What he gave me was a load of horseshit about needing a change in his career path, if you can make any sense out of that. Said he's spent twenty-two years in the newspaper business, and now he wants to do something else for a while."

"Like what, astronaut training?"

"He didn't say."

I tried the reasonableness of that on for size, and decided I didn't like it. "Did you ask him about Lambert?"

"Are you kidding? I kept after him for better than an hour, but all he'd tell me was that the Lambert story was a dead end."

"So then, is he still looking for Darlene Munson?"

"He says not."

"Then what the hell did he hire me for?"

"Good question. Maybe you can ask him when you see him. What he said to me was, he decided finally that, as far as the story he was working on goes, there was no there, there."

"Did you believe him?"

"I don't know what I believe," he said, just before the light overhead flashed '11' and the elevator doors slid open. "But I'm positive something bigger than we thought is going on with this Lambert thing."

"Then I guess the answer is no, you didn't believe him." I started to ask him what Carver Dickinson wanted with me, but he shook his head as if to shush me and stepped quickly off the elevator.

We wound our way through a maze of as-yet unoccupied fabric-and-glass-walled cubicles toward an office on the far side of the building. From the absence of early morning activity and the fact that there were no telephones ringing, I supposed the eleventh floor must have been home to the accounting department, or some other non-editorial function. That far removed from the action seemed like an odd location for the publisher's office, but then, as I said, I didn't know what to expect.

Dickinson's secretary, a handsome, fiftyish woman wearing a blue business suit, met us at his office door. "He's waiting for you," she said, more to Dick than to me. She smiled when she spoke, but her tone was cool, as if Dickinson wasn't a man in the habit of being kept waiting. To her credit, she didn't make a show of looking at her watch.

Dickinson was talking on the telephone when Dick and I walked in. Without interrupting his conversation, he motioned us both into a pair of visitor chairs facing his desk.

"They're here now," he said softly into the mouthpiece. He nodded to no one in particular and said, "Yeah, both of them. They came in together." Then, "Don't worry about it. I told you I'd take care of it, and I will."

He listened for another minute or so before hanging up. "Thanks for coming on such short notice, Mr. Gamble." He rose from his chair and extended his hand. "Most mornings, I'm not here this early myself."

"No problem." I shook his hand and took a seat.

Dickinson was a compact man, standing perhaps five-eight or so, and I doubted he weighed more than a hundred and fifty pounds with jogging weights strapped to his ankles. He was dressed in a gray three-piece pinstriped suit, a pink shirt with narrow red stripes, a white collar and cuffs, and a dotted maroon bow tie. His hair was black and parted near the middle. He wore gold wire-rimmed glasses, a gold collar pin, and gold cufflinks. He spoke with just a hint of an accent that sounded more like Texas than Tennessee.

As if to compensate for his smallish stature, Dickinson seemed to crackle with nervous energy that filled the office all out of proportion to his physical size. Even seated at his desk, he was in continuous motion. While he talked, he smoothed his hair, fiddled with his tie, inspected his fingernails, and drummed his pencil on his pad.

"You want a cup of coffee or something?"

I thought asking for a Diet Coke might be pushing my luck. "No, thanks."

He glanced at his watch. "Then, if you don't mind, I've got a full morning ahead of me, so I'd like to get right down to business. Do you know why I wanted to talk to you?"

"I can guess," I told him.

His pencil started tapping again. "Well then, to save time, you should know Dick has brought me up to speed on this story Albert Glass has been working on. Frankly, I'm more than a little concerned."

"Concerned about the paper, the Hermitage Group, or Albert?"

"All three. I understand you're working on some sort of an investigation that involves them all."

"I was. I'm not anymore. Albert fired me last week."

"Did he tell you why?"

"He said I fucked up the job he hired me to do."

"Right. That sounds like something Albert would say. Did you fuck up the job?"

"More or less, yeah, I guess I did. The job wasn't exactly what I was led to believe. I had to improvise. There were complications."

"I see," he said, brushing at a spot of lint on his lapel. "So, since you're off the case, you won't mind my asking what you found out for him."

"I don't mind you asking," I said.

"But you aren't going to tell me." He permitted himself a small smile, as if an important psychological point had just been made between Dohrn and himself. "Dick warned me you'd probably say something like that. Any point in trying to bring you to your knees with money?"

I glanced over at Dick. He had a look on his face like a rabbit that's just figured out what the pot of vegetables boiling on the stove is all about.

"You probably have a pretty good idea what my income is, Mr. Dickinson, so I won't sit here and pretend money isn't without its attractions. But there are a few too many things wrong with this case for me to let myself get bought off just yet."

"In other words, you don't believe what Albert's been telling you."

"Let's just say before I take your money or anyone else's regarding this investigation, I'd like a little better idea of what I'm getting involved in."

He nodded and leaned back in his chair, causing the air in his seat cushions to exhale in protest. "You seem to be a reasonably intelligent man, Mr. Gamble. I like working with intelligent people." He nodded meaningfully in Dick Dohrn's direction.

"Resourceful, too," I threw in.

"No doubt." He permitted himself a small smile. "Did Dick tell you Albert has quit the *Times*?"

"He did, just now. I gather it was quite a shock."

"We'll survive. People come and go all the time. And anyway, Albert signed a no-compete contract. That means we won't be hearing anything more from him anywhere in our circulation area for at least three years, so no worries there." He paused, as if to gather his thoughts. "Listen, Mr. Gamble, you and Albert are in a somewhat similar line of work. Does his story make any sense to you?"

"About why he quit, you mean?" I shrugged noncommittally. "Twenty-two years is a long time to be sifting through any city's garbage. After a while, I imagine it gets pretty hard to wash off the smell."

"Yes, it does, but that's not what I meant. What do you make of the investigation he was working on?"

"Hard to say. He didn't share very many of the details."

"I see." He went back to tapping his pencil. "Mr. Gamble, what would you say to letting me put you on the *Times* payroll?"

"I'd say it depends on what you want me to do. I should warn you, though, I'm not much of a writer."

Dick interrupted. "I didn't have time to discuss this with him, Mr. Dickinson."

Dickinson seemed not to hear. "It's like this." He leaned forward again and folded his hands on his desk. "Albert Glass is a damn fine reporter, make no mistake about it. And we're all very sorry to lose him. But as publisher of this newspaper, I'd be a whole lot sorrier to lose the good reputation the *Times* has built for itself within this community."

"Okay."

"Now, I don't know myself all the details of what Albert has gotten himself into, but I'm convinced, and so is Dick, that this investigation he's had you working on is part of the reason he resigned last Friday. I want you to find out what the hell's going on, and I mean everything, and report back to me. I don't give a shit one way or the other about the circulation value of Albert's story. It won't be the first time we've taken a pass. But if he was involved in something illegal while a member of this newspaper's staff, I want to be the first one to know about it."

"Why would you think he was involved in anything illegal? As far as I can determine, he was working on a perfectly legitimate story."

"Maybe he was. And if he was, I just want to know what it is. I think you're the right man to find out for me."

"And when I find out, then what?"

"Dick and I and the rest of the senior staff will decide what course of action to pursue, if any."

I said, "You understand that I can't divulge anything I might have come across while I was working for Albert unless I get his permission?"

"How you go about this is your business. Mine is the hundred and sixty-seven thousand readers who depend on this newspaper to give them an honest accounting of the events of the day. It may sound quaint to you, but I feel as though I have a responsibility toward them. You do what you have to do to get this thing cleared up. We'll pay you twenty-five hundred dollars a day until you do."

I didn't even have to think about that. "Nothing doing."

Dickinson's eyebrows shot up. "That isn't enough for you?"

"No. It's too much, and we both know it."

"I don't understand."

"Sure, you do. If I let you pay me that much, you'll figure you own me. Then, at some point, you'll feel justified asking me to violate a confidence or to look the other way at something I shouldn't for the good of the newspaper. I'll be happy to work for you, Mr. Dickinson, but if I do, it'll be by my rules. And I'll charge you a thousand dollars a day, which is double my regular rate. Not to put the squeeze on you, but because I figure it's going to take a lot more time than usual, and because it's more than a little possible, I might end up getting killed."

"Jesus, we just got rid of one prima donna. Now we're getting another one. Okay, send me a bill for whatever you think is right."

"Also, I want to know about the Hermitage Group."

I had hoped to catch him off guard with the question, but he fielded it without a hitch. "There isn't anything to know. We're a group, of business people working to bring new investment dollars into the community. Every city has an organization just like ours."

"Does every civic organization have a fund-raising chairman—excuse me, a recently deceased fund-raising chairman—who was in hock up to his armpits in gambling debts? And a district attorney whose campaign for governor is being backed by a newspaper publisher who claims his only

134

concern is for the well-being of his readership?"

He said blandly, "I don't see any conflict there. Newspapers endorse candidates for office all the time. It's part of our responsibility to the community."

"Your responsibility, right," I said. "Your paper ran a story a while back about an investigation into organized crime in Nashville. I may have missed it, but I don't recall ever reading about any outcome."

"Pending a summary report from the district attorney's office, we haven't published a final installment."

"Don't you mean pending a report that reflects favorably on Roger Seacrist's campaign for governor?"

"I think," Dickinson said pointedly, "that you would do well to concentrate on the problem at hand. Leave politics to the people who are good at it."

"People like Charlie Lambert and Roger Seacrist, for instance? Or like you?" I was beginning to get irritated. Maybe it was the early hour, or that I had the distinct feeling I was led down the garden path. I said, "You know the gist of Albert's story is that Charles Lambert appears to have, what shall we say, temporarily borrowed money from the Hermitage Group to prop up a failing business and then repaid the loan with organized crime money?"

"There is no evidence I know of that would support that."

"I think there is, Mr. Dickinson. I think that evidence is what Darlene Munson has in her possession and Albert is chasing after. You do know, do you not, that Ms. Munson is holding out for a hundred thousand dollars before she turns that file over to Albert?"

For the first time since I'd shaken hands with Carver Dickinson, his face showed genuine surprise. "I did not know that, no." He turned to Dick Dohrn. "Were you aware of that, Dick?"

"First I've heard of it." Dick kept a straight face, but I got the definite impression he was enjoying his boss's obvious discomfort.

I said, "Let me ask you something, Mr. Dickinson. If Darlene were to approach either the *Times* or the Hermitage Group with the same demand, do you suppose either organization would be willing to pony up to meet that demand?"

135

"Absolutely not." He paused, considering, I supposed, what he was going to say next. "I'll be honest with you, Mr. Gamble, because I'm paying you to be honest with me. The Group certainly knew about our friend, the late Charles Lambert's financial problems. Between you and me, if he hadn't had his accident, he would have been asked to tender his resignation at the earliest opportunity. Unfortunately, as it turned out, his death made it a moot point, so that's the end of that. As far as Roger Seacrist's campaign is concerned, I happen to believe he's the right man to lead our state for the next four years and I'm within my prerogatives as publisher of the *Times* to say so."

"Fair enough," I said. "But suppose when all the rocks are finally turned over, Albert's story turns out to be right. How is the paper going to handle that?"

"My answer to that is we'll do the right thing when the time comes."

"You're saying you'll publish the truth?"

"The truth is what you make of it, Mr. Gamble. In complicated situations like this, it's never a simple matter of black and white."

"Are we talking about alternative facts here, Mr. Dickinson?" When he didn't answer, I said, "Right, got it." I got up to leave. "I'll be in touch."

"Just a minute, please." He wrote a telephone number on the back of his business card and handed it to me.

"From now on, I don't want you talking to anybody about this except me. This is my private line, and I know it's secure." Then he added, "I'll keep Dick posted on your progress. I'm not trying to shut anybody out, but I want to make sure there aren't any leaks." He gave me a small smile. "Also, try not to get shot."

This was a hell of a time to start worrying about that. I could have told him. But all the same, I found his concern touching.

Chapter Twenty

I drove from the *Times* offices back to the office and left my car in the parking lot. From there, it was a short walk to the Stahlman Building at the corner of Second and Union. I wasn't looking for exercise, but I did have a sudden urge to talk with James Austin Gannaway, the attorney who had represented both Charles Lambert and Talent Management Associates during the sale of Black Strap Music Corporation. Following my sit-down with Carver Dickinson, I was feeling sleek, sassy, and ready to kick ass and take names. Having a client with deep pockets has that effect on me.

I found Gannaway's office on the fourth floor. With a client list that included Robert Edward Cherry and Charles Lambert, I expected an upscale layout. Instead, I found a one-man operation similar to my own, with a waiting room and a private think-tank for Gannaway himself. The main differences between his setup and mine were that the attorney had better quality waiting room chairs, a television set tuned, not surprisingly, to Fox News, and a living, breathing receptionist. She was a bottle blonde, attractive in the right light, and a few years on the downhill side of forty. The nameplate on her desk said her name was Glenace Rowe. When I walked in, she was sitting at her desk with her left shoe in one hand and the heel of that same shoe in the other.

She held the shoe and its truncated heel out for me to inspect. "You have any idea how to fix this?"

I shook my head. "Gorilla Glue? Otherwise, not the first idea."

She frowned in discouragement. "Me neither. I caught it in a sidewalk grate this morning. I don't know how I'll be able to walk to the parking lot tonight."

"Very carefully," I suggested. "Is your boss in?"

She put down the shoe and flipped open her appointment calendar. "You are?"

"In a hurry," I said, handing her a card.

"I don't see your name, Mr. Hurry," she said, overlooking my attempt at humor. "Is Mr. Gannaway expecting you?"

"I'm sure he's not. I only need a minute."

She snapped the book shut again. "Then you'll have to come back another time. Mr. Gannaway is very busy right now, and I'm afraid he never sees anyone without an appointment."

"I don't mind waiting," I offered.

"He's going to be tied up all day." She smiled with the bottom half of her face, showing me a row of teeth that would have made a barracuda blush. I got the message.

"In that case, I wonder if you could give this to Mr. Gannaway." I took my business card out of her hand and wrote a name on the back. "Tell him I'll wait five minutes."

It was a heavy-handed approach, but as heavy-handedness sometimes does, it prompted action. Glenace Rowe excused herself and hopped lopsidedly on one shoe into Gannaway's private office. I heard a few words of muffled conversation, then a man's voice shouting something I couldn't quite make out. In another moment, the office door opened again, and Glenace stood to the side, looking flushed.

"Mr. Gannaway will see you now, Mr. Gamble."

I gave her a smile as I passed. "My advice? I'd try to break the heel off the other shoe if I were you. It'd be a lot easier walking that way."

Gannaway's office turned out to be more upscale than the waiting room suggested. There was a wealth of dark wood paneling, chairs upholstered in olive-and-burgundy needlepoint, and a glass-faced cabinet filled with volumes of Tennessee statute law. A framed diploma from the University of Texas School of Law hung on the wall by the bookcase. Next to that was a photo of Gannaway's graduating class and a certificate affirming that he was a member in good standing of the Tennessee Bar Association. There were also framed photographs of Gannaway mugging it up with some of his clients and various other individuals. I recognized Charles Lambert, a couple of past Nashville mayors, several city councilmen, my old boss Roger Seacrist, and a few others. Gannaway, it seemed, was a man who knew the right people. He was a round-faced man of middle years with a receding hairline and an advancing waistline. He was dressed for a funeral in a black suit, a crisp white shirt, and a navy blue tie with red stripes. He smelled strongly of Old Spice and Old Granddad, as if he'd applied a liberal dose of each just prior to my arrival.

Gannaway sat without speaking until Glenace had closed the door and taken a seat on one of the two chairs facing the desk. I noticed that she had a stenographer's notebook in one hand and a ballpoint pen in the other. Her boss continued to wait until Glenace clicked the end of her ballpoint and nodded she was ready for whatever was coming next.

I sat down without waiting for an invitation. "I appreciate you squeezing me in on such short notice."

"You're welcome." He fingered the edge of the card I'd given Glenace. "I'm going to ask Glenace to take a few notes during our conversation. I hope you won't mind. Nothing personal. It's just a precaution, in case questions arise later."

"Always a good idea," I said.

"Yes, well, since you're here because you evidently know my client, Mr. Cherry, I'm guessing you either know something or you want something. However, I'm due in court in a little over an hour, so why don't we skip the pleasantries for now, and you just tell me which one it is?"

"We're getting a little ahead of ourselves, aren't we? I mean, aren't you supposed to say something like 'I never heard of anybody named Robert Edward Cherry and I don't have time to waste talking to you'?"

"What I don't have, sir, is time to cock around playing games with you. Pardon me, Glenace. If you've got something to say, let's hear it. Otherwise, get out before I call building security and have you thrown out."

We sat trading hard looks for a few seconds, but it was never a real contest.

He dropped his eyes. "Let's try this again," he offered. "Your card mentions the name Cherry. Do you have a connection with Mr. Cherry, or was that just something to get in the door?"

"Mostly to get in the door," I admitted. "But even so, you'd be doing us all a favor to hear me out."

"You talk," he said. "I'll decide about favors."

I said, "About a week ago, I was hired for what started out to be a routine investigation into an unrelated matter. In the course of my inquiries, I ran across the names Black Strap Music Corporation and Talent Management Associates. One of my associates did some digging and discovered that Black Strap was bought out by TMA not long ago, and that both parties were represented by you. That seemed a little unusual, so I thought before I drew any wrong conclusions about it, maybe I ought to drop by and get a few more of the details."

"Why do you need details? Are you working for either of the parties to the transaction?"

"Not at this time."

"Then you already know I can't divulge any information relating to either of my clients, or about the deal itself. You could have called me here at the office, and I would have told you the same thing. It would have saved you a trip."

"And would you have taken my call?"

"Probably not. And the fact you're sitting here doesn't mean I'm going to tell you anything more than I would have on the telephone. Mr. Gamble, I assume you have a legitimate interest in asking me about all this?"

"Trust me."

He laughed harshly. "Now that's something that's hard to come by in both of our businesses, wouldn't you agree? And anyway, I couldn't tell you anything even if I wanted to. What you're asking for is privileged information. I can't discuss any dealings on behalf of any client without talking to them first, or at least without having some idea what you want it for."

I knew I had him then. Any attorney on the up-and-up would have simply told me to buzz off, that the water I was fishing in was strictly off-limits. The fact that Gannaway was doing a little angling of his own confirmed that Quail and I had guessed right. There was something more to the Black Strap deal than just a simple business transaction. Gannaway was worried about how much I knew.

I said, "Look out that window behind you and tell me what you see. This is the Bible Belt, Counselor, not Hollywood Babylon. And we're not talking about some alt-rock or hip-hop label. Black Strap produces and markets gospel and C&W music. If I have to spell it out for you, that kind of music sells to a very socially conservative audience."

"And that's supposed to mean what to me?"

"Just this. My client has influential media connections. Do you have any idea what would happen to Black Strap's record sales—or at least what's left of them—if word got out the new owner was actually a gangster named Red Cherry? Or, if that's too strong a word for you, let's call him an individual with suspected underworld connections. The TV and newspaper people would be swarming over you like crows on roadkill. I don't know what that would do for your practice, but I think I know what it would do for Black Strap's record sales, or whatever is left of them. I also have a pretty strong hunch Red isn't looking for that kind of publicity."

"I think," he said evenly, "that you're skating on some very thin ice here, Mr. Gamble. I'd advise you to be careful what you say next because it's starting to sound perilously close to extortion."

"With respect, Mr. Gannaway, if I wanted to squeeze you or your client, you'd feel it. Are you getting this, Glenace?"

"Every word," she said, giving me a smile that said she was enjoying the conversation immensely.

Gannaway drummed his fingers on the arms of his chair. "Your funeral," he said finally. "I can tell you this much. When Mr. Lambert sold Black Strap, he was in a pinch for cash. The only buyer around able to bail him out without asking a lot of questions was my client, Mr. Cherry. I handled the deal because it was a straightforward buyout, and a lot of additional legal advice wasn't needed. Also, to put it bluntly, Mr. Lambert didn't have much choice. My client made a take-it-or-leave-it proposition."

"Like an offer he couldn't refuse? How much was the offer?"

"Jesus, Gamble, what do you think? I can't discuss that with you. Besides, I don't carry every transaction I'm involved with around in my head."

"I'll bet Glenace has it in her files. Should we ask her to check?"

"All right," he sighed. "To the best of my recollection, it was in the neighborhood of one point three million. In addition, Talent Management assumed the obligations for Black Strap's secured debt which, I might add, was substantial."

"That's all? A million three doesn't sound like much for a company that size."

"That's because what you see isn't always what you get. Black Strap is actually two companies: a recording studio and a publishing house, and their operations are quite different."

"Give me the short course."

"It's like this. Say you've got a studio and a publishing house. The studio is where music is actually recorded. Unless they're big-name artists and own their own studios, they pay a fee for the use of its facilities whenever a recording is made. That includes use of the studio itself, on a per-hour basis. It also includes recording and mixing equipment, plus union scale for however many session musicians or backup vocalists are required. It costs more if you want A-list session people, but all that is spelled out ahead of time. Once the basic tracks are recorded, there's post-production work, adding additional overdubs and sound effects like car horns, birds singing, whatever. It's all spelled out ahead of time, same as if you hired a plumber, or took your car in for service. It can get expensive in a hurry."

"Okay."

"But the publishing house makes its money from the sale of records, CDs, or these days, downloads, plus royalties from radio airplay and streaming services, like Spotify. That can be real money as well, because even fractions of a cent per play on a popular song can add up to a big number. If the song is ever covered by another artist, or if it's used in a movie soundtrack, or as a jingle in a commercial, there are separate royalties for that. Plus, whoever

142

holds the rights to the song gets paid for radio airplay. And best of all, from an investment standpoint, the rights to songs can be bought and sold, just like patents or stock certificates."

"Like when Michael Jackson bought the Lennon-McCartney catalog."

He nodded. "Paul and John should have read their original contract, but that's another matter."

"Go on."

"Well, in Black Strap's case, the difficulty was that Lambert had been selling off his song catalog piecemeal for a number of years. The popular songs were just about gone, and the new material they were putting out wasn't nearly as marketable. So, to make a long story short, what TMA actually got for its money was the studio, the rights to the Black Strap name, and a handful of songs that, to be honest, weren't all that strong. But even that wasn't free and clear. There was a second mortgage on the office and the studio for more than twenty million dollars. When you take all that into account, Lambert actually got far more than just a million three."

"You mean in the sense that he got out from under the accumulated debt. How was the payout handled?"

"About three hundred thousand was paid in the form of a certified check to Lambert himself."

"Made out just to Lambert," I interrupted, "or Lambert and his wife?"

"Just him. Her name was not on the incorporation filing. The rest was assigned to a creditors' committee for the purpose of liquidating outstanding personal loans Lambert had made using the business as collateral."

"So, for all intents and purposes, he was flat broke." I had to smile at the simplicity of it all. "Let me guess. One of the biggest creditors on that committee was TMA."

"After the sale was finalized, Talent Management Associates was represented, yes. Of course, TMA also assumed the obligation for the second on the office and the studio."

"Sure, it did. What better way to launder Lambert's gambling debts to Cherry than to have their respective businesses assume the obligations? What's the next step, bankruptcy and a massive tax write-off?"

Gannaway shifted uneasily in his chair. "Not my area. I wouldn't have any knowledge of any financial plans subsequent to the transaction."

"Or maybe a late-night fire or a boiler explosion? Would anything like that be in the offing?"

"I won't dignify that with a response one way or the other."

"No, of course you won't. Having knowledge of that kind of goings-on could get you disbarred, couldn't it?"

He suddenly sat up straight.

"Now, that does sound like a threat."

"Just thinking out loud. So, what Lambert actually ended up with was three hundred grand and a figurehead job as president of the new company. I wouldn't say that's much of a tradeoff for twenty years work, would you?"

"Under the circumstances, I'd say he was very lucky. He still had his reputation, and he still had a job that paid exceptionally well. That's not bad for a guy who was thirty days away from being forced to close his doors, in which case he would have gotten next to nothing."

I dropped my hole card on the table. "Are you aware that the money Charley Lambert received from Robert Edward Cherry—or do you call him Red? Are you aware that that money very likely found its way into the campaign fund supporting Roger Seacrist's candidacy for governor?"

There was a pause. "I don't get involved in politics."

"Okay, let me ask you this, then. At any point during the course of your meetings with Charley Lambert and Red Cherry, was Roger Seacrist either present or represented by anyone in his employ?"

"Now you're losing me, Mr. Gamble. What am I missing here?"

"Why don't you tell me? My information is that the money Lambert borrowed from Red Cherry went straight into the Hermitage Group accounts to replace the money he'd siphoned off earlier to try to prop up the recording company when it was on the verge of collapse. I'm thinking you helped our friend Mr. Cherry engineer this buyout so he'd have something on Seacrist after the election. Either that or Seacrist was in the loop from the get-go. Maybe his involvement would be enough to forestall any further organized crime investigations, at least until Roger was safely off to the governor's mansion. Tell me, counselor, is that the kind of law they taught you at the University of Texas?"

Gannaway's face got suddenly red, and I thought for a moment he might collapse right there in his expensive leather desk chair.

"You like fishing, Mr. Gamble?"

"It's a manly sport," I told him.

"That's a good thing, then, because if you think you can just walk in here and talk to me like that, you're going to wind up face-to-face with the biggest fucking catfish you ever saw. Only it'll be him fishing for you, not the other way around."

I said, "Now who's making threats?"

"I want to know where you got that information."

"Forget it," I said. "I'll talk to Red."

"I'm pretty sure he won't want to talk to you."

"But I'll bet you can arrange it."

"Not a chance."

"Then I guess that's where we leave it. I'll keep following this up on my own, but all the same, you might want to mention to him I stopped by. You never know what he'll say."

"I know what he'll do if you start spreading that story around."

"Well, now we know who's holding the other end of your leash, don't we, Counselor?" I said and showed myself out.

Chapter Twenty-One

O ne thing about swatting at a hornet's nest with a short stick. The result tends to sharpen your focus.

I was a block from the office when I remembered something that I should have followed up days earlier. It was a detail really, something that had fallen through the cracks during all the excitement the morning I got carted off to the Harding Hoosegow. Trouble is, when everything's said and done. It's usually the little things that make the biggest difference.

As soon as I got back to my office, I telephoned the state Department of Motor Vehicles and asked for Drew Little in the data processing section. Drew was a guy I'd once helped straighten out an especially messy divorce. That had been several years earlier, before I stopped accepting domestic cases. I was counting on him still being grateful.

"This is Gamble," I said when he came on the line. "I need a favor."

There was an easy laugh in my ear. "Imagine my surprise."

"I know, but this really is easy. I need a make on a license plate." I recited the number I'd memorized in Harding a few days earlier. "It's registered to a Ford sedan. A Crown Vic, blue. I'd say it's at least fifteen years old."

"No problem, just take a minute." The line went dead while he put me on hold. After a suitable interval, he was back.

"That plate is registered to Davidson County. It's a motor pool license. The car could be used by just about anybody from a building inspector to somebody from the health department."

"Cops?" I asked.

"No. Police cars are registered differently."

"How about the district attorney's office? Do they use county cars?"

"Sure, I guess so. I don't see why not." So that answered that. The guys who'd followed me to the Rustic retreat were detectives working for the district attorney's office. That meant Roger Seacrist had been wise to whatever Albert Glass was working on from the very outset.

My next call was to the answering service to pick up my messages. There were two. The first was from Mrs. Delilah Liggett, calling to find out whether I'd made any progress locating her daughter, Amelia Anne. She left a number where I could call her back, so I did.

She picked up on the second ring. "Mrs. Liggett, this is Jackson Gamble, returning your call. We spoke at my office yesterday. I assume you were calling about your daughter."

"Yes."

I decided to suck it up. "Mrs. Liggett, I'm sorry to have to be the one telling you this, but your daughter is dead. She was killed twenty years ago. The man who murdered her—I don't have his name—but the man who murdered her is in prison. He's on death row, awaiting execution. The police did tell you that, didn't they?"

"Of course, they did. Don't you think I relive that day every moment of my life?"

"Then what…" I started to say.

"I just want someone to care. I want someone to listen to me when I tell them what a wonderful girl she was, how full of life. How beautifully she played piano. I want somebody to understand that she had a future and that she would grow up, get married, have children of her own, and have a happy life. I want someone to know how much I loved her."

Got it. I said, "Mrs. Liggett, do you have pictures of your daughter?"

"I do. I have whole albums filled with pictures of my Amelia. She was a beautiful girl, Mr. Gamble. Everybody who knew her said so."

"Then how about this? Why don't you bring that album down to my office next week? If you'd like, I'll make you a cup of coffee. We'll look at the pictures together, and maybe you can tell me all about Amelia."

There was a long silence. I said, "Mrs. Liggett?"

"You would do that?"

"Absolutely. Next week. Just give me a call, and we'll pick a time."

"Thank you." Another silence, shorter this time. "You are a decent man," she said and hung up.

Some days, I hate my job.

The second message was from Dave Quail. He had called early that morning to tell me he was sorry we had missed connections and that I should stop by his house to talk about some information he had turned up since yesterday. I copied down the address, let the service know I would be going out again, and locked up the office.

Half an hour later, I pulled up outside Quail's house. It was a small brown brick bungalow in the middle of a long block of well-kept brick bungalows in the older part of Donelson. No consequential money had ever lived on this block, and none ever would. But despite his obvious handicaps, that hadn't prevented Dave from keeping up appearances. Consistent with the overall tenor of the neighborhood, the lawn was neatly mowed, the paint on the trim was fresh, and the driveway had been recently resurfaced with a coat of shiny black sealant. An aging but freshly washed Ford Focus was parked there.

I left my own rolling museum piece at the curb and walked across the lawn to the house. A note stuck in the screen door read, "Office in the garage, come on back," so I hopped down off the porch and followed the driveway around to the rear of the property.

My first thought was that I'd missed him. The one-car garage Dave had converted into a workstation was locked securely. I climbed up on an overturned wheelbarrow and peered through the window. Nobody home. The lights were off, and the monitor of Quail's desktop computer was dark. I had already dropped back down to the ground before it struck me what else I had seen. It was the flesh-toned plastic of a prosthetic leg, still wearing a shoe and a sock, sticking out from behind the desk. It took three tries before the service door yielded to the weight of my shoulder. Then the frame split apart, and I was inside.

Dave Quail was lying on his back behind his desk. He hadn't gone easily.

There was blood covering the front of his shirt from the bullet wound in his neck, just below the right ear. His face was purple and swollen. His prosthetic lower leg had come partially detached and was bent at an odd angle away from the rest of his body. The tan linen jacket he was wearing both times we had met previously was draped over the back of the desk chair.

Discovering a dead body is never pleasant, no matter the circumstances. Sometimes, people die peacefully in bed, either from old age, a long illness, or a bolt out of the blue like a stroke or a heart attack. Sometimes, they're killed in an automobile accident, or they fall off a roof, cleaning leaves out of the rain gutters and break their necks. Once in a while, they go fishing, have a few beers too many, and then fall out of the boat while pissing over the side. And sometimes, like now, somebody kills them.

There are procedures for cops to follow when securing the scene of a homicide, including photographing the body *in situ*, as well as the area in which it was found. Equally important is not disturbing anything until the proper personnel are on hand, which means a medical examiner and trained homicide detectives. I was neither of those, so I followed the only rule I was absolutely certain applied to me, and that was not to touch anything where I might leave a fingerprint.

At first glance, it didn't appear as though anything of a physical nature was amiss, at least if I could manage to overlook a dead man on the floor. No drawers had been pulled out, and their contents dumped on the floor. The computer did not appear to have been tampered with, although the hard drive could have been wiped or removed altogether, or individual files deleted. I had no way of knowing about that. What I did not see, however, was the notebook Dave was carrying the last time we'd been together, nor the notebooks he had appropriated from Albert Glass's file cabinet. Whoever had killed him must have taken those with him. What I did find was a bottle of prescription pain pills and a small bag of marijuana. I left those where they were.

If the still-damp blood on his body was any indication, Dave had been killed no more than an hour or so earlier. The answering service said he'd called at eight-fifteen. It was eleven forty-five now. I'd left Gannaway's office at nine-thirty. That would have given him more than enough time to relay my message to Red Cherry, and for Red to put out a contract on Dave.

But why go after Dave? And except for Dick Dohrn, who else even knew he was involved? I hadn't mentioned his name to Gannaway, or to Carver Dickinson, or anyone else I'd talked to since our meeting the previous evening. Dick knew that Quail and I had talked, but I doubted he would have said anything about our conversations to anyone who might have represented a threat. So. Had Quail decided he had taken his research on Albert as far as he could and started digging into Cherry's operation on his own to try to confirm whatever leads he had developed? I'd gone out of my way to warn him against trying something like that. But even at the time, I recognized the fire in his eyes when he realized he might be chasing an important story, and I knew there was no way I could have stopped him.

I took a deep breath and forced myself to take a closer look at the body. Quail's eyes were wide open, as if the bullet had been a complete surprise. He'd been shot from behind with a small caliber weapon, probably a .22, and at very close range. The entry wound was just beneath the jawbone. As there was no exit wound, the slug had evidently deflected upward and into his brain. The concussion had spilled him over backwards in his chair. He was almost certainly dead before he hit the floor, although his heart had continued to beat for a few moments after his brain had been scrambled into an omelet. With the extensive damage inside his skull, blood was able to accumulate within tissue and underneath the skin. That explained the swelling and discoloration of his face.

I knew from my time with the cops that professionals tend to favor small caliber autoloading pistols, because those are the only ones that can be silenced reliably. On the off chance that Dave's killer ran true to form, I got down on my hands and knees to see whether the shell casing might have been ejected and lost under the desk. There was no sign of it, but I did find something else: a single piece of note paper with a telephone number I remembered seeing before.

I picked up the phone on the desk and began dialing. Then I stopped, because that was all the time it took before the sequence of digits registered, and I remembered where I had seen that number before.

Chapter Twenty-Two

On a light traffic day, it's an easy forty-minute drive from Donelson to Fox Park Circle in Hendersonville. Today, I broke every traffic law that's ever been written and made it in twenty-eight minutes flat. I had strong reason to hurry. There was a lot that I still needed to do, and not much time before I figured to be out of circulation for a while.

On the way, I got on my phone, blocked caller ID, and called the cops. I told them I was one of Dave Quail's neighbors and that I wanted to report a prowler nosing around his garage. Once they got there and found the body, I knew it wouldn't take long for them to put me at the scene, but there was nothing I could do about that. I couldn't just leave him for some neighbor kid to find hours or days later.

I leaned hard on Audra Lambert's doorbell and kept on leaning until the opening chords of "What a Friend We Have in Jesus" played at least a half-dozen times. Finally, Elvis Preston came to the door. Today, he was wearing a pair of white gym shorts and a red knit pullover shirt. I wouldn't have thought it was possible, but free of the loose folds of his sweatsuit, he looked even bigger than I remembered.

"Back again?" His tone of voice made it sound like I was a rat trying to get in through a hole in the screen door. "I guess you don't remember what I said would happen next time I saw you."

"Save that for some other time, will you? I need to talk to Audra right away."

"You mean Mrs. Lambert, don't you?" He stationed himself squarely in the doorway and folded his arms across his chest. "I don't think she's expecting you."

I heard a humming noise start to build inside my head and could feel the tingling sensation of a rapidly rising adrenalin rush. My field of vision began to narrow so that the only thing I could see clearly was the big man standing in the doorway. It was the same sensation I'd experienced when I was on the job, and it looked as though somebody was about to start shooting. It meant that one of us was about to get hurt, maybe badly.

"Okay, Elvis," I said. "Here's how it is. You can show some manners and stand aside. Or else, I will give you exactly five seconds to get out of my way, and then I am going in to talk to the lady of the house. I can either go around you, through you, or right straight over you. One way or the other. It makes no difference to me."

He looked at me the way a predator sizes up an easy meal. Then, with a lightning movement, he reached out and slapped me hard on the right ear.

"'Less you want to really get hurt, you best run along now." His other hand flashed out, and he slapped me again, this time on the left ear, near where Roydell Jones's cantaloupe-sized fist had knocked me flat the week before. A white-hot flash of pain shot through my still-tender jawbone, and I could taste fresh blood seeping into my mouth. The pain left me momentarily dazed, and I took a step back to clear my head.

Preston moved in for the finish. "Okay, pal. You want to see the lady so bad, it's just like you said. You can go over me, around me, or through me." He clasped his hands behind his back and stuck his chin out defiantly.

"C'mon, buddy, give me your best shot. Let's see what you got."

That was his mistake. I am no street fighter, although I have won a few and lost many more. If Elvis had pressed his advantage and just kept on swinging, he could have easily finished me there and then. But for some reason, he didn't. He gave me a second to consider what to do next, and I am not above getting down in the dirt.

I took a short step sideways and backward, as if to put a little maneuvering room between us. But instead of throwing the punch he no doubt expected, I pivoted on my left foot and kicked him squarely in the balls. It was a solid shot, hard enough to lift him partway off his feet. He gave a strangled cough and doubled over, gasping raggedly for breath. He crawfished backward through the doorway, both hands covering his wounded testicles. Before he could straighten up, I stomped down hard on his left foot, in the process, I was sure, breaking two or three metatarsals. Then I grabbed him by the collar and the waistband of his shorts and ran him head-first into the door frame. Staggered but still game, he made a swiping motion at my legs, but I cut that short with a hard right hook into his ribs. Then I knee-walked him out onto the porch and, with another well-placed kick to his backside, sent him sprawling down the steps onto the front sidewalk.

"Big possums walk late," I said to nobody in particular.

I stood in the open doorway for a moment, waiting until I could clear my head and get my breathing under control. Then I went looking for Audra Lambert.

* * *

I retraced my steps from my previous visit, down the hallway and toward the sitting room at the back end of the house. Audra wasn't there, but General Forrest was, still scowling darkly down from his perch on the wall. I threw the look right back at him.

"The hell with you, too, bub."

A movement by the swimming pool caught my eye, so I walked outside to take a look. Audra was sunning herself on a white vinyl lounge chair, stretched out full-length, like a great, elegant cat. She was dressed in a black, form-fitting bathing suit that would have done credit to a woman half her age. At another time, under other circumstances, the effect would have been heart-stopping, but today was not that day. Much as I might have enjoyed pausing a moment to take in the view, this was a business call.

She didn't notice me approaching until I was almost next to her. Then she heard my footsteps on the pool apron and looked up.

"Gamble." She stared at me with astonishment. "How did you get in here?"

"The door was open. I let myself in."

She sat up, wary. "I don't understand. Where's Elvis?"

154

"Don't you mean, how did I get past him without getting my neck broken? Elvis has left the building." When that got no response, I said. "Why, is there a problem? Didn't you say you hoped you'd see me again?"

"Yes, of course I did. It's just…I wish you had called first. I might have been busy."

"Are you busy? You don't look busy."

"Gamble, why are you acting like this? Is something wrong?"

"You could say that, yes. Something is wrong." I pulled one of the deck chairs around and sat down so that I was directly facing her. "It's truth time, Audra. No more holding back. No more games. No more lies."

She pushed her sunglasses up so that they rested on top of her head. "I don't understand any of this. Has something happened?"

I reached into my pocket for the piece of paper I'd found under Dave Quail's desk. I held it out for her to see.

"You know what this is?"

"My phone number."

"Say it again."

She looked at me, uncertain. "If this is some kind of a joke, I'm afraid you've lost me."

The humming noise inside my head was starting again. "I'm not fucking around, Audra. Tell me what this is."

"Damn you, it's my telephone number. So what?"

"So, this is what. A reporter named Dave Quail had it. You remember that name, don't you? I asked you about him the other day, and you said you didn't know who he was."

"I remember. I still don't."

"Well then, let me tell you. I just came from his house. He's dead. He was murdered. Somebody put a gun under his ear and blew his brains into applesauce. I don't think he even saw it coming."

"Oh, God, no! How terrible."

"Terrible for him, anyway. And maybe for you, too, if I don't get some straight answers."

"What are you saying? You think I killed him?"

"No, I don't. But I do think you're a big part of the reason he's dead." I folded the paper and put it back in my pocket. "I'm assuming from this that he called you. What did he want to talk to you about?"

"I don't know what he wanted. He telephoned here last night. He said he was working with you on a story, and he hoped I might have some information he needed. I didn't have time to talk with him just then and said so. I told him if he wanted to give me a call back this morning, I'd try to find a few minutes to spend with him."

"What else?"

"That's it. That's all there was to it."

"Are you sure? He didn't tell you what he was working on?"

"No. He was very vague, but with everything that's been happening, I assumed it must have been something else to do with Charles."

"But he didn't actually say that?"

"No. If he had said any more, I'd tell you."

"Would you? I wonder." I got out of my chair and walked over to the side of the pool. I looked down into the cool blue water rippling in the breeze and then up into the sky, bleached white as death by the mid-afternoon sun. My shirt was sweat stuck to my back, and I could feel the beginnings of a headache.

I went back to where she was sitting and pulled my chair around. "Okay. What happened after that?"

"Nothing happened. He didn't call back this morning, so I assumed that whatever he wanted, it must not have been important. When you asked me before if I had met him, I was telling the truth when I said no. And except for that one telephone call last night, I still haven't. So, if you or the police or anybody else thinks he can implicate me in his murder because of one telephone call, you're welcome to try. My attorney will have you laughed right out of court."

"He might," I allowed, "if that's all there was to it. But it's not, because even if what you say about Dave Quail is right, that you only talked to him the one time, there's still a problem with your relationship with Albert Glass."

"You're losing me again. I don't have a relationship with Albert Glass."

156

"Then you tell me what you'd call it. After I left here the other night, I drove over to Darlene Munson's apartment. I wanted to see if I could find anything that might give me an idea where she'd gone."

"And did you?"

"I never had a chance to look. When I got there, the door was open. I found Albert inside, tearing the place apart. I almost shot him before I realized who he was. Albert didn't want to tell me where he'd been, or what he'd been doing. But I told him I was going to go to the police unless I got some answers, and that made him jumpy enough to finally start talking. Can you guess what he had to say?"

"No, and I don't think I care, either."

"Maybe you should. Piecing together what he told me with what Dave Quail and I had already figured out, it looks very much as if your husband was involved in a scheme with an organized crime figure named Red Cherry. A scheme that wound up funneling mob money into Roger Seacrist's campaign fund."

She shook her head doggedly. "That makes no sense. Charles did some foolish things in his life, but he was not involved with criminals. I doubt he even knew this Red Cherry you're talking about."

"Oh, he knew him all right. I'm absolutely sure that's what's in the file Darlene got from your husband. That's why Albert wants it so badly. I didn't know it when I took the case, but I now believe it shows that your husband owed Cherry big money, likely millions. It's how he kept his recording company afloat for as long as he did. Selling Black Strap to one of Cherry's front companies for dimes on the dollar was how he finally paid him off."

I searched her face for a reaction and got nothing. "Is any of this starting to get through to you, or do you want me to keep going?"

"Go ahead and say what you've got to say. You obviously think you've got everything worked out already."

"Not quite everything, I don't. At least, not yet. When I heard about your husband and Cherry throwing in together, I wasn't sure what to make of it, either. I'd never met your husband, so I didn't have any particular reason to think he would be above that sort of thing, except that the story didn't feel quite right. On the other hand, I didn't have any way to prove or disprove it."

"It doesn't sound to me as if you have any evidence of anything, do you?"

"Maybe I do. After I left Albert at Darlene's apartment, I decided to see where he was going next. I didn't have anything particular in mind. I was just curious, so I tailed him. I thought that maybe after the shaking-up I gave him, if he was going to get careless, this might be the time he'd do it."

I said, "Do you want me to tell you where I followed him, Audra, or is that not necessary?"

There was a long pause. "No, not necessary," she said, finally. "He was here." She made a small movement with her hands. "My robe is on the back of the chair there. Would you hand it to me, please?"

I retrieved it and held it open for her to slip into. Then, I steered her toward one of the pool chairs and got her to sit down.

"Okay, let's try this again, shall we? Albert came by to see you the other night. What did he want, money?"

"Money? No. He wanted to get a look at Black Strap's financial records. He said he had lined up a forensic accountant to examine them."

"Then, you did know there was something going on between your husband and Cherry."

"No. Not until Albert was here the other night. It was then that he told me what he was working on. He said he thought if he could get a look at the books, there might be something that would help keep Charles in the clear."

"More likely it was to hand him his story on a silver platter. Did you let him take them?"

She shook her head. "I didn't have them to give. Black Strap was a private company, so there were never any public filings. And anyway, there are no books as such. All the company's financial records were on a computer in our accountant's office."

"Not quite all of them. I'm betting that whatever moves your husband was making with the Hermitage Group's campaign funds were in a separate file, and that's the one that Darlene Munson somehow made off with. The same file that Albert is so anxious to see."

CHAPTER TWENTY-TWO

She sat, thinking. "So, what happens now?"

"Good question. On my way over here, I called the police to report finding a dead body. Here's going to be the sequence of events, starting right about now. The cops are going to find Dave Quail's body, and then they'll find out he worked for the *Times*. After that, they'll get in touch with his bosses and ask what's the last thing he was working on. They'll also dump his phone. Those two things will connect him to me, and also to you, since he called you yesterday.

"After I leave here, I'm going to go back to my office to wait for the police. Might as well make it easy for them. They'll take me to headquarters for questioning. Unless they already know more than I think they do, your name probably won't come up, and I will not volunteer it. Even so, my guess is before the day is over, there'll be a couple of homicide detectives knocking on your door. They're going to ask you how you knew Quail and what did you talk about when he called."

"If they do, what should I tell them?"

"As little as you can. Tell them Quail called yesterday and asked to meet with you today, but that he never called back. Other than that, you've never spoken with him before or since." I gave her a hard look. "That is true, isn't it?"

"Yes."

"Okay. But depending upon who they talk to at the *Times*, they might already know more than we think. If they start asking about anything else, especially if they want to talk about your husband's business dealings, or if Albert's name comes up, tell them they should talk to your attorney. The cops don't like it when people lawyer up, but you'll be within your rights, and refusing to talk to them without your lawyer present won't incriminate you in any way."

"I understand."

"Good. And for God's sake, whatever you do, don't talk to anybody else. Especially, don't talk to Albert Glass. Don't take any of his calls. Don't let him come to the house. Don't agree to meet him someplace. Tell him you're sick, get Elvis to break both his legs if that's what it takes, but absolutely stay away from him. Right now, as far as you're concerned, he's radioactive, you understand?"

She nodded. "When will I hear from you?"

"I don't know. It might be a day or two. I'll be in touch."

* * *

Driving back into the city, all I could think about was my conversation with Audra and the mess we were both in. Every instinct in my body told me she was mixed up to her eyebrows in whatever financial shell game her husband was running with Red Cherry. And even if she wasn't involved, she had to at least have had an idea what was going on. At the same time, I didn't really think she had anything to do with Dave Quail's murder. But even so, she was about to be in a very tough spot, and I came close to feeling sorry for her. And then I remembered a seventeen-year-old girl wearing a white robe and her first pair of high-heeled shoes, singing in a gospel choir in Rock Hill, South Carolina, and how far she had come since then.

And I had to wonder all over again.

Chapter Twenty-Three

I got back to the office around three-thirty. If you were a teacher or a stockbroker, you might have already called it a day. If you were a salesman, or a truck driver, or an employee in almost any other line of work, it might be time for an afternoon coffee, or a cigarette break. For me, though, it was just another hour in another long day, and I was pretty sure it was about to get a great deal longer. My suspicion was confirmed the moment I stepped off the elevator.

Halfway down the corridor, I could see the door to my waiting room standing open. I don't keep it locked during business hours, but I distinctly remembered pulling it shut on my way out that morning. I thought about turning around and heading back down the elevator, then decided I might as well go ahead and face the inevitable.

There were two of them. There are always two of them when detectives make a business call. I knew them both. The older one I met during my time on the job, and we had reconnected a few times after that, including two years earlier, when I had been forced to fatally shoot a man while working on a case involving a runaway teenaged girl.

All things considered, for a cop, he was a pretty decent guy. His name was Detective Sergeant John Spillner. It had taken him just short of three decades to work his way up through the ranks, and was the second most senior man working homicide out of Central Division. He was well into his fifties, tall and angular, with a face like a sad old coon dog. He wore a tan suit, which could have used a pressing, and a blue shirt that was worn around the collar and cuffs and faded from too many trips through the washing machine. He looked tired and bored, and I guessed that the minute the clock ticked past his retirement date, he'd put in his papers, take the money, and never look backward.

The other detective was younger and harder-looking, with deep-set, piercing eyes and dark hair cut short like a Parris Island drill instructor. Although our paths had crossed once or twice, I knew him more by reputation than by actual contact. At that, it was enough for us to develop an intense, mutual dislike. His name was Gardner, and he was one of those cops who, for two cents, would cheerfully push you down a flight of stairs and then kick you in the teeth if you complained about how hard it was to get back up again.

Both of them stood up when I walked in. It's a habit with cops, but not out of politeness. At some point in every policeman's training, they're taught they have a more commanding presence on their feet than sitting down, and some of them actually believe it. The toughest cop I ever knew could scare the hell out of you lying in a hospital bed with both his legs in traction. More important, though, and as a practical matter, it's much more difficult to reach your weapon, or to fight off an attacker, if you're parked on your backside in a chair.

"Well, well, Gamble, nice to see you again," said Gardner, starting the conversation off on a cheerful note. "Still operating the same fancy setup, I see."

"Hello, Gardner. When did they start letting you out without a leash?"

The older officer spoke up. "Since you two seem to be old pals already, I guess there's no need for introductions."

"None at all." I walked across the waiting room and unlocked the door to the inner office. Both cops followed me inside. Spillner folded his bony frame into the customer's chair. Gardner hung behind long enough to make a big production out of checking out the new door.

"This is some pretty heavy-duty security here, Gamble. What are you trying to do, keep the bill collectors out?"

"Squirrels in the attic. Up until just now, I thought we'd gotten rid of them." I sat down behind my desk and waited. When nobody spoke up, I said, "You guys here for anything in particular, or are we just wrapping up a slow afternoon razzing the gumshoe?"

Spillner said with practiced offhandedness, "A newspaper reporter named David Quail. Know him?"

I nodded. "A little."

"Exactly how much is a little?"

"A little is not a lot. Like this." I held up my thumb and forefinger so they were about an inch apart. "I met him last week through a mutual friend who works at the *Times*. We shared a couple pitchers of beer, and he reminisced about his days as a session musician. After that, I can't tell you for sure what we talked about."

Spillner frowned. "Can't tell us, why?"

"Oh, wait," I said. Did you not hear the part about the beer?"

"And you never met him before that?"

"Like I said, I met him for the first time last week. I stopped by the *Times* to do a little background research on a case I've been working on. Quail helped me locate a couple of articles that turned out to be useful. I bought a few rounds as a thank-you for the help. Why, have we got a problem here?"

Gardner piped up. "Let us ask the questions, will you, Gamble? You just be a good citizen and answer. What did you talk about when you saw Quail last time? Besides music, I mean?"

"I told you. We talked about being a session musician, and then he told me about getting injured during a NATO exercise in Eastern Europe. He was all nostalgic about the old days, before he got part of his arm and leg blown off. Oh, and he asked me if I knew where he could hire a clown to hand out balloons at his church picnic." I paused and gave him my warmest smile. "Don't tell me he hasn't called?"

Gardner clenched his fists and took a step toward me. "The city doesn't pay me enough to put up with that kind of shit from a smartass like you, Gamble."

"The city wasn't paying you to pick lint out of your navel while Mickey Horshak was running poker game nights over on Elliston Avenue either, but I didn't notice it bothering you too much when you were working vice.

Guess somebody else must have been picking up the tab for your time on that one, huh?"

The color drained from Gardner's face like oil from a busted crankcase, and his lips contorted into a primal snarl. "On your feet, Gamble. You and me are going to get a few things settled right here and now."

"Not on my shift, you're not." Spillner backed Gardner off with a wave of his arm. "You two lovebirds want to carve your initials in each other's chests; it's okay with me, but do it later. Right now, we got business to take care of.

"Speaking of which," he said, turning his attention back to me, "I don't recollect hearing you say anything about what case you're working on that you had to go digging through a newspaper morgue."

I said, "That's because I didn't. And I think before I answer any more questions about anything, somebody better tell me what the hell's going on here. Otherwise, you can call my lawyer."

Gardner shot a sideways glance at his partner. The lanky detective just shrugged. "Go on. Might as well fill him in, as if he doesn't already know."

"Your friend Quail has been knocked off," Gardner obliged, sounding very much as if he was enjoying being the one to break the news. "Somebody left him dead in his office. Kind of a dirty trick, him being a disabled vet and all, don't you think?"

They were looking for a reaction, and even though I'd known it was coming, I didn't have one to give. So, I bluffed. It was a marginal tactic at best, but I hoped it might buy me time to figure out how much they actually knew.

"There are murders being committed in this city all the time. Why try to pin this one on me?"

"It wasn't our idea," said Spillner. "It was the deceased's neighbor. Seems patrol got a call to check out a prowler at the victim's address. We don't know who phoned it in. The guy didn't leave a name, so it could've been anybody. Anyway, our boys get there, and they cruise the block a couple of times. There's no prowler they can find, but the second time around, they notice a garage that's been broken into. So, they check that and, what do you know, there's a dead guy on the floor inside. While they're waiting for the detectives, which turns out to be me and Sparky here, one of the uniforms starts canvassing the neighbors. He doesn't turn up much, except for one old-timer across the street. He's not sure, but he tells our guy there might have been somebody snooping around the house a little before lunchtime."

"Maybe it was somebody from the gas company reading the meter."

"I guess it could have been, but meter readers don't usually drive around in prehistoric Thunderbirds. Anyway, the description he gave us wasn't much good, but he did have the presence of mind to write down the license number of the car the guy drove away in. So, we ran it through DMV, and much to the surprise of absolutely no one, your name came up. Considering the line of work that you're in, we thought it might be worth stopping by to see whether there was anything more you could tell us."

"I'm not sure what it would be but go ahead and ask your questions."

"Okay, how about this for starters? We tell you we found a dead guy. Turns out to be somebody you've already admitted you knew. We also tell you that your car was seen driving away from the victim's residence about the time it appears he was killed, and you don't show any reaction at all. Why is that?"

"What did you expect me to do, fall over in a dead faint? When homicide detectives show up, it's generally because somebody's gotten dead. Of course, I'm sorry to hear it was Quail. The little I knew him, he was a nice guy, and I liked him. But the way you two have marched in here and pretty much accused me of pulling the trigger hasn't given me much chance to work up any kind of normal emotions."

"Right." Spillner picked idly with his thumbnail at a spot between his front teeth. "In all the excitement, I must have forgotten to tell you he was shot. So how did you know that?"

"Just a lucky guess," I said. "It could have just as well been Colonel Mustard in the drawing room with the candlestick."

"I told you we wouldn't get anything out of this joker," Gardner growled at Spillner. "Let's just escort him over to Division and find a nice quiet spot in the basement where we can help him think things over."

"Hold on," Spillner said. "You mind telling us where you been all afternoon?

We've been sitting here better than two hours."

"You should have called first. That's what I pay an answering service for."

"Next time, we'll do that. For now, just answer the question."

I said, "I can't tell you, Sergeant, I'm sorry. I'm working on a case that's highly confidential, and I have an obligation to protect my client."

Gardner chimed in. "This is bullshit, Sarge. Let's take him downtown."

Spillner ignored the younger cop. "Does this client of yours have any direct connection with Quail?"

"If I said no, would you take my word for it?"

"Probably not." Spillner looked at me with his big, sad eyes. "Come on, Jackson, think about how you're making things look. We come by to ask you some perfectly routine questions about a homicide, and instead of cooperating like a good citizen, you give us a runaround. Now I'm telling you straight, and I'm telling you one last time. Either you talk to us, right here and right now, or we got no choice except to take you in."

"On what charge, failure to cave under pressure?"

"How about interfering with a homicide investigation? How about suspicion of murder? I already told you we got a witness can put you at the scene of the crime."

"Some judge will get a good laugh out of that, unless you have more proof than you've told me so far. You got a witness who saw me shoot somebody, or did I leave a signed confession pinned to the victim's shirt?"

"I never said we could make it stick, but we can sure make you wish we hadn't tried."

I didn't know what to tell him and said the same.

"Okay, I give up. I guess we're done talking." Spillner climbed wearily to his feet. "Assume the position, Jackson. We're going downtown."

Chapter Twenty-Four

They had me turn out my pockets. They took my gun and my license, read me my rights, and clamped me into a pair of handcuffs. Then they rode me down the elevator and frog-marched me through the lobby of the building like I was Public Enemy Number One, on his way to the death house. I half expected Gardner to slip me a kidney punch when nobody was looking, but it never happened. Maybe the guy's skin was a little thicker than I'd thought, or maybe he was taking Spillner at his word about staying away from rough stuff on city time. Whatever the reason, I arrived at police headquarters in one piece and in good health.

After that, things got interesting.

I was photographed. I was fingerprinted. I was read my rights. I was strip-searched. I was cavity-searched, given an orange jumpsuit, and then escorted to a holding cell, where I was left to reflect on the wisdom of my life's choices for the next two hours. For company, I had a couple of rough-boy male prostitutes and a junkie huddled in the corner, shivering uncontrollably.

About halfway through my time doing penance, a familiar face appeared on the other side of the bars.

"Mister Gamble. I heard you were here." The voice belonged to Detective Lorraine Proctor, a homicide cop who sometimes partnered with Detective Spillner. "What brings you here this time?"

"The usual," I said. "Trying to do my job. Your guys had other ideas."

One of the leather-clad Lotharios took notice of Proctor. "Hey, mama," he called out in a loud voice. "Get me outta here, and I'll give you the ride of your life."

"Right," she said, ignoring him. "Got it. You figure to be here a while?"

"Not likely. They're trying to connect me to a body, but that's just for the suckers in the cheap seats. Unless they can get a warrant to hold me as a material witness, I'll be out pretty soon. This whole 'Book 'em, Dan-o,' thing is just to see if they can shake something loose."

"Something, like what?"

"They've got a body. They know I didn't kill the guy, but they think they can scare me into telling them who did."

"Sometimes it works," she said. "How's your lady?"

"Getting over the rough spots. And I never did thank you for what you did for Maggie."

The reference was to the days and weeks following Maggie's abduction and torture by a lunatic named Bobby Fury, who was involved in the disappearance of fourteen-year-old Gabrielle Hawkins a couple of years back. After Maggie was treated for her injuries and released from the hospital, Detective Proctor stayed in close touch with her until the worst of her nightmares went away.

"Happy to help," she said. "You want me to give her a call? Maybe let her know you might be running a little late?"

"I'd appreciate it. And I think she'd be glad to hear from you."

"Will do. Anything else?"

"No, I'm good, thanks."

Around six o'clock, a couple of uniforms came to collect me. My street clothes were returned, and I was escorted to an elevator. Then, the accompanying unis rode with me up three floors. The elevator doors slid open, and we stepped out into a long hallway punctuated with overhead fluorescent lights and wooden benches positioned outside interview rooms.

"In here," one of the cops said and pointed to a hard wooden chair at one end of a table in a windowless, twelve-by-twenty interview room. At the other end sat Harry Roodhouse, the central division homicide skipper. He glanced at me before returning to the contemplation of his hands, which were folded quietly on the table in front of him. His face wore an expression of weary patience.

I knew Harry Roodhouse reasonably well from my time on the job, and we'd had occasion to cooperate on cases once or twice in the ensuing years. Like Spillner, he was a good cop and an okay human being. He was honest, thorough, and strictly by the book. Rich or poor, white or black, with or without hooks, you could count on getting a fair shake from Harry Roodhouse, no more and no less.

At that moment, I was getting mine.

Also seated at the table was a man dressed in a close-fitting three-piece suit, white shirt, and a green necktie accented with what looked like red seahorses. He appeared to be about the same age as me and could have been the poster boy for "average height, average weight, medium build." He had a squarish pink face punctuated by a pair of red-framed glasses. His close-cropped hair was light brown, going to gray in places and receding noticeably at the temples. There was an open briefcase on the table next to him that he was shuffling papers rapidly in and out of. Nobody had passed out scorecards, but from the way Roodhouse sat quietly waiting, it was obvious the man in the suit was in charge of the proceedings. We all sat and waited while he rattled papers around in his briefcase.

After a few more minutes of fiddling, he found what he was looking for. He glanced rapidly over two sheets of typewritten paper, then threw the report back into his case and slammed the lid shut.

"Okay," he said finally. "Let's get this show on the road."

Roodhouse cleared his throat. "Gamble, this is…"

The other man cut him off. "Save the introductions. I can talk for myself." He got out of his chair and walked slowly around the table in my direction.

"My name is Priest, Mr. Gamble. Christopher Priest. I'm senior assistant district attorney for Davidson County. I work for Roger Seacrist."

"Congratulations," I said. "Tell him he can count on my vote."

Roodhouse chuckled out loud. "You'd do well to mind your manners, Jackson. Mr. Priest is here at the specific direction of the Great Man himself."

"Let me guess. Roger wants me to join the campaign and hand out flyers at his rallies."

"You're a very funny man, Mr. Gamble," Priest said. "If it was my call,

169

I'd have you locked up so far back they'd have to feed you with a slingshot. Captain Roodhouse, however, has persuaded me that you are a reasonable man and that, like all reasonable men, you'll be only too happy to cooperate once you understand the seriousness of your situation."

"And just what is my situation?" I stared blandly at them both. "All I understand is that two of your detectives rousted me a couple hours ago on an unsubstantiated charge of suspicion of murder. Since then, I've been strip-searched, mug-shot, fingerprinted, and thrown into a holding tank with the cast of a gay porn film and a junkie foaming at the mouth from withdrawal symptoms. I don't know how that kind of treatment sits with either of you, but it tends to take the reasonableness right out of me."

"Be thankful that's all that happened," Priest blinked at me through the thick lenses of his glasses. "You don't seem to appreciate yet how much trouble you're in."

"I don't see where I'm in any trouble at all."

He leaned across the table until our faces were nearly touching. "Don't shadowbox with me, smart guy. There's a dead man in the morgue you've already admitted you knew. We have a witness can put you at his house at the approximate time of death, and we're pretty sure it was you who made that phony call about the prowler. That was a cute stunt, by the way, calling the police the way you did and then bugging out. Now, I want to know where you've been since eleven-thirty this morning."

"Working. I don't feed at the public trough like present company, and even though I don't expect you to understand what I'm talking about, there are some of us who have to earn our livings the old-fashioned way."

"Is that so? Well, just how do you go about earning that living, anyway? You've got a license, so as far as the state is concerned, that makes you legal. The only thing is, I never saw a PI that operates the way you do, so now I have to wonder whether you're something else."

I said, "If you've got a point, make it."

"The point is, you're just a little too willing to bend the law to suit your own purposes. Oh, right, you were on the job, I know all about that. I've seen your service record and your personnel file. I've also seen the file on you since you went private. Believe me, my friend, it doesn't make good reading."

"Then don't read it. I can recommend any number of good books."

Roodhouse coughed nervously. "I warned you once about cutting out that smart mouth while you're ahead of the game."

"And I asked you once, Harry, ahead of what game? You boys are having the time of your lives trying to frame me for killing a guy I barely knew, and for reasons I can only guess at. At the very least, somebody ought to give me a phone so I can get hold of an attorney."

Roodhouse said, "Look, Jackson, be sensible. We know you didn't kill that reporter. We aren't trying to make you say you did, and we aren't trying to fit you into a frame. But you know how it goes when some newspaper or TV guy gets himself killed. No matter what we do or how many men we assign to the case, there won't be a minute's peace until it's cleared up. All we're asking you to do is give us the information you have and let us take it from there."

"Is that all?" I let a note of sarcasm creep into my voice. "Well, that raises an interesting point. I listened to the news on the radio a good three hours after your men said Quail's body was found, yet I didn't hear the first word about it. Considering the guy worked for a newspaper and you're all worried about publicity, I'd say you're doing a pretty good job keeping the peace."

"Maybe you weren't listening to the right station," Priest offered.

"And maybe you're feeding me a lot of crap," I said to Roodhouse. "Who's screwing the lid down on this investigation, Harry? Is it Priest here, or is it coming from someplace higher up?"

Roodhouse's face reddened, but his voice stayed even. "You dumb son of a bitch. Don't you know when somebody's trying to do you a favor?"

"I know when somebody's trying to sing me a song. This little session doesn't have anything to do with who killed Dave Quail, or even that he got killed, and all three of us know it. What we're talking about here is making sure nothing happens that will derail Roger's campaign for governor."

There was a silence that filled the room the way a fat man fills a middle seat on an overbooked flight. Roodhouse wrinkled his brow ominously in the direction of ADA Priest.

"Or is it possible that everybody in the room doesn't know it?" The question was directed at Roodhouse, but I didn't wait for him to answer.

"Ask Mister District Attorney here why his office is so interested in a deceased record company executive named Charles Lambert. And while you're at it, have him tell you why a couple of his men have been snooping around a fleabag motel out in Harding, asking questions about a former secretary of Lambert's named Darlene Munson."

I turned to Priest. "It was your people that followed me out to the Rustic Retreat, same as it was them that tapped me on the head and upended Darlene's cabin later that same night. Or don't you know anything about that, either?"

"We weren't sure whose side you were on. We didn't want you getting in the way."

"But I did get in the way, didn't I? And unless I miss my guess, I'm still in the way. What are you looking for, Priest? What's in that file Albert Glass wants that's making everybody so nervous?"

"Albert Glass? The newspaper columnist?" asked Roodhouse. "What's he got to do with this? And what's this about a file?"

"Albert Glass is a person of interest in an ongoing investigation by the district attorney's office. I've got my people out on the street right now, trying to round him up."

He looked at me meaningfully. "As far as anything else might be concerned, I'm not at liberty to discuss. And if Mr. Gamble is even half as smart as he thinks he is, he's not at liberty to discuss it either."

It wasn't the most subtle layoff speech I'd ever heard, but it got the message across. It also cleared up one point I'd been wondering about. Roger Seacrist hadn't sent Priest to find out what I had to say. He sent him to make sure I didn't say anything. That meant somebody downtown was worried about the Lambert investigation and was pulling out all the stops to make sure the story didn't hit the media until it had been sufficiently sanitized.

Roodhouse glared at Priest over the half-moons of his reading glasses. "I think we need to talk."

Priest shook his head. "There's nothing to talk about, Captain. I'm sorry. The Quail investigation has been reassigned to our office. As far as your department is concerned, until you're informed otherwise, it never happened. The official notification from the Chief of Detectives should be landing on your desk just about now."

He turned to me. "And as far as you're concerned, Mr. Gamble, it never happened either, and that includes this meeting. If you want to keep your shingle hung out, as of this minute you're off the Quail case, off the Lambert case, and if there even is one, off the Munson case. My advice to you would be to go home, get drunk, and then tomorrow, find yourself a nice juicy divorce you can chew on for a few weeks. Near as I can tell, that's more your style anyway."

"Now that's just priceless," I said, "talking about style after you've just shut down a murder investigation because it's politically inconvenient."

He started to say something, but I kept going. "You want to splash around in this cesspool, Mr. Priest. You just have at it. It's your career. But I've got a client who's paying for results. I've also got a legal right to pursue my occupation, and I don't take orders from you."

His face registered neither surprise nor anger, only mild amusement, as if my refusal to go along had been exactly what he had expected.

"That's the way you see it? Fine." He opened his briefcase again and took out a large brown manila envelope. He dumped the contents out on the table and picked up an undernourished-looking billfold. It was mine, and I didn't need three guesses to figure out what was going to happen next.

Priest flipped though the wallet until he found my identification card and my private investigator's license. He removed both and dropped them back into the envelope. He tossed the wallet indifferently toward my end of the table.

"According to the officers who brought you in, you have knowledge of the activities of a gambler named Mitchell Horshak, AKA Mickey the Horse. You may not be aware of it, but the district attorney's office is now seeking indictments against Mr. Horshak for violation of a number of illegal gambling activities. You've also implied having knowledge of alleged police corruption."

"So?"

"So, under the circumstances, I don't think it would be too difficult to have you detained under a material witness warrant along with Mr. Glass once we locate him. And that's exactly what I'll do unless I have your word that you'll steer completely clear of any further involvement in the Quail investigation."

"What about my license?"

"Think of it as my insurance policy, just in case you have an attack of conscience and decide to change your mind later. You behave yourself, and you'll get it back in a week or so. Get in the way, and I'll see you're out of business for good."

He had me cold, and we both knew it. I picked up my belongings and walked out, closing the door behind me.

Chapter Twenty-Five

A brisk wind had picked up, and there was a promise of rain in the air as I hurried out of the police station to catch a cab back to my office. Most other times, I could have gotten a lift from any of a dozen cops I knew. Tonight, though, I didn't see any familiar faces, and I didn't want to risk running into Harry Roodhouse while I waited.

If it had been up to Harry, I'd have been right back in the slammer, cooling my heels or going three-on-one with a wrecking crew in the station house basement. Harry had gotten backstabbed by the D.A.'s office, and he wasn't one bit happy about it. If he couldn't get answers from Christopher Priest, he was damn sure going to try to get them from me. Priest's threat to hold me as a material witness had been an obvious bluff. Seacrist and Priest wanted me back on the streets, visible and available, but out of the reach of the cops. They'd get around to telling me their reasons why when they were good and ready.

In the meantime, there was the problem of my gun, license, and ID. Not surprisingly, Priest hadn't returned them. And although we both knew he couldn't keep them forever, it could take several days of legal maneuvering before I'd be able to get them back. Until that time, I was effectively out of business.

The bank building lobby was nearly deserted as I passed through on my way to the elevator. Except for a couple guys in suits talking with the guard at the security desk, everybody had long since given it up for the night. I had one phone call to make, and then I was going to do the same. It had only been since this morning, but it seemed like a month ago that I'd met with

175

Dick Dohrn and Carver Dickinson at the *Times*. Besides feeling vaguely responsible for Dave Quail's death, I still didn't know what Albert Glass was doing, or where Darlene Munson was, or even how I would be earning a living come tomorrow morning. All in all, it hadn't been one of my better days.

The telephone was ringing when I walked into the office, but it stopped before I was able to reach it. I was pretty sure I knew who it was, so I sat down at my desk, propped my feet up and waited. Five minutes later, it rang again.

"Am I speaking to Jackson Gamble?"

I recognized the voice. "How are you doing this evening, Mr. Dickinson?"

"How should I be doing? You were supposed to check in with me, remember?"

"I remember. I've just been a little busy." When he didn't pick up on that, I added, "The cops wanted to talk to me about Dave Quail. I assume they've informed you what happened."

"They have. Do they know who killed him?"

"No, but the cops and the D.A. both think I know."

"And do you?"

"I have an idea, but I'd rather leave it at that for now. It won't help the case to see what amounts to nothing more than speculation on the front page of tomorrow's paper."

"Then speculate for me privately."

"I don't think I'm ready to do that, Mr. Dickinson. And I don't think you're ready to hear my ideas on that subject."

There was a silence on the line that in polite circles would have been termed a pregnant pause. Call it intuition, but before he said it, I knew what he was going to tell me next.

"The *Times* has agreed to downplay the Quail story for a few days," he said carefully. "It's not the kind of thing we like to do, but the police believe it will help speed up the investigation. The situation being what it is, we were persuaded we had no choice except to go along."

"That makes Seacrist three, Quail nothing."

He said irritably, "I thought we settled all that this morning. We are simply cooperating with the police in their investigation of a homicide. Roger Seacrist had nothing to do with our decision."

"No? This afternoon, the cops pulled me in on a charge of suspicion of murder. It didn't mean anything. It was just to shake me up and to give them a chance to ice me down for a few hours in case it turned out I had anything to tell them."

"Have you been charged with anything?"

"Not yet. I had a session with a homicide captain named Roodhouse and an assistant district attorney named Priest. They started out asking me about Dave Quail, but that was only a fishing trip. When the conversation drifted around to Darlene Munson and Charles Lambert, Priest suddenly decided he didn't want to hear anything else I had to say. He didn't want anybody else to hear it either, because he took the case away from the cops and threatened to hold me on a material witness warrant if I didn't keep my mouth shut."

"And did you agree to stand down?"

"What do you think? I can take a certain amount of heat, but at the end of the day, I'm still a one-trick pony. I've got no friends and no connections in high enough places to do me any good. If somebody like Priest wants to bench me, I have to sit down. But Harry Roodhouse is no pushover, and I wouldn't have figured your newspaper was, either. Yet Seacrist has us all sitting on our hands, and none of us knows why. I guess it just goes to show how easily one man's life can get lost in the shuffle of big-time politics."

Dickinson sighed. "That's one of the harshest realities life can throw at us. Sometimes, things happen the way they do for a reason, but we can't always see it at the time. We just have to trust they'll work out in the end."

I laughed out loud. "Save the mysteries of faith for Sunday morning, Mr. Dickinson. You and your paper have been dancing with the devil since the day you got behind Roger Seacrist's campaign for governor. This is hardly the time to start complaining that you don't like the music."

There was a sound on the line like someone sucking air through his teeth. "You should make sure you have all the facts before you rush to judgment,

Mr. Gamble. You may find you have sold me painfully short. I told the police I'd hold off printing this story for a few days, and I will. But that doesn't mean I can't take steps of my own in the meantime." He took what sounded like a deep breath before letting it out slowly.

"I don't care how much it costs. I want you to drop whatever you were doing before and find out who killed Dave Quail. Until I tell you otherwise, that is your number one priority."

"Which is it, Mr. Dickinson? Find Albert or track down a killer?"

"I have a feeling we're talking about two pockets in the same pair of pants, Mr. Gamble."

"Well, that may well be," I said, "but there's a problem. Our friend Priest is holding my license. Without it, I can't lift a finger, regardless of my priorities or yours. If I so much as make a phone call on behalf of a client, the D.A.'s office will shut me down for good. And to get back to harsh realities, having the means to make a living is still where it begins and ends for me."

The line was silent while he thought that over. Then he surprised the hell out of me.

"Let me worry about that. It may take a little doing, but I think I can convince Roger that getting your license back is part of the price of my cooperation. It's too late tonight, but I'll get on it first thing in the morning. If you don't hear from Priest by tomorrow afternoon, give me a call here at the office."

I told him I'd be sure to do that, and we said good night. Then I called Maggie.

She sounded worried. "Lorraine Proctor telephoned earlier. She said you were in jail. Again. Is this getting to be a habit with you?"

"There ain't a jail been built yet that can hold me, little missy." My attempt to channel a worn-out line from countless B-movie westerns fell flatter than a fritter.

"I'm serious. Are you okay?"

"I'm fine, Maggie. They wanted to shake me up a little. Get my attention."

"And did they?"

"In technicolor." I gave her a quick recap of how my day had gone, beginning with my early sit-down with Carver Dickinson and continuing through finding Dave Quail's corpse, meeting with Audra Lambert, and ending up with a trip to the city lockup.

The line was silent for a moment. "Will I see you tonight?" she asked, finally.

"You have no idea how tempting that sounds, but I don't think I would make very good company. How about if we shoot for tomorrow?"

And that was where we left it. I went home and spent a restless night, wondering what the hell I was going to do next.

Chapter Twenty-Six

I spent the next morning at the office, waiting for the telephone to ring. I was expecting to hear from Carver Dickinson, telling me he had straightened out my license problem with the district attorney's office. I would have been happy with a call from either Christopher Priest or Harry Roodhouse. I would even have been happy to hear from Delilah Liggett. At least that would have broken the monotony, and sitting with her looking at photos of her daughter would have made me feel a little virtuous. As it was, though, the telephone remained resolutely silent, leaving me with nothing to do except read the newspaper and wait until lunchtime. Finally, around twelve-thirty, I decided to head out to grab something to eat. Just to be sure there would be no surprises waiting for me upon my return, I made sure to lock the outer office door before leaving.

I was walking down the hallway toward the elevator stop. I was tired, hungry, frustrated, and angry. Nothing about the case was breaking the right way, and now I had the added problem of trying to decide how far I could trust Carver Dickinson. An hour earlier I would have said about as far as I could throw my car. Now, I wasn't sure whether that might be giving him too much credit.

Two guys dressed in ill-fitting, off-the-rack suits were waiting for the elevator as I came around the corner. I mumbled a greeting, thinking at first, they must be the two accountants from down the hall, heading out for a bite of lunch themselves. Then I looked again and realized they were the same pair I'd seen talking to the security guard the night before. At the same moment, I glanced at the elevator call button and saw it wasn't lit.

I was about to have a problem.

They each grabbed me by an arm and flung me like a rag doll up against the elevator door. My forehead cracked hard metal, and just for a second, I heard a bell ringing. It wasn't the telephone, but it was definitely for me.

Experienced hands patted me up and down and found nothing of interest. They spun me around so that I was facing them, but still braced against the elevator door.

The shorter of the two laid a Smith & Wesson 9MM auto along the side of my cheek. His smile showed teeth stained the color of cinnamon sticks. His breath was sour enough to peel the paint off a battleship.

"This can be hard, or it can be easy, boy. Makes no never mind to us."

"What's the beef?" I asked, bees buzzing in my head.

"You might say we're an escort service," Cinnamon Mouth grinned. "Way we hear it, y'all said you wanted to see Mr. Cherry. Turns out, he wants to visit with you, too. We're just here makin' sure y'all get together."

Another bell rang, only this time it was a real one, as the elevator dinged to a stop on our floor and the doors slid open. The tall goon turned me around again and forced me inside. The short one thumbed a button, and we were on our way.

The elevator reached bottom and they shoved me out into the semi-darkness of the underground parking garage. An engine roared to life from somewhere outside my line of sight. In another moment, a white Cadillac Escalade with heavily tinted windows all around rolled to a stop next to where we were standing.

The driver got out and walked around to open the rear door of the Escalade. Probably, it was the memory of too many bad gangster pictures, the ones where some poor sap steps into the back of a big, black Packard limousine where George Raft or Jimmy Cagney is waiting to take him for one last ride. But in that moment, so help me, I saw my life flash before my eyes.

I felt a hard nudge on my backside, and the short goon growled at me impatiently.

"Come on, boy, hop on in. Mister Cherry ain't got all day."

I climbed into the back seat of the Caddy and heard the door close behind me. Then the two goons and the driver positioned themselves like sentries around the outside of the car.

Until that moment, I had never seen Robert Edward Cherry in the flesh. I knew who he was, of course, and I'd heard one or two stories about him. But here and now, coming face to face with a real live underworld boss, and one at that who had good reason to feel I'd tweaked his nose, was an encounter I now understood I'd been less than judicious in seeking.

In fact, Red Cherry was part of the new breed of mobster, like the late John Gotti, the "Dapper Don" of New York City's Gambino Mob, before he finally took a hard fall in 1992. Despite their somewhat sketchy resumes, Cherry and his ilk were highly sought after in certain circles as dinner guests, patrons of the arts, and supporters of worthy civic causes. And like Charlie Lambert and his pals, Red could be charming and quotable. He was a conspicuous contributor to such worthy local causes as the Performing Arts Association, the Middle Tennessee Historical Society, and even the National Organization for Women. I didn't think he'd managed to get himself invited to join the Hermitage Group just yet, but if they'd announced that one of the local colleges was planning to name a new wing after him, it wouldn't have surprised me a bit.

Despite his veneer of glossy sociability, however, Red was a far cry from a renaissance man. According to legend, he had made his bones before he was old enough to vote. By the time he was thirty, he had gained control of most of the gambling, loan sharking, and vending machine action between New Orleans and Pensacola. Unofficially, Red was believed to have personally killed a half-dozen people, including one who was found impaled on a seven-foot steel pipe on the front lawn of his own home. Before he died, the victim's hands and feet had been hacked off with a machete. His genitals were found stuffed halfway down his throat.

As Dave Quail had reported, Red had only been convicted once, of conspiracy to commit murder in New Orleans. However, after Red had been incarcerated at Louisiana's Angola prison farm for no more than a few months, his lawyers managed to get his original conviction overturned on a technicality. A retrial was scheduled. Unfortunately, the key witness in his original trial, who had been relocated to Sandpoint, Idaho, as part of his witness protection deal, was killed in a somewhat suspicious automobile accident involving a collision with an Amtrak passenger train traveling at speed at an unsignaled grade crossing in rural Washington State. Without a witness, a retrial was not possible, and so the original conviction was vacated. Red walked away without so much as a traffic stop on his record.

Red in real life looked pretty much like Red in the newspapers. He was about fifty-five, trim, tanned, and handsome in a carefully packaged, blow-dried sort of way. He was dressed in a black silk shirt, a gray Armani suit, and black Samuel Hubbard Frequent Traveler loafers, no socks. On his left wrist, he wore a Rolex the size of a Faberge egg. On his right, he sported a gold bracelet heavy enough to use as a towing chain. He had a pair of Wayfarer sunglasses propped stylishly on top of his head and was chewing casually on a wad of bubble gum.

He folded his arms on the back of the jump seat where he sat facing me.

"So, is this customer service, or what? I got a message you wanted to talk to me, and here I am. You can't beat that."

"You didn't have to go to this much trouble. I could have come to you."

"Next time, we can meet for lunch. My treat. Today, let's just visit for a bit." He blew a lopsided bubble with his gum and popped it loudly. "How do you like this for a tough guy? My wife made me promise to try to quit smoking. Her women's club, had some expert come in and talk about addictions, and she got on me like white on rice about nicotine. I feel like Archie Andrews chewing this shit, but what are you gonna do? For better or worse, right?"

I nodded.

"There a woman in your life, Mr. Gamble?"

"There is. She thinks I should consider another line of work. She says it's too risky."

"She's probably right. But then, where's the fun if there's no risk?"

I didn't have an answer for that, so I just kept my mouth shut and waited for him to get around to what he had to say. He started me off with an easy two-hopper.

"I understand you been asking a lot of questions about me and my business.

I wonder if you can tell me why."

I said truthfully, if not precisely, "I'm not at all interested in your business. I don't even know for sure what you do. I was hired to help out locating a young woman who's gone missing. Your name came up in conversation."

"Me?" He pointed to himself and arched his eyebrows in an expression of surprise. "My name came up? What, do you think I'm operating a safe house for runaway housewives?"

"The woman I'm looking for is nobody's battered wife. She's a former employee of the late Charles Lambert. According to my sources, she disappeared about two weeks ago. She took with her a highly confidential file that had belonged to her boss. Nobody can tell me what's in it, but every indication is that it has something to do with Lambert's financial dealings with you."

"And you figured I might be worried it was going to be a problem and snuffed her." He gave me a wondering look, as if I'd just accused him of the Kennedy assassination. "Who do you think you're talking to here, Louie Lepke? This isn't Murder, Incorporated. The business doesn't operate like that anymore."

"I'm relieved to hear it," I said.

"I'll bet you are. You like country music?"

"I can take it or leave it," I said, not sure where he was going with the question.

"Personally, I hate it. I was brought up in this part of the country, but I never liked listening to that shit. Stan Kenton, you know who he is?"

I did know. He was talking about a progressive jazz musician and big-band leader who was popular in the 1940s and 1950s.

"Stan Kenton once called country music ignorant and decadent, did you know that?"

I remembered reading about the incident and the stink that it raised some years earlier, when Kenton came to town for a concert date.

"As I recall, it nearly got him run out of town."

"He should have left on his own, but then, I guess maybe he needed the payday. The point is, I didn't buy out Charlie Lambert because I liked his music. If he was Harry Connick, or Aaron Neville, or even Winton Marsalis, somebody with more of a New Orleans flavor, it would have been different. Guys like that have talent. I'd pay good money just to sit in the studio with them while they rehearsed. I bought Black Strap because it was the only way I could get back the money Lambert owed me. If he'd been running a used car lot or a string of dry-cleaning stores, I'd have done the same thing. My experience? A dollar doesn't care where it comes from."

"So, you're just another investor looking out for his money, is that it?"

"That's it exactly," he said in a tone of voice you'd hear a teacher use to encourage a child struggling with his multiplication tables. "It's all in how you look at it."

The thought came to me that I should just leave it at that and thank Red for his time. The smart move would have been to get the hell as far away from him as I could while both my knees still worked. But then I remembered the look on Dave Quail's face as he lay dead on the floor of his office, and decided, fuck it, let's go for broke. I was careful, however, to keep my tone of voice strictly neutral. No sense, I figured, in provoking him unnecessarily.

I said, "Then as long as we're looking at things, if you've got a few minutes, let's look at this the other way around and see what we've got. First, Charlie Lambert comes to you looking for a loan to try to save his failing record company. Okay, that keeps the wolves away from the door for a while, but in the end, it's hopeless, and before you know it, he's back again with his hat in his hand. Only this time, there is no loan, just an offer to buy him out for a fire sale price. That clears the books, but it leaves Charlie with his business gone and very little money to show for it. Do I have it right so far?"

He shrugged, said nothing.

"That's an interesting way to build a conglomerate. Or am I missing something here?"

"What you're missing is, you don't know what you're talking about. Charlie Lambert showed up on my doorstep when he couldn't get financing anyplace else. All the bankers, all the stockbrokers, all the shit-kicker yodelers he turned into stars, when he needed help, none of them wanted to know him from the man in the moon. So, he came to me. I gave him a fair price for what he had to sell, and maybe even a little bit more."

"You're a generous guy, Mr. Cherry."

"Not generous, just looking out for my own interests." He rolled down his window and spit his gum out. "Let me ask you something, Mr. Gamble. Do we know one another? Have we ever done business together?"

"No, sir, we have not."

"Well, then, before today, before right this minute, have I ever done anything to cause you to have a problem with me, even indirectly? Maybe I cut in front of you in a ticket line, or I ran over your dog and didn't stop?"

"Not that I can think of."

"That's what I thought. You know, if we had a problem, I could maybe understand you wanting to shake things up a little bit. But since we don't, I want to understand why you're running around asking questions about me. I mean, I can't imagine what your missing woman investigation would have anything to do with me."

"With respect, what would you say if I said I couldn't tell you?"

He unwrapped another stick of gum and popped it into his mouth. "Gum? It's Blackjack. Good stuff. I have to order it special."

"No. Thanks," I said.

"Well, then, to answer your question, I guess I'd want to ask you why not."

I weighed my next words carefully, aware that for all his seeming affability, Red Cherry was nobody to monkey around with. Say the wrong thing now, and my suspended license would suddenly become the least of my worries.

"It's like this. When I took this case, I thought all I was doing was helping to locate a woman who had gone into the wind with some stolen property in her possession. A computer file, or maybe a notebook. A flash drive, I don't know. Some damn thing. And I didn't care. Still don't. But now it's turned into something much more complicated. Somebody has already gotten hurt, and I don't want that to happen to anybody else. The only way I can be sure of that, especially in the present circumstances, is to not answer your question."

"By 'hurt,' you mean somebody was killed?"

"Yes."

"And you think, what? You think if you tell me who this woman is, I might decide to make her dead to keep whatever she's got from getting out into the open? Is that what you're worried about?"

"I wouldn't have said it quite that way, but the thought had crossed my mind."

He considered that. "I understand. This person who got dead, who are we talking about?"

I said, "A newspaper columnist named David Quail. I met him right after I began this investigation. He didn't have any connection with the case. But he did with the person who hired me, who coincidentally had also gone missing. Out of loyalty to that person, he asked if he could help me. I can always use a little extra manpower, so I let him. Yesterday morning, I found him on the floor of his garage with a bullet in his brain. I don't know who killed him and believe me when I tell you I'm not suggesting you had anything to do with it. But I don't want to be responsible for anyone else getting hurt, either. And, no disrespect, the only way I can be sure of that is by not naming any other names. If that means you and I have a problem, then that's the way it is."

He closed his eyes. "This newspaper guy who got shot. Was he a friend of yours?"

"A friend?" I shrugged, realizing that until that moment, I'd never thought much about it. "I don't know. He was a good person, a brave man. He was seriously injured serving his country. I guess I'd like to think he could have been a friend."

"And you're wondering if I know something about what happened to him?"

"I was more hoping you might have an idea."

"Uh-huh. You also said you wanted to ask me about this missing woman. I don't know for sure who you're talking about, but from what you're telling me, I believe it might be this little gal who worked in Charley Lambert's office a while back. Her name is Darlene or something like that. Am I right?"

When I didn't say anything, he said, "I'll take that as a yes." He looked at his watch. "Is there anything else?"

"Just one more thing," I said, "It has been suggested that you may have known when you loaned Charles Lambert the money he got from you, that those funds ended up being earmarked for Roger Seacrist's campaign fund. I'm just wondering if you thought a left-handed contribution like that might help you buy your way out from under whatever organized crime investigation Roger claims he's ready to take public."

"Now, that's the kind of talk that could get you into some very serious trouble." Cherry wagged an admonishing finger under my nose. "I made a loan to Charley Lambert. What he did with it after that is his own business."

"Just thought I'd mention it," I said. "In case it comes up again later."

Cherry looked at me for a long moment, as if he were trying to make a decision about something.

"You know, Mr. Gamble, when I was a boy growing up in southeast Arkansas, my father had a business working on people's cars. He was a good mechanic, and he did all right. But with four kids there wasn't any money for any of us to go to college, so I ended up joining the army. After that I took some night school classes, and then I went into business for myself. Now, sometimes in the course of conducting my business, I had to do some things I know I shouldn't have, but even so, I managed to make a decent amount of money and build up a fairly profitable operation. But then I ran into some trouble down in New Orleans over something I didn't do, but which the law mistakenly said I did. Well, it took a little time, but we got that all straightened out, and now I'm on my feet again. You following me here?"

"Yes."

He shook his head slowly. "No, I don't think you are. I'd say you're probably wondering where we're going with this, so I'll just turn up the wick a little bit and then we can go off on our separate ways. I started out with nothing, maybe less than nothing, but I worked hard, and kept at it, and things have turned out pretty well. And now that I've got a chance to put a little something back, call it for the good of the people of Tennessee, who have welcomed me warmly, I want to do it." He paused to let the point sink in. "You see now what I'm getting at?"

"I think so."

"You're a smart guy, so let me just say something here. What you're doing now, what you're poking your nose around in? You're in way over your head. You want to feel bad for your friend, that's okay. You want to do something about it, that's okay too. But you don't want to be where he is now, you know what I mean? You don't want to be there just yet."

"I appreciate your concern."

"Not concern. I just met you, and you seem like a nice enough fella, working hard to make a living in a business that's not likely to make you a rich man. Other than that, to be blunt, I don't much care whether you live or die. So, unless something goes wrong in the next minute or two, you can walk away good as new soon as we're done talking. Call it my end of the deal. Your end is that this foolishness about me trying to buy an election stops right here. Even if I was involved in something like that, which I am not, I would never risk fucking up my livelihood by doing something as stupid as letting myself be blackmailed by an amateur. Which, as I understand it, is how I think you've connected your missing woman to me. As to that reporter that got killed, I had nothing to do with that, either. You have my word. Now, I want your word that since that's settled, you don't have any other interest in me or my business."

"There isn't anything else."

He nodded and offered his hand. "Then we're done here. And Mr. Gamble? Unless you've got a good reason, don't come looking for me again."

Chapter Twenty-Seven

I t was one of those wild and windblown summer storms, the kind that can be enormously entertaining to stand at the window and watch if you're inside, safe and dry, but intimidating and even dangerous if you're out in it. It took better than an hour to cover the usual thirty-minute distance from the office to my house. Rain was coming down in sheets, and even with the windshield wipers going full-out, it was all I could do to see past the edge of the hood. The staticky radio said trees and power lines were down in many areas around the city, and there were flash flood warnings for low-lying areas. Malfunctioning stoplights at a number of intersections were flashing red in all directions. Cars were pulled over to the roadside, their drivers waiting for the rain to let up, and water was flowing hubcap-deep in the streets, where over-matched storm drains couldn't carry it away fast enough.

Lights were out as far as I could see in either direction when I turned down my street. I got the 'Bird into the garage and myself into the house without getting much wetter than a drowned muskrat. Stumbling around in the semi-darkness, I hung my jacket and pants over the back of a kitchen chair, peeled off my shirt and underwear, and stepped into a shower that I hoped would help me calm down enough to get some sleep. Twenty minutes later, with just a towel wrapped around me, I was stretched out on the couch, listening to heavy raindrops drumming insistently on the roof.

It might have been midnight, or it might have been four in the morning. I'd been dozing, and without my watch, which I'd left on the kitchen table, I had no way of being sure of the time. The wind and lightning had moved off to the east, but the rain hadn't slowed at all, and the power was still off. I had been dreaming that I was running down an unlit alley, chased by a white Cadillac SUV. The Caddy was rocking from side to side on the uneven pavement, and gangsters dressed in fedora hats, hand-painted neckties and chalk-striped double-breasted suits were leaning out the side windows on both sides, shooting at me with World War II-era Tommy guns. The staccato noise from the gunfire grew steadily more insistent until it finally woke me up. And then I realized it wasn't machine guns I was hearing. Somebody was knocking on my door.

The cops had hung onto my Colt, but experience sometimes really is as valuable as it's cracked up to be. When I was on the job, I bought a Charter Arms bulldog .44 to carry as a throw-down piece. After I left the force, I had no further use for the bulldog and stowed it on a shelf in the hall closet. It's impractical as hell, small, light, and not accurate beyond the distance you could wind up and throw it at somebody. But at ten feet, if you don't let the recoil scare you, it'll blow a boxcar out of the middle of a moving train.

I slipped into a pair of jeans and a t-shirt, checked the load in the bulldog, and tiptoed across the front room. Then I yanked open the door.

"Maggie?"

Maggie is not tall, and she doesn't carry much weight. And standing on my doorstep with the rain still coming down, she seemed even smaller than she actually is, with her wet hair hanging limply and her dress clinging to the curves of her body. It took me a few seconds to realize she was waiting for me to say something. "What are you doing here?" was the best I could come up with.

"When we talked yesterday, you said tonight, and then you didn't call. And then that detective called, and then it got late, and I didn't hear from you, and I thought, well, that's just like you to get busy with something and forget. But then this storm blew up, and my power went off, and—I just didn't want to be by myself, that's all."

She looked up at me, and when I just stood looking back at her, she said, "So, are you going to let me in, or are you hiding another woman in there?"

"I stashed her behind the couch," I said, "but you can come in anyway. And how did you get so wet? Don't you have a raincoat?"

"I live in a condo, remember? I don't have a garage. And then I had to stand out here on your porch until you answered the door."

"Maggie," I said, "you have a key. You could've let yourself in."

"And wake you out of a sound sleep and get shot as a home invader? Gamble, it's after midnight. And before you ask, I did try calling. It went straight to voicemail."

"My phone is turned off." I palmed the bulldog so she wouldn't see it and tucked it into the back pocket of my jeans. "It's been a tough couple of days."

I went into the bathroom and brought back a clean towel. While Maggie sat on the couch drying her hair, I sat down next to her and told her about how the last thirty-six hours of my life had gone, beginning with my sit-down with Audra Lambert, meeting Carver Dickinson, finding Dave Quail's body, then losing my license and my gun after a short trip to the city lockup, and finishing with a most unusual—and in hindsight, probably ill-advised—come to Jesus meeting with Robert Edward Cherry."

She stopped toweling her hair and gave me a look I couldn't quite read. "You know," she said at last, "every time you tell me about what you've been doing, I can't help thinking the next time I see you, it will either be through thick glass on visiting day or else laid out in a coffin."

"You have an overactive imagination," I said. "How about something to eat? It'll be daylight in a couple of hours. I can fry us up some breakfast."

"That's a tempting thought, but I'm not very hungry." She moved over from her end of the couch to mine. "Would it be asking too much for you to let me stay here, just until morning?" Her voice got soft, and she extended a slender finger and gently traced an invisible line down the middle of my chest. "If you're tired and you don't want to share the bed, I don't mind sleeping on the couch. I know you've had a rough couple of days. I promise you won't even know I'm here."

"Actually," I said, "I'm pretty sure I will."

I cupped her face in my hands and kissed her softly on her mouth. Then I let my hands drift down to the buttons at the top of her dress. I unfastened one, then a second, and a third. As my fingers reached under the fabric and felt the warmth of her skin, she gave a little shrug of her shoulders. Her dress fell away and dropped to her waist.

Maybe for Maggie, it was nothing more than a letting go of the fright-bordering-on-panic that comes from being home alone on a stormy night, especially considering her recent history. For me, as always, it was something else. Maggie Totten was the best thing that had happened to me, maybe in my entire life. She was smart, honest, and resilient, and even though she wasn't blessed with the classic beauty of an Audra Lambert, she was far and away the most desirable woman who'd ever set foot in my house.

Much later, we were nestled on my narrow couch, watching the darkness outside the window brighten into orange and pink dawn. I felt her body stir against mine.

"Gamble?"

"Hmm."

"There's something I've been wanting to ask you. The first time we met, when you were telling me about the kind of work a detective does, you said you didn't take domestic cases."

"I remember."

"Well…you never told me why."

"It isn't a very pretty story." I leaned over and kissed her behind the ear. "And it isn't important anymore, either."

"I'd still like to hear it."

"Why?"

"Because I've been thinking about it and because you made a point of it at the time. I have a feeling it's got something to do with the person you are now, and I'm still learning who that person is. I know he's more than just a roll in the hay, although that was very good, too."

"You weren't so bad yourself, lady."

"I'm serious." She threw a sharp elbow that caught me squarely in the ribs. "Unless, of course, something happened that's so terrible you can't talk about it."

I said, "I can talk about it, but remember you asked." I turned to face her and propped myself up on one elbow.

"When I was first getting started, I took a few matrimonial cases. It was part of the business when the divorce was contested, or there was a lot of money or custody of children involved. In those situations, it helped if you could prove somebody did something to somebody else, or was adulterous, or had an addiction, or whatever. If two people couldn't just agree to split up and let that be the end of it, things could get complicated in a hurry.

"I was working on a case where the wife was suing the husband. She was claiming infidelity, and she wanted nothing short of the whole package. We were talking alimony, custody of the kids, child support, the house, the 401K, all of it. The problem was, he was contesting the suit, and her attorney wasn't sure she had a strong enough case to get everything she wanted.

"To seal the deal, the lawyer hired me to follow the husband around, see what I could find. Well, sure enough, he was doing a little tomcatting, although I'd seen a lot worse. It took a couple of weeks, but finally, I tailed him to an apartment rented to a woman who turned out to be working in the guy's office. I got pictures of him going in with her and coming out by himself, which at that time was more than enough to make the case. We had him cold.

"The lawyer and I met with the guy over lunch the next day and showed him the photos. The idea was to get him to be more cooperative so we could get the case settled out of court."

"What did he say?"

"He said that he'd need some time to think about it. Then he went home, took out a 12-gauge shotgun and shot his wife and kids, and then himself. A neighbor found them there a couple days later."

"My God."

"Yeah, that's pretty much what I said."

She looked at me intently. "Surely you don't blame yourself for what that man did."

"Not at all, and it doesn't have anything to do with blame or guilt. Those are just words. I believed then, and I do now, that the only thing you can do is take care of what's in front of you the best way you can and hope to make things better a little bit at a time. Helping people trash their lives that way didn't seem to fit."

She was quiet for a long time. "Is that why you do what you do? You want to make things better?"

"Hard to say. I don't have the talent to be a doctor or the conviction to be a priest. And I'm not cut out to sit behind a desk and shuffle papers or greet shoppers at some discount store. Not often, but every once in a while, this job gives me the chance to set something right that might otherwise not be. It isn't much, but right now, it's the only thing I've got."

"Well, not the only thing," she said. "You've got me."

"Yeah, but that's a pretty sharp elbow you've got there. You're going to need to do something to make up for that."

"I have just the thing," she said. Then she hooked her arm around my neck and pulled me close. We didn't talk anymore after that.

Chapter Twenty-Eight

The category was rock and roll trivia. The question was, what singer who later went on to be a country and western superstar played and toured briefly with the Beach Boys? The answer was Glen Campbell, only none of the three dimbulb contestants on the show I was watching knew that, so nobody won the vacation in Las Vegas or the matched set of luggage that went with it. On the other hand, with a prize like that, maybe none of them wanted to win, especially since it was all taxable. I turned off the television and walked into the kitchen to look for something to eat.

Maggie had left sometime around the middle of the morning, a couple of hours after the power came back on. I was sleeping like a baby. No more Cadillacs or gunfire on a darkened street. This time, I was safe and warm in a land of fragrant flowers and soft green grass, and when I woke up, she was showered, dressed in clean clothes, and ready to go. I took a shot at coaxing her back into bed, but she shook her head and said she had a can't-miss appointment with one of her clients but would check back later. Then she kissed me one last time and was out the door. Before she left, I promised I'd call her that evening and let her know if there were any new developments.

Afterward, I took a shower of my own and got dressed. Then I sat down on the couch and mentally walked back through the goings-on of the last couple of days to try to make sense out of everything that had happened. Inevitably, I found myself circling back to the question of who had killed Dave Quail. It didn't take long before I realized that, if I included my short encounter with Albert Glass on the night that I found him tossing Darlene

Munson's apartment, I had been in contact with at least four people who might have had a motive to kill him, including Albert himself, Red Cherry, Audra Lambert, and Roger Seacrist. And then, just to round things out, I added Carver Dickinson to the list, although I couldn't really think of a reason why he'd do it.

My thinking went something like this: Start with the original proposition, which was that *Times* investigative reporter Albert Glass had hired me to track down and surveille a woman who he was convinced was in possession of a file of some sort that was the foundation of a story about some unspecified political corruption. I mishandled my original assignment, which eventually led me to bring Dave Quail, another *Times* staffer, into the picture. Quail managed to get hold of Albert's notes on the case. The notes connected Albert to a man named Charles Lambert, who had died some months earlier in an auto accident. Lambert, the founder of a record company that had recently gone bankrupt, was also a member of a quasi-civic organization called the Hermitage Group. Other members of the Group included Davidson County District Attorney Roger Seacrist and *Times* publisher Carver Dickinson. The Hermitage Group and the *Times* were pledged to support Roger Seacrist in the upcoming gubernatorial election. And that's where things began to get tangled up.

Moving forward, Charles Lambert had embezzled a sizable amount of money from the Hermitage Group's election fund to prop up his own failing recording business. Lambert was forced, first to borrow money and then later sell his business to a known racketeer named Red Cherry in order to replace the funds that he had stolen from the Group. That meant several million dollars of mob money was now mixed into Roger Seacrist's campaign fund. It also meant that, if Seacrist were to win the election, he would have no choice except to curtail his long-running investigation into area organized crime, which almost certainly included Red Cherry's activities. Meanwhile, Lambert's wife, Audra, was eager to preserve and protect her husband's reputation as a respected country music impresario. To that end, she had threatened to go to court to suppress the story before it reached the front page of the newspapers. In short, everyone except Albert Glass had a vested interest in making sure the story never found its way into print. Albert, on the other hand, almost certainly would have wanted to keep Dave Quail from hijacking the investigation and getting his own name in the by-line. And still, nobody knew what had happened to Darlene Munson or the file she had in her possession. And I couldn't do anything about any of it because my license had been revoked.

Speaking of which…

It was after lunchtime when I remembered that I hadn't heard anything from Carver Dickinson about getting my license back. I called the number he'd given me and wound up talking to his coolly efficient secretary. No, Mr. Dickinson wasn't in the office. No, she couldn't say if he'd be returning this afternoon, and no, he hadn't left any message for me. I could almost see her sitting at her desk, tapping her pencil impatiently on her notepad. If I cared to leave a message, she'd be sure he saw it first thing in the morning. I thanked her and said to tell him I called. He'd know what for.

I was thinking about trying to reach him at home when I heard somebody giving my doorbell a workout. I was hoping for Maggie and more or less expecting Spillner and Gardner, but what I got was Christopher Priest, the last guy in the world I was looking for. He had two uniformed cops with him. None of them seemed particularly happy to see me.

Without preliminaries, Priest said, "We need to talk."

"About what?" I asked him, making no move to step out of the doorway. "Have you found another dead body you want to leave on the sofa?"

He turned to the two uniforms. "Wait here. I'll call you if I need you."

I was about to tell him to take a hike unless he had a warrant, but before I could even get my mouth open, he brushed past me into the living room.

I said, "The usual procedure is to wait to be invited in. Or doesn't Roger require his employees to observe the rules of common courtesy?"

He gave me a hard stare. "I don't have time to do a lot of explaining right now. Just go put on a clean shirt and do it fast. You've got work to do."

I grinned and shook my head. "You've got me mixed up with somebody else. I'm out of business, remember?" I turned and started to walk back toward the couch. "There's beer in the refrigerator if you or your guys want one."

He was across the room in two steps. He grabbed me by the shoulder and spun me around so that our noses were no more than a couple of inches apart. His fingers dug into my arm like the jaws of a steel trap.

"Now you get this straight, because I'm only gonna tell you once. First, I'm in a hurry and don't need any of your horseshit. And second, you're out of business when I say you're out of business. Right now, I say you're about to have a grand reopening."

He took my Colt out of his coat pocket and shoved it into the waistband of my pants. "It's still got a full clip. Try not to blow your dick off with it." He followed the Colt with my license and identification. "Not that I wouldn't as soon do it myself, but if I don't get some fast cooperation from you, I'm going to have those two officers outside pick you up by your ankles and bounce your head off the sidewalk until you understand I'm not fooling around."

Okay, then. I said, "Give me five minutes."

I changed into slacks and a blue button-down dress shirt. I put my license and ID back into my wallet, returned the Browning to the holster on my shoulder rig, and put on a gray, summer-weight sport coat.

Priest was pacing impatiently back and forth when I came out of the bedroom. "If you've got a tie, wear it."

The uniforms were waiting in the front seat of a Metro blue-and-white. Priest and I climbed into the back seat.

With the blue lights flashing, we made a right off my street onto Nolensville Pike, heading toward the city. Five minutes later, we were doing eighty-five on the Interstate. Nobody had said where we were going, or why, but the uniform behind the wheel knew, and he was weaving through traffic like a broken-field runner in sight of the goal line to make sure we got there in a hurry.

I struggled to coax the tie I'd brought into a presentable Windsor, then gave up in frustration and threw it in a heap on the seat. "Anybody here feel like telling me what's going on?"

The two uniforms pretended they hadn't heard the question. Priest grunted something that sounded like, "Wait and find out," and stared out the window.

We followed the expressway through the city, then exited at Charlotte and turned west. This close to downtown, traffic was beginning to pick up, and the cop driving had to make frequent use of his lights and siren to clear the right of way. We ran two red lights that I saw, the second time narrowly missing a battered Ford pickup truck whose driver ended up losing half his load, swerving into the curb.

"Goddamn kudzu cowboys," the cop driving swore. "Don't anybody know what the hell a siren means?"

We stutter-stepped through traffic like that for two more blocks before turning suddenly into the parking lot of a boarded-up tourist motel called the Music City Manor. A faded sign hanging crookedly near the curb promised rates by the day, week, or month. A second, newer sign next to that one announced that this site was the future home of the Charlotte Pike Assembly of Christ.

For a place that had been out of business for some time, the Music City Manor was busier than a Walmart on Black Friday. The parking lot was crowded with Davidson County sheriff's cars, Nashville Metro police cars, an ambulance, and even an Eyewitness News van. Scattered among the vehicles was a crowd of perhaps a hundred people, including uniformed officers, people from the medical examiner's office, plainclothes detectives, and an assortment of the simply curious. Most of the action seemed to be taking place outside a ground-floor unit near the back. The door was open. The two cops posted outside looked shaken to the soles of their shoes.

Priest said, without enthusiasm, "Let's go see what all the excitement's about."

Despite the door and the window both being open, the odor inside the tiny motel room was staggering. It might have been the sour stench of vomit coming from the bathroom, or maybe it was the ghastly, decaying thing on the bed. I felt my knees start to give way and steadied myself against the dresser.

"Mother of God," I heard Priest whisper under his breath.

The woman on the bed was naked. Her wrists and ankles were bound to the bed frame with Venetian blind cord. The gaily colored butterfly tattooed on her right ankle stood out in ghastly contrast to the deteriorating condition of the rest of her body. Her mouth and nose were covered with a wrap of heavy gray tape. The rest of her face was a mass of bruises, and her breasts, belly, and thighs had been slashed repeatedly and then burned with a lighted cigarette. Her eyes were open, and staring in horror at something only she could see.

Darlene Munson was no longer a woman in the wind.

After giving me a moment to take in the scene, one of the detectives asked me if I could make a positive ID. But since I had never seen Darlene alive, I could only say that the body appeared to match a description I had been given the week before. Priest made a motion to one of the medical examiner's men, who began to cut at the Venetian blind cord with his folding knife.

In a voice straining to sound natural, Priest said, "I've seen torture-murders maybe three times in my life. I don't think I've ever seen anything quite like this."

I knew what he meant. I'd seen one or two banged-up bodies while I was with the cops, mostly the victims of traffic accidents, but never one as savagely brutalized as this. Darlene was an image from my worst nightmare, and the impression of her terror-filled eyes was something that would stay with me for a long time. I hoped that if there were truly a compassionate God, He would accept Darlene's last agonized hours on earth as payment in full for any sins she may have committed during her short time on earth.

One of the detectives came over to Priest and me and flipped open a notebook. "A couple of drifters looking for copper pipes to steal found her just like this about two hours ago. The M.E.'s best guess puts the TOD at least four or five days ago. Given the condition of the body, it's kinda hard to tell. The cause of death appears to be asphyxiation, but looking at what we've got here, who knows? I'd say when whoever did her got tired of cutting her, he just put some more tape over her nose and watched her suffocate." He closed the notebook and dropped it back in his coat pocket. "What kind of a sick son of a bitch does a thing like this?" he asked nobody in particular.

Before I could say anything, Priest took me by the elbow and led me back outside. "I know what you're thinking, Gamble. I'm thinking the same thing, but right now, we don't have time for that, so I want you to just listen for a minute. Please. At this moment, for the record, we've got no motive, no suspects, no witnesses, and no evidence, aside from what you see here. Nobody heard anything, nobody saw anything. My guess is that by the time the evidence team has finished shaking down the room, it'll turn out to be some kind of a drug-related incident. Unless we get lucky and somebody talks, we'll probably never know who did it."

I turned on him. "What the hell are you talking about? For Christ's sake, this killing isn't about drugs, and this isn't some Jane Doe here. We know who she is, and we know why she was murdered."

Priest shook his head. "We didn't find any ID with the body. You already admitted you've never actually seen Darlene Munson, nor even a photo."

"Albert Glass has seen her. Audra Lambert has seen her. Red Cherry has seen her. Hell, he probably had her killed. With as much blood as there is all over that room, whoever cut her is bound to have gotten some on him. Let's just pick up everybody who works for Red and have forensics check every scrap of clothing they own."

Priest shook his head slowly. "There's a sizable stash of cocaine under the mattress. As soon as the coroner's men move the body, the detectives will find it. Once they do, they'll chalk this one up as a drug-related homicide committed by a person or persons unknown."

"While they're at it, will they find the killer hiding in the closet, or is that what I'm here for?"

Priest said, "You just flat ass refuse to see what's in front of your face, don't you? I'm not telling you this because that's how I want it. I'm telling you that, at least for now, that's the way it's officially going to go into the books."

I started to argue with him, but he cut me off.

"Unofficially, this investigation is very much alive. But whatever we do, and I want to emphasize the word 'we,' it's got to wait until things are settled. After that, we can haul in anybody you want, and you have my word. I will give you all the help you need and more, even if it means you and I have to handcuff the bastard to the bumper of my car and drag him down the Interstate." He started walking toward a car parked across the parking lot. "But not now. We still have a job to do."

"Where are we going?"

"You're the detective," he told me. "You figure it out."

Chapter Twenty-Nine

I n fact, it was a no-brainer, and I had it wired before we were halfway there. But I kept my mouth shut and pretended to be surprised when Priest turned off Cottonwood Lane and drove in past the mailbox with the name Seacrist on it.

The house looked very much like the one owned by Hank Williams before his death: a rambling, brick ranch painted white, with lots of windows, a three-car attached garage, and a circular turnaround in the front. It was a nice home, upscale, but not too much so. It was the kind of house appropriate for a respected and ambitious public servant not wishing to appear to be living overly high on the taxpayers' hog. However, in a nod to upper-middle class ostentation, there was what landscapers call a water feature, a fountain located in the center of the lawn surrounded by the circular drive. Colored lights played gaily on the cascading water. In the gathering darkness, the lights created a festive atmosphere starkly at odds with the events of the past two hours.

Priest and I appeared to be the last to arrive. Several cars were already parked around, including a white Escalade I remembered seeing only the afternoon before. Priest pressed the doorbell, and as we waited on the porch, I threw a questioning glance his way.

"You wanted in on this, Gamble. Now you're in all the way."

"Who else?"

A shrug. "Could be some surprises. Why don't we wait and find out?"

A uniformed policeman opened the front door and motioned Priest and me inside. He gave Priest a nod of recognition.

"If you all will just hold on for a minute, I'll let them know you're here."

After he had disappeared down the hallway, Priest turned to me. "Let me give you a word of advice, if you'll please, just for once in your life, take it. You'll be on your own in there, so I can't help you. But whatever they want you to do, just do it. No arguments. No questions. No backtalk. Just do what they ask. It'll go much easier that way."

While I was considering the advisability of that, the officer returned. "They're ready."

The room where he took us was furnished like an ordinary family room in an ordinary suburban home. There was light tan carpeting, comfortable-looking furniture a cut above what could be found at Williams-Sonoma, and neutral-colored walls decorated with family pictures and photos of landmark events in Roger Seacrist's career as he rose through the chairs in the district attorney's office.

At the far end of the room was a stone fireplace. In front of that, four dark blue leather chairs had been evenly arranged around a circular glass-topped table. On the table was a large, zippered nylon bag. Three men were seated around the table: Carver Dickinson, Red Cherry, and Roger Seacrist. Except in newspaper photos and occasional television news features, I hadn't seen Seacrist in a few years, but not counting a few more wrinkles and maybe ten extra pounds around his middle, he hadn't changed much from his days as Assistant D.A.

Seacrist rose to greet Priest and me. "Gentlemen, come in."

Roger Seacrist looked every inch a man who was captain of his own ship and knew it. He was about sixty and dressed in country club casual, as if he'd just walked off the eighteenth green at Pebble Beach. He was half a head taller than me, with wavy black hair-going-to-gray, piercing brown eyes, and a practiced, professional smile. Everything in his manner said that, barring a major political upset, I was shaking hands with the next governor of Tennessee.

An invisible signal of some sort passed between Seacrist and Priest. The Assistant D. A. gave a curt nod, turned, and left the room. Seacrist took me by the arm and led me over to where the others were sitting. He took the chair between Cherry and Dickinson and motioned me into the remaining empty chair.

"I think you already know everyone here," Seacrist said to me, "so why don't we dispense with the introductions and get right to the purpose of the meeting?"

"It's your bat and your ball, Roger." I leaned back in my chair and crossed one leg over the other. "I have to say, though, this is quite a gathering you've got here. All we need now is a priest and a tenor, and we can have ourselves a regular Irish wake." Red Cherry laughed out loud, and even Carver Dickinson allowed himself a small smile.

"You're a piece of work, Gamble," said Seacrist. "It's a wonder you're still running around with your head on top of your shoulders."

"You're pretty amazing yourself. Thirty years in public service, and you still can't tell the difference between ethics and expediency. You'll make a wonderful governor. Hell, Roger, you ought to run for president. You couldn't screw things up much worse in Washington than you already have right here."

"I'll take that to mean you know why we needed to meet with you this evening."

"You're going to invite me to take Charlie Lambert's place in the Hermitage Group?"

"I'm afraid not, although I have pointed out to my associates that you are possessed of a certain resourcefulness that we hope will prove useful." He leaned forward in his chair and gave me his best I-need-your-vote look. "As a matter of fact, we were hoping you might be willing to handle a small delivery for us."

"Why me? Why not have Priest, or Red, here take care of it?"

"That's a good question," Seacrist answered. "Personally, I don't trust you with an assignment like this. No offense, but you never could follow instructions worth two hoots. In this instance, however, the person you'll be meeting to make the delivery specifically requested you. It has to be you—just you—or there's no deal. Your job will be to exchange that bag on the table there for an item that is the rightful property of this Committee."

"Right," I said. "That would be the file Darlene Munson stole from Charlie Lambert's office. I imagine you know she doesn't have it any longer."

"We do know, yes. And let me assure you, when the time comes, justice will be served."

"So, not counting two dead civilians, how much are we paying for it? And what's in it?"

Dickinson, who had been sitting quietly to this point, found his voice. "I don't like this, Roger. I think we need to find another way."

Seacrist said quietly, "I thought we agreed this was our only option." Then, to me, he said, "Despite what I said earlier, we can trust you, can't we, Gamble? After all, it's important not just to us, but to all the citizens of this state that we have your cooperation."

I had to laugh at that. "Oh, bullshit. At least half the people in this state couldn't care less who the next governor is. And half of the ones who do care will vote for the other guy anyway."

"Does that mean you're not willing to do what we're asking?"

"That means answer my question first."

Seacrist exchanged looks with Cherry and Dickinson before taking a deep breath. "The bag in front of you contains three million dollars in used, non-sequential fifty- and hundred-dollar bills." When I raised my eyebrows at that, he said, "Oh, don't look so surprised. A few million doesn't make up as big a bundle as you might think. You'll be exchanging it for a small notebook, about ten by seven inches in size."

"A notebook? I was expecting something more like a flash drive."

"Safer on paper and harder to copy. Miss Munson was the old-fashioned type."

"You should mention that when you deliver her eulogy." When that got no reaction, I said, "How will I recognize the book? Whoever is on the other end could be turning over recipes for corn fritters. I wouldn't know the difference."

"You'll see dates, numbers, and names. The names I'm sure you'll recognize. The book contains records of certain financial transactions connected to the Hermitage Group. You should see notations of money received and disbursed going back about two years."

"Three million dollars for a notebook," I whistled softly. "For that kind of a trade, it's going to cost you."

"Now, just a minute," Cherry began.

Seacrist cut him off with a wave. "Let's hear him out, Robert. What's your price, Gamble?"

"So now, you two are on a first-name basis? You should get all this down, Mr. Dickinson. I'll bet your readers would be fascinated."

Dickinson said, "The district attorney asked you your price, Mr. Gamble."

"Fine. I want three things. First, a day's pay, at my regular rate, plus expenses. I also want your absolute assurance that when this is over, nobody comes looking for me. That includes you, Priest, Harry Roodhouse, Red here, and anybody else you can think of to send after me. Also, I don't want to hear anything else about anybody fucking around with my license. What I do may not seem like much to you, but it's how I make my living, and I'd like to keep on doing it."

Seacrist nodded his head. "Agreed."

"I'm not finished yet. Before I carry that bag of yours anyplace, I want to know what's going on here, and I mean all of it. Otherwise, you can just get on the phone to FedEx and let them deliver it."

"Now you're barking up the wrong tree, Gamble. Name something else. A job, for instance. I haven't discussed it with my staff, but I'm sure there'd be no problem offering you chief of security for the upcoming election campaign. Maybe even after. Despite your all-too-frequent lapses in discipline, you are a useful person to have around."

"Thanks, but as we both know, I already have a job. I don't need another one." I leaned forward in my chair as if to leave. "I think it's time I said good night, gentlemen. Maybe I could use your phone to call a cab?"

"Walk out of here now, and you'll be making the biggest mistake of your life."

"Come on, Roger, who's kidding who? You going to shoot me in the back? Every day I turn the key in the office door, I'm making some kind of a mistake. What the hell difference is one more going to make?"

Seacrist glanced at Cherry, who shrugged as if to acknowledge it was my funeral.

"Very well. The notebook we want you to retrieve can prove conclusively that more than eight million dollars received and subsequently earmarked for election campaign expenses were laundered funds obtained from sources that were, well, out of the ordinary."

"Now we're talking about Red here. I wondered when he got elected to the Executive Committee."

"I got elected to shit," Cherry said with a sour grin. "By the way, Gamble, I heard my employees scuffed you up a little bit yesterday afternoon. I want you to know that I didn't tell them to do that. I owe you one."

Seacrist went on. "I don't have to tell you, Gamble, if what we've been talking about here tonight were made public, it would ruin the careers of everyone associated with the Hermitage Group. But more than that, it would undo a lifetime of service to our city and our state. That work is continuing even as we speak."

"Is that a marching band I hear coming up the driveway?"

He let that pass. "Obviously, you're aware that Tennessee is electing a new governor this November. And although I don't claim to know your political affiliations, I'm confident you will agree it's important that the people send the right man to the state house."

"And that man would be you," I said.

"In this instance, yes, for a certainty. My opponent is a well-meaning, public-spirited individual who is utterly lacking in the political skills needed to manage our state for the next four years. And if the polls are correct, I will be elected in November. But if word got out that our efforts were financed even in small part by..." His mind refused to provide him with a politically correct term.

"By a gangster," I finished for him. "Shucks, Red doesn't mind if you call him what he is. It's certainly a more honest job title than public servant."

Cherry gave me a blank stare, said nothing.

"The point is," Seacrist continued, "if this story were to get out, the election could very well break the wrong way. Look, Gamble, the Hermitage Group didn't deal this mess. Certainly, we never had any idea about Charles Lambert's fundraising irregularities, but what's done is done. All we want to do now is clean things up the best way we can."

"And Mr. Dickinson here is just the right man to see that the hundred and sixty-seven thousand readers—that is the right number, isn't it? The hundred and sixty-seven thousand readers who depend on the *Times* to give them an honest accounting of the day's events remain blissfully in the dark."

"I'm afraid, in this instance, that's the way it will have to be," Dickinson said.

I said, "Let me make sure I've got this straight, Roger. Charlie Lambert had been diverting the money he raised for the election campaign to pay debts he had piled up trying to bail out his record company?"

"Unfortunately, yes, and even more unfortunately, he wasn't able to make good on his, what shall we call it? His unauthorized loan. So then, to make up the shortage in the Group accounts, he had to seek funds elsewhere."

"Which made Red an unwitting, but very major contributor to the cause." I had to shake my head at the stupidity of it all.

"I'm afraid that's correct, and the notebook you will be retrieving contains the record of all the payments and receipts Charles Lambert made during this unfortunate sequence of events, including names, dates, and even bank account numbers."

"I got that, but even after you get the account book back, Red's money still stays in the campaign coffers, doesn't it? Because it has to. And that means Red's got all you upright citizens by the short hairs. Because from what I've been told, Black Strap Music isn't worth anything like eight million, so there has to be something more to this. Hell, Red, you're holding all the aces. If I were you, I'd hold out for lieutenant governor." And then I had a thought. "Or are they offering you something even better?"

Seacrist rubbed his chin distractedly. "An exchange of favors has already been arranged, though not without some compromise."

"Ah," I said, enlightenment coming in a blinding burst of clarity. "Let me guess. The organized crime investigation?"

"My office is preparing a statement announcing that we have found no evidence linking our friend Mr. Cherry to any kind of illegal activities within our jurisdiction."

I laughed out loud at that. "That press release ought to make you look like a real gangbuster, Roger. Or has Red agreed to throw you a sacrificial lamb so your campaign for governor doesn't wind up down the toilet?"

"Mickey Horshak," said Cherry. "He's a good soldier. He knows how to go along. We feed him to the TBI. Figure twelve, eighteen months at the outside at Clifton, and then he's back home again and in the clear."

"Along with a sizable monetary expression of the Group's gratitude to compensate for the inconvenience?"

"He's counting on it," said Cherry.

"And the *Times* will no doubt run that story on the front page?"

"It will," said Dickinson.

"Well then, that's it. You've thought of everything."

"Except for Charles Lambert's carelessness, I'd have to agree," said Seacrist. "But because he failed to secure his records properly, they fell into irresponsible hands after his accident. Now, all of us in this room are forced to pay once again for his sloppy work."

I thought about that. "Let me ask you something. All of you, and you don't have to answer if you don't want to. But if Charley Lambert hadn't crashed his car back in April, would he be sitting around the table here with us this evening?"

"Sadly, no," Seacrist said. "And he would have been missed. But his lack of judgment was simply too costly for all of us to overlook."

"My sympathies all around. But if you'll pardon my saying so, it's going to be a lot less costly for you than it has been for Dave Quail and Darlene Munson."

Carver Dickinson spoke up. "I have a feeling you still don't understand what's at stake here, Mr. Gamble, so let me try to draw it out for you. This election represents much more to Tennessee than just a new face in the governor's mansion. Under energized leadership, it will mean additional Federal money coming back to our state. That means new jobs and new construction, and increased funding for a whole variety of civic betterment projects. All of that can only make Tennessee grow and prosper. Think about that before you start passing judgment. With your help, we can truly make this a greater place to live and work than it already is. Nashville will become a world-class city."

"And keep you and your Group from looking like a pack of world-class idiots."

"Now, look here…"

"No. You've had your say, now you listen to mine. You've been sitting here, the newspaper publisher and the district attorney, both of you respectable men, spouting a lot of high-minded bullshit about civic betterment and world-class cities and wringing your hands about how awful it was to find out you'd taken money from a man like Red Cherry. But let's put it into plain English and see how it sounds then.

"What you're about to do—what your Group is already doing—is conspire to perpetrate a fraud on the voters of this state, and in doing so, indirectly causing the deaths of two people. And you didn't do it for the good of the state, or for jobs, or whatever else you're telling yourselves is so important. You did it to paper over your own incompetence and to make sure Roger here gets elected in November. That's what this is all about. It's just politics.

I shook my head. "As far as I can see, Red is the only honest man in the room, because he's the only crook who isn't pretending to be something other than what he is."

Cherry said, "You really know how to pay a compliment, Mr. Gamble. Remind me not to invite you to my Knights of Columbus testimonial."

I said, "As far as the Hermitage Group is concerned, you all can go to hell. The more I think about this, the more I think I should just walk away and let you sort things out for yourselves."

If Seacrist was knocked off stride, he did a good job hiding it.

"Nicely spoken, Gamble, and, knowing you, just about what I would have expected. Therefore, let me remind you that you're already a part of it, including the two homicides you mentioned. Put the right spin on the facts of those two cases, and you will find yourself spending a very long time in front of a grand jury. At the very least, license or no license, it will be a long time before you ever work in this state again."

"I don't think you can actually make that happen," I said, knowing full well that he could easily do just exactly that without breaking a sweat.

"I wouldn't be so sure if I were you. People will believe anything they read if they read it often enough. We have the power of the press and the prestige of the office of the district attorney. What have you got besides two dead witnesses? To put it bluntly, sir, and with apologies, you're a nobody." He paused to let the point sink in.

"But I don't think any of that will be necessary, because there's something else. I have a feeling that, no matter what you say, you want to see this thing through to the end. How else are you going to find out who murdered all these poor innocent people you're so concerned about?"

He was right. Whatever else might happen, I knew I wouldn't rest until I'd exhausted every possibility of squaring accounts with the person or persons who killed Dave Quail and Darlene Munson. That's what Priest was talking about when he said don't ask questions, just do. He knew when all was said and done, Seacrist would have no choice except to give me a hunting license, and I would have no hesitation about using it.

I said, "I want your word, Roger, that when this is over with, you will do whatever you have to do to settle accounts with the person who killed Dave Quail and Darlene Munson. No deals, no plea bargains, no parole dates in exchange for a confession. Agreed?"

He nodded. Reluctantly, I thought. "Agreed."

"All right. What do I need to do?"

"You're a good man," Seacrist said. He pushed the bag with the money across the table.

"Christopher will give you the details. Just be sure you follow them to the letter. Oh, and Gamble, one more thing. For what it's worth, I want you to understand something. I know you think I'm nothing but an ambitious politician and the only thing I care about is winning the upcoming election. Well, you're partly right. Winning is important to me, and I will move heaven and earth to make sure I win in November. But human life is also important. I deeply regret what happened to those two people, and I want as much as

213

you do to see that their killer is brought to justice. Win or lose, when the time comes, there will be an accounting. You can believe it or not, but that's the truth."

"Those two people have names, Roger." I looked at him for a moment, searching for something in his eyes that looked like comprehension. He held my gaze for a couple of seconds. Then he turned away, as if I'd never been there.

Chapter Thirty

My instructions were to drive to a public telephone located at a 24-hour coffee shop at Seventh and Commerce and to wait in the car until something happened. Priest didn't seem to know if that meant I'd be getting a call, or if a naked lady on a white horse would ride past and make the exchange. It didn't take much brainpower, though, to figure out that the reason for that particular location was that it was a public place that still had a conventional outdoor pay phone. That meant a caller could contact me and still watch from a safe distance to make sure I was alone.

Priest handed me the keys to his car. "I got a lot invested in you," he told me. "Try not to fuck this up."

"I appreciate your confidence."

"I mean it. You do anything other than exactly what you're told, both our nut sacks will be hanging from the courthouse flagpole." It was a graphic image, but given the circumstances, probably pretty close to the truth.

I got to the coffee shop about nine o'clock and found the phone I was told to look for. Most of the surrounding businesses were getting ready to close, and except for a few kids hanging around outside a convenience store passing around a brown paper bag with a bottle inside, I had the place pretty much to myself. I switched off the ignition, turned on the radio, and waited.

Two hours later, I was still waiting. The kids were long gone, and traffic had dwindled down to nearly nothing. Now and then, a car would drive by, but none of them slowed, and none of the drivers showed the remotest interest in me. I passed the time wondering whether Roger had put a tail on

215

me, and, if so, where he might be hidden. When I got tired of that, I thought about Maggie and the kind of life we could have together if the money on the seat next to me were mine to keep. We would never have to work again, never have to worry about paying a bill, or making a car payment, or even filing an income tax return. In fact, all we would ever have to do would be to keep looking over our shoulders, waiting for one of Red Cherry's guys, or Roger Seacrist's detectives to bring our sweet dream crashing down on top of our heads.

My own sweet dream was interrupted by the telephone. I was out of the car and on the line before the third ring.

An electronically altered voice said, "Gamble?"

"Yeah."

"You're driving a police car. With a radio."

"No radio," I said. "It's a D.A.'s car. It's clean."

The line went dead.

Five minutes later, it rang again. Same electronic voice. "Okay, it's a D.A.'s car. It's eleven-fifteen. Look under the phone, then wait ten minutes."

"Wait," I started, but the connection was already severed.

I felt beneath the coin box and touched a small piece of paper attached with tape. I peeled off the tape and took the paper back to the car. It was a pencil-drawn map that showed a route leading toward a spot outside the city, along the Stones River. As instructed, I waited ten minutes, then started the car. The map led me west on Bell Road, then south on Route 41. Five miles outside a little town called Smyrna, I spotted my turnoff. As I pulled off the main highway, I could see the lights of the big Nissan assembly plant, glowing like the back door of hell against the midnight sky.

The road petered out from two-lane blacktop to two-lane gravel, and finally to a pair of muddy ruts that ended at a wooden barricade about a hundred yards short of the river. I had to hand it to whoever picked the spot. If it was seclusion he wanted, he'd gotten it. We were a good mile and a half from the nearest house, and with nothing but moonlight to illuminate the scene, any other car approaching could be spotted well enough in advance for an entire army to vanish into the trees.

I stayed inside the car and waited, for what I didn't know. There was no sound except for the rhythmic lapping of the river and the whirring and clicking noises of locusts calling to one another in the trees. For a moment, I was back in my own car, waiting outside a cabin at the Rustic Retreat Motor Court. That had been what seemed like a lifetime ago. As my eyes adjusted to the darkness, I began to get a better look at my surroundings.

Directly in front of me was a section of wooden fence painted with zebra warning stripes. Beyond that was a path that led into a clump of trees. The area was littered with beer cans, Styrofoam live bait containers, and used condoms, suggesting this was a popular fishing spot during the daytime and other activities after the sun went down.

The trees continued around to my right and crowded up to within about ten feet of the car. Behind me was the cow path I'd driven in on. To my left was an open field of wild grass and horseweeds that stretched maybe fifty yards toward still more trees. If somebody was there waiting to meet me, that figured to be where he'd come from.

Sure enough. By concentrating on the tree line, I managed to pick out an opening where another path broke through. A minute or two passed, and then there was the wink of a flashlight, flickering in my direction. I didn't know what I was supposed to do, so I flashed the headlights once in response, threw the bag over my shoulder, and got out of the car. I kept both hands in plain sight, or as plain as could be under the circumstances, and started walking toward where I had seen the signal.

When I was within a few steps of the trees, a voice said, "That's far enough, Gamble. Just hold it right there." I froze in my tracks and watched as my old friend Albert Glass stepped out from behind a tree. He was carrying a large flashlight in one hand and his revolver in the other. I'd seen that revolver before, and just like the last time it was pointed directly at my chest.

Albert said, "Put the bag on the ground and open it. Then put your gun and car keys inside and step back."

I did as I was told, keeping my hands well away from my body. Albert moved cautiously toward the bag. In the darkness on uneven ground, he was having trouble walking and keeping his eyes on me.

217

"Is it all there?"

"How the hell would I know? You have any idea how long it takes to count to three million?"

He waved me back a couple more steps with his gun hand. "Now, don't move." He looked quickly inside the bag. Then he took my gun and keys and put them into his coat pocket. With the same hand, he took out Charles Lambert's notebook and tossed it in my direction. I let it lay where it fell.

"I hope this isn't research for another one of your penny-ante exposes, Albert, because if it is, it's a loser."

"You're wrong, Gamble. This time, it's a winner, and so am I. I've got the money, and I've got the gun."

"You'll be dead by this time tomorrow, Albert. You've got nothing."

"You mean I had nothing. For twenty-two years, I had nothing, working for one editor after another who didn't know news from newsprint. It was me that made the *Times* what it is. Not Dohrn. Not Dickinson. Me. I uncovered the corruption. I dug in the dirt while Dickinson and others like him ran around to cocktail parties and political fundraisers. I built the circulation, and they took all the credit." He paused to take a breath.

"Well, okay, I could live with that. But what I couldn't live with was being stabbed in the back by my own newspaper. That's when I made up my mind it was time to get a little payback."

I took a small step backward, hoping to put a little more distance between me and the gun in Albert's hand.

"What are you talking about, Albert? Who stabbed you in the back?"

"Dickinson. The *Times*. They're getting ready to endorse Seacrist, aren't they?"

It hit me in a flash. "You were really going to write the Charles Lambert story, weren't you? But because the Hermitage Group didn't want the bad publicity it was going to bring down, Dickinson wasn't going to print it."

"You got it."

"Why didn't you just take it to another newspaper?"

"Because I wanted to teach them a lesson. And because I finally realized that no matter whether this story got printed or not, there'd only be another

Dickinson and another Seacrist right behind them to kill the next story. I didn't care anymore, Gamble. I just wanted out." He tucked the flashlight under his arm and zipped the bag shut.

"Well, now I'm out, and I'm taking this with me."

"Mind telling me where I fit into all this?"

"You? You don't. You never did." He picked up the bag and hefted it to test its weight. "I just needed you to draw attention away from me until I could finish putting this deal together."

"About that deal," I said. "When you showed up in my office the first time, were you still planning to write a story, or had you already made up your mind to turn the whole thing into a money grab? At what point was it all just bullshit to string me along so that I would draw the attention away from you?"

"In the beginning, it was real, but then when I figured out that the paper wasn't going to run with it no matter what, I decided I might as well get something back for all the work I had done. I couldn't tell you I didn't need you on the case anymore, because I knew if I did, you might start nosing around on your own and screw things up."

"Then you might have had to kill me, is that it? The same way you killed Dave Quail and Darlene Munson." I took another step away from where he was standing. "Tell me something, Albert. Now that you've got your money, was it worth killing two people to get?"

"I never wanted any of that. Dave Quail found out about the connection between Cherry and Lambert and tied it back to the Hermitage Group. If I hadn't done something, he would have gone to Dick Dohrn and told him the whole story."

"Quail wasn't interested in any stories, Albert. Neither was Dick. They were worried about you. They both thought of you as a friend and didn't want to see you get hurt."

"Well, that's too bad, then. I did what I had to do. I couldn't afford to take a chance on anybody screwing things up by getting in the way."

"What about Darlene? Was she getting in the way, too?"

"That bitch," he said bitterly. "She was screwing Charlie Lambert. He was stupid enough to tell her about what was going on between him and Cherry, and so she knew about the notebook. I guess maybe he thought she'd be impressed.

"After Lambert died, she thought there might be some money in it for her, either by blackmailing Lambert's wife or by selling the notebook to the highest bidder. I convinced her it would be suicide to try offering it back to the Hermitage Group, or to Cherry, but as you already know, she still wanted a hundred thousand dollars before she'd turn it over to me. I knew I couldn't get it from the *Times*, so I hid her out until I could raise the money on my own."

"Only she double-crossed you by bugging out."

"That's right. After I promised to get her the hundred thousand, she decided it wasn't enough. I told her there was no way to get more until we made the exchange, but it made no impression on her. She wanted the money now, and she thought she could shake me down by refusing to hand over the notebook until I paid up, so I had to—well, I had to persuade her to tell me where it was."

"Just out of curiosity, Albert, how did you think you were going to raise a hundred grand? I mean you couldn't just walk into a bank and ask for a loan." I had a sudden flash. "Or were you planning to pay Darlene out of the proceeds of what's in the bag?" I had to laugh at the stupidity of it all.

"What a mess. You couldn't get the money until you had the notebook, and you couldn't get the notebook without the money. I don't know who's more incompetent here, you or the guys you're shaking down."

"I've got the money," he said. "I don't see what else there is to say about it."

"Yeah, well, I hope you've got some way to spend that money fast, because you don't figure to be around for very long after all this."

"That's where you're wrong. All the Group is interested in is the notebook. Now they've got it. If they try to come after me, it'll just raise more questions. That's why I know I don't have to worry about you. You make any move to bring it up again, and they'll step on you like you were an insect."

"I don't have three million dollars of their money, Albert. You do. You think all they want is that notebook, but you're wrong. They want something

220

a lot more important, and if you can't see that, you're a dead man already."

"I don't know what you're talking about."

I said, "Listen to me. You're fooling around with powerful men, Albert. Men who are used to getting their way with everything they do. They won't let you get away with this because they can't. If they did, you'd be beating them at their own game, and that's something they just won't abide. Don't you see that?"

"All I see is that you're trying to put something over on me, and if you keep it up, I'll have no choice except to kill you."

"That's exactly what they're counting on, you dumb bastard. Why else do you think they let me come out here? They figure you'll kill me, and then they'll get rid of you and that'll be the end of everybody."

"Not everybody," he said. "I'm surprised you haven't figured that out yet." He stepped back toward the opening in the trees. "Now get down on your knees and put your hands through your belt."

"I'd rather die standing up."

"That's just what'll happen if you don't do what I tell you." He waved the gun up and down to indicate where he wanted me. "I don't want you following me after I've gone."

I dropped to my knees and stuck both wrists underneath my belt. "I saw Darlene's body after you finished with her, Albert."

"So?"

"I don't know how it was with Dave Quail, but I think you enjoyed what you did to Darlene. You couldn't have worked her over that badly if you hadn't. And I'll bet you had the notebook in hand long before you finished her off. So, I want you to know even if this is over as far as the Hermitage Group is concerned, it's not over with me. Hide where you want, and enjoy your money while you can, because I'm going to come looking for you, and I won't be alone. And when I find you, Albert, so help me, I'm going to kill you."

In the bright moonlight, I could see him shaking his head from side to side.

"That's what I figured you were going to say." He hesitated just for a second before he raised his gun and fired. Then he took off running for the trees.

Chapter Thirty-One

I don't know how long I remained on the ground after Albert took off. Maybe it was a minute, maybe two. The bullet had torn through the sleeve of my jacket and taken a chunk of my upper arm with it as it exited. And although it hurt like hell in the moment, it had luckily missed the bone and most of the muscle. The explosion half a heartbeat away had left my ears ringing and my eyes seeing brightly colored lights dancing in space. A split-second before Albert fired the shot, I had thrown myself over to one side and played dead. Whether that bit of acting fooled him and saved me, or whether he had suddenly lost his appetite for any more killing, I'll never know. Either way, I buried my face in the weeds and whispered a silent prayer of thanks that Albert didn't move in for a kill shot.

When I could no longer hear footsteps retreating into the woods, I untangled my arms from my belt and sat up. I felt around on the ground for Charles Lambert's notebook and stuck it in my inside jacket pocket. Then I started after Albert.

It probably wasn't the smartest thing to do, especially since he still held most of the cards and both of the guns. He also had the flashlight, and he knew where he was heading. All I had was the memory of Darlene Munson's lifeless, terrified eyes and a massive surge of adrenalin that was racing through me as a result of coming near as dammit to having my head blown into the weeds. I was also the only one of us who knew for certain I was still alive. I hoped that might be advantage enough.

The path through the woods followed a fairly straight line for perhaps two hundred yards, and in bright moonlight, the going wasn't too difficult. After that, the undergrowth got thicker, and the ground got rockier as it began sloping downward toward a small creek. I picked my way cautiously down the bank, searching for handholds among the weeds to keep from tumbling headlong into the water. I reached the creek in good shape and was trying to find an easier route up the opposite side when I heard the shots. There were two, followed a minute later by the sound of a car driving away, fast. I dropped down on all fours and, favoring my injured arm, scrambled like a clumsy, oversized lizard toward high ground.

Once there, I took off running full-tilt in the direction of the shots, ignoring the brush and low-hanging branches that clawed and slapped at my face and clothing. Once, I tripped over the root of a big hickory tree and landed on my hands and knees in the dirt of the forest floor. A spasm of red-hot pain shot through my arm.

A few yards to my left, I spotted a break in what had at first appeared to be a solid wall of trees. I scrambled through the opening and felt the ground drop like a trap door out from underneath me.

I tumbled ass-over-armpits down a steep gravel embankment and skidded to a stop on my face in a narrow ditch alongside another road. I froze in place, sure that the next sound I'd hear would be the shot that would finish me. When it didn't come, I opened my eyes and looked around.

Albert Glass was there, no more than two feet away. Like me, he was on the ground, but unlike me, he was dead. There was a dark hole in his neck, and part of his face was missing. A thick pool of blood was forming near the spot where his chin used to be. I opened my mouth to scream, but the only sound that came out was a ragged, croaking noise.

I rolled over on my back and stared up into the sky. I used the last of my self-control to block out the image of the human refuse that had been Albert and to force myself to inhale and exhale in deep, rhythmic breaths. When I thought I could stand up without keeling right back over again, I climbed to my feet and took a look around.

Albert and I were alone, or, more precisely, I was alone with what used to be Albert. His car was parked a few feet away with the engine off. The door was open on the driver's side. I looked inside and all around the car, but couldn't find any sign of his keys, or the bag with the money. I patted Albert's body down and found my own gun and car keys. And then, with nothing left to do, I sat down by the side of the road and waited. The adrenaline rush that had propelled me to this point was wearing off, and the bullet wound in my arm was beginning to hurt like hell. There was no question I was going to need medical attention soon.

I don't know how long I sat there by the side of the road with Albert's lifeless body at my feet. I didn't have the haziest idea what I should do next, and to be honest, I was past the point of caring. All I did know was that I was hurt, tired, and sick down to the pit of my soul. In the past few days, I'd tripped over one dead body, had been forced to look at a second, and was now in the company of a third. I'd been hired, fired, hired again, knocked unconscious, jailed twice, lied to, shot, and used as a fall guy to cover up for who knew how many illegal acts. And I'd done it for a little less than three thousand dollars all in, and the promise of another day's pay from a group of men who had every reason to figure I'd be dead before the bill came due. Well, the hell with them all, I thought. I was still alive, and so far, none of them had been able to do anything about that.

I looked down the road and saw the faint white glow of headlights approaching in the distance. I stood up and racked a round into the Colt. At that moment, if it had been a truckload of Ku Klux Klansmen coming to tar and feather me, it wouldn't have made the slightest difference. I was ready for anything anybody could throw at me, and I'd kill as many as I could before they finished me.

The lights grew larger and brighter until they were almost on top of me. I took two-handed aim at a spot just above the one on the right and held my breath until the car came into handgun range. At the last moment, the car slowed and stopped, barely a hundred feet away. A lone figure got out and started walking in my direction, arms in plain sight. In the backlit glare of the headlights, I recognized the outline of Christopher Priest.

He held out his hand with the palm up. "I'll take the notebook, Gamble. And put that damn gun away before one of us gets hurt."

I handed him the book. He glanced at it briefly and then shoved it into his coat pocket without looking inside.

"You look terrible," he said, offering me his handkerchief. "Try to clean yourself up if you can." I looked myself over in the light and saw what he meant. My hands and knees were caked with red dirt and dried blood. My slacks were in tatters, and the front pocket of my jacket was torn almost completely off. Blood from the bullet wound had seeped through my coat sleeve and was running down my arm onto the back of my hand.

"How bad?" Priest asked.

"Hurts like hell," I said, "but I don't think there's any permanent damage."

I used the handkerchief as a compress against where my arm was bleeding. "I wasn't a very good errand boy, Christopher. I warned Albert that Seacrist would come for his money first chance he got. He just wouldn't believe me."

"You think that's what happened?" He shook his head in wonder. "Christ, I don't know why I stick my neck out for you. You're more trouble than you're worth."

I looked at him uncomprehendingly. "Then who? And what happened to the money?"

"I don't know," he said, pausing for emphasis after each word. "And if you're smart, you don't want to know, either." He stood very close to me, so that his eyes were directly opposite my chin.

"Listen to me, Gamble. It wasn't easy keeping you alive, so if you don't mind, you can return the favor by letting me give you yet another piece of advice. Go see a doctor and get yourself patched up. Then go home. Get some rest. Get drunk. Take a vacation and send me the bill. I don't care. But whatever you do, try to forget any of this ever happened, hear? Trust me, it's better that way."

"You're right, Christopher," I said, understanding at last. "It is better that way."

Chapter Thirty-Two

Having no other means of transportation, I rode back to town with Priest. On the way, we stopped by Roger Seacrist's house. It was nearly two in the morning when we got there, but even at that hour, there were enough lights lit to make it obvious that we—or at least Priest—were expected. Not so sure about me.

Priest said he thought it might be better if I waited in the car while he talked to his boss. I agreed that was probably a good idea.

"You gonna be okay for a few minutes? I don't think this will take long. Then we'll get you squared away."

I told him I'd try not to die before he got back.

I was dozing lightly when he came out of the house. The door slamming on his side of the car snapped me back around. Priest slid in behind the wheel and stared at me with a look of utter amazement.

I said, "What's the matter?"

"Roger." He shook his head. "I told him what happened, you know, with you and the money and everything."

"Yeah?"

"He said tell you thanks for a good job and that if you're interested, the position he offered you earlier is still open."

"Anything else?"

"Yeah. He said don't forget to vote."

I yawned and tried to stretch out a kink in my back that had been there since yesterday. "Tell him...tell him I'll think about it."

"You can tell him yourself, you asshole. You thought you were a dead man."

He let his face relax into a grin. "He also said be sure and tell you to send your bill to him personally."

I said, "That notebook, Priest. That notebook that cost three people their lives, did Roger tell you what's in it?"

"No. He didn't have to. I already know it's a dumpster fire. It could kill Roger's campaign and maybe even get him disbarred."

"So then, you do know. Do you care?"

"Do you? And do you think it makes any difference?" He turned on the seat to face me. "Look, do you seriously believe anybody outside of politics gives a shit who's the next governor, or how that person gets elected? People get up in the morning, go to work, come home, have supper, watch TV, go to bed, maybe go to church on Sunday, and do it all over again the next week and the week after that until they finally fall over dead. So what? If it isn't Roger that gets elected, it'll be somebody else, and people will go right on doing what they're doing now."

I tried to think of an answer, but couldn't, so I said nothing.

"Come on," he said. "Let's get you fixed up."

Priest drove me right up to the door of the emergency room at Vanderbilt Hospital. He badged us in past the usual questions and forms that are required by law to accompany admissions resulting from a gunshot wound. The ER doc summoned a specialist who cleaned the wound and stitched me up. Then, I was given a heavy dose of antibiotics and a tranquilizer and admitted to a private room in the surgery wing, where I was kept overnight for observation. Late the next morning, I was re-examined by a resident physician, and over her objections, I was released with a prescription for more antibiotics and, no surprise, Hydrocodone. The resident wanted to keep me for another day just to make sure there was no infection, but I told her there was something I needed to do, and I was pretty sure that after today, I wouldn't have another chance to do it. Christopher Priest, suddenly a most thoughtful individual, had retrieved my car during the night and left it parked in the valet lot at the hospital. When I checked in, I was told not to worry, that the hospital had been instructed to send the bill to the district attorney's office.

Chapter Thirty-Three

That police captain back there in Harding had it exactly right. Taking a bullet, even when it results in a middling flesh wound like I suffered when Albert Glass tried to kill me, is a massive insult to the body. More often than not, it requires a considerable amount of time and medical attention before the victim feels anything like normal.

In my own case, I was exceptionally lucky. If Albert's bullet had struck me one more inch to the right, it would have shattered my humerus and likely left me without a working left arm for some time to come. A couple inches further, and the slug would have torn into my lung, almost certainly with fatal results. But even so, the bullet took a divot out of my upper arm that the ER resident at Vanderbilt needed almost two hours to cleanse, suture, bandage, and then administer a tetanus shot. After that, she cleaned up the multiple cuts and contusions I'd acquired chasing Albert through the woods.

On my way home later that morning, I checked my phone and saw there were two calls from Maggie and one each from Carver Dickinson and Christopher Priest, all of which had gone straight to voicemail. I knew I should at least call Maggie to let her know where I was and that I was okay. But then I'd have to explain everything that had happened since we were together last, and that meant telling her I'd gotten shot. And if I told her that, there would be no telling how she would react, except that I knew it wouldn't be good. That was a conversation we would need to have in person. So, instead of calling Maggie, I checked in with the answering service. I was thinking there might be a call from Audra.

* * *

By mid-afternoon, and after a couple hours of sleep, a shower—one arm in a plastic sleeve—and a shave, I had made myself more or less presentable. I had serious reservations about meeting with Audra Lambert again. I almost decided to just let it go, particularly since the two jobs I had been hired to do—track down Darlene Munson and retrieve Charley Lambert's secret ledger—were essentially finished. But in the end, there was one more question I needed to have answered. So, tough guy that I am, I swallowed a couple of Hydrocodone capsules and headed out, driving as carefully as I could, but loaded with painkillers and only one fully functioning arm. On my way, I stopped by the district attorney's office to drop off a bill addressed to Roger Seacrist for my services the night before. Counting my fee, plus estimated expenses for my ruined clothes, it came to around nine-hundred and fifty dollars. I worked it out later. At current rates, it was equal to a little more than two days' interest on the three million dollars.

* * *

A light rain was starting to fall as I drove the short block down Fox Park Circle and turned into Audra Lambert's driveway. I parked my car right behind the red Panamera, which had been pulled up close to the front steps, as if someone was planning to make a quick getaway. I rang the bell once, and, as before, "What a Friend We Have in Jesus" chimed inside. I waited for a minute or two, and when nobody answered, I tried the door. It was unlocked, so I let myself in.

The place looked pretty much the same as it had the previous two times I'd been there, except that the house seemed eerily quiet. Elvis Preston was nowhere to be found and there were two matching Hartmann suitcases standing at the foot of the stairs leading up to the bedrooms. Audra was on the move. She was leaving. Today. This afternoon. Right the hell now. And she was traveling light.

I went up the stairs to the bedrooms and then down the hallway toward an open door, where I heard a voice coming from inside. Audra was there, sitting on the bed, her cell phone in her hand. She was dressed in dark slacks, a long-sleeved white blouse and low-heeled shoes. Her makeup was perfect, and her hair was pulled back into the same little ponytail she'd worn the first time I met her. In all, a perfect getup for traveling. I stood in the doorway until she looked up. When she saw me, she gave a short gasp of surprise and let the phone drop to the floor.

"Gamble! I didn't expect to see you. I thought you were...." She let the sentence trail off.

I said, "Let me help you, Audra. I think the word you're looking for is dead. You thought I was dead."

She looked at me with what was supposed to be a mix of surprise and relief. It didn't work. Not even when she ran across the room and threw her arms around me, causing a spasm of pain to shoot up my arm and into my shoulder. Then she saw the look on my face.

"You're hurt."

"Hurt, yes, I got hurt. In fact, I got shot. Albert shot me, but it's no big deal. I'll survive, which is more than I can say for Albert. But then, you already know that, don't you? Because when you left him last night, he was lying in the road with half his face shot away."

"What? No. What are you talking about? I've been trying to reach you since last night. I tried to leave a message. I wanted to tell you—"

"What were you going to tell me? Goodbye? Good luck? Have a nice afterlife?" I shook my head. "There were no messages, Audra. Not on my cell and not on my office phone. So, I wonder, what were you using to call me? Gabriel's trumpet?"

"I don't understand," she said. She looked into my eyes, and for just an instant, I thought maybe I was mistaken. Maybe she really didn't know anything about what had happened the night before, that Albert Glass had been shot and killed, and that somebody else, maybe Roger, or Christopher Priest, or one of Red Cherry's goons, had scooped up the bag full of money and returned it to wherever it had come from. That's how good she was. There was exactly the right note of sincerity in her voice, and her eyes held the perfect look of innocence. But all the same, something was off. Maybe it was her manner or in the tone of her voice. I couldn't have said just what it was, but I knew it wasn't right. And for some reason, it made me feel sad.

I pushed her gently away from me. "What did you do with the money?" I asked. "Is it in one of those suitcases downstairs, or have you already sent it ahead?"

She hesitated for just an instant and something that might have been resignation flickered across her face. I thought for sure she was going to deny everything. She didn't even bother to try. Instead, she said, almost casually, "Is that why you're here? Is Roger paying you a little something extra to retrieve his precious bag of money? Or are you on your own now?"

"If I were working on my own, I would have killed Albert myself. I would have kept the money and skipped town last night with a very hefty nest egg. I came here today because there was something I needed to know for sure. Now, I do."

"Well, then. Since you've come all this way, go on and ask your question. What did you need to know?"

"That it was you who killed Albert. That was the plan all along, wasn't it? Get Albert to put the squeeze on the Hermitage Group. Let him think you were going to split the money with him and then get rid of him the minute he got his hands on it."

"Gamble, you have no idea what you're talking about. You can't know how it was."

"I know how it is now, though." I walked over to the window and looked out at the rain, which had begun falling harder. In the distance, the clouds had grown darker, reaching all the way down to the ground. It seemed to me to be an appropriate backdrop for the conversation we were having.

I said, "Last night, when I agreed to be Roger Seacrist's bag man. I knew it was a risk. But I was willing to take it because I wanted to see this thing through to the end. I didn't care one way or the other about Albert's front-page story, or Roger getting elected governor, or any of the other distractions that seemed to keep popping up. But it bothered me that I'd had an indirect role in Darlene Munson and Dave Quail being murdered, and if I could, I wanted to make sure somebody would pay the price for that. And even though I never really believed your story about your concern for your husband's legacy, I thought I'd at least give you the benefit of the doubt on the off chance that I'd misjudged you and that maybe you were nothing more than a victim of your husband's bad business sense."

When she didn't say anything to that, I went on. "But you're not a victim, Audra. You're a liar and an extortionist. And now you're a killer. I don't think when you were cooking up this scheme with Albert Glass that you gave five minutes' thought to anything other than getting your hands on the money in those two suitcases downstairs. You said it yourself, the first time we met. You wondered whether there ought to be something more than memories to compensate you for the struggles you went through with your husband. Do you remember? I asked you if you were talking about money, and you said, of course, you were talking about money.

"I didn't think much of it at the time, because I didn't know you, and I didn't really understand what was going on between you and Albert Glass. I thought you were just feeling alone, and angry, and frightened. And maybe you were. But you were also very much involved in a plan to get the money you thought you deserved.

"Well, now you've got it all to yourself, but somehow, I don't think you're going to get the chance to enjoy it."

She took a step backward and glared at me. "You're talking like somebody born yesterday. All I've done is take back what rightly belonged to me. I worked just as hard as Charles, making Black Strap a success. Just because he was irresponsible and lost everything we worked for, that's no reason why I should be left with nothing."

"It's not a question of getting back your money, Audra. You probably did deserve more than you thought you were getting. The problem is how you went about it. I don't know what you said to him, but somehow, you convinced Albert that he could get away with shaking down some very powerful people for three million dollars in exchange for Darlene Munson's file. But in order to do that, he had to kill Darlene and then Dave Quail. And then, once Albert got his hands on the money, you took him out so you wouldn't have to share it.

"What a fucking mess." I shook my head at the stupidity of it all. "My advice? Get a lawyer and turn yourself in to the cops. Maybe you can call that shyster Gannaway. I hear he's pretty good. If you do, and if you hand back the money, they'll go easy on you. Because if you don't, I'll turn you in myself. I'll tell them the whole story, and you can throw yourself on the mercy of the court. Maybe you can claim severe emotional distress and get off with a light sentence."

She made a noise that could have been a laugh. "Suppose everything you've said is true. What do you think you're going to do, march me into police headquarters in handcuffs? I don't know what kind of a story you're planning to tell, but I guarantee you won't be able to prove a word of it."

"Are you sure? Let's take this from the top and see what we've got. I think Albert Glass started nosing around into your husband's death, at first, probably with nothing special in mind. Maybe he was curious about his connection with the Hermitage Group. After all, the night he was killed, he was coming home from one of their meetings. That by itself would have provided him with an incentive to make a deep dive into the workings of the Group. Or, who knows, maybe he just wanted to write a human-interest story. We may never find out what got him interested in the first place.

"Either way, though, he would have needed to talk to you and, at some point, to Darlene Munson as well. For a reporter, interviewing the deceased's widow and his former assistant would be pretty much standard procedure. He even asked Dave Quail to dig up background material to help flesh out the story. Dave was a logical choice since he had longstanding relationships within the music industry.

"And then, somewhere along the line, Darlene told Albert her story about your husband's notebook, and she showed him enough of it to prove that mob money had gotten mixed up with Roger Seacrist's election campaign. But she wasn't about to hand it over for nothing, and when she demanded a hundred grand from Albert, he was stuck. He knew the story was a big one, but he didn't have that much cash, and he couldn't very well ask the *Times* to advance it to him. I think that's when he came back to you, maybe still with the idea of buying the notebook to support what he thought would be a hot news story. But you had no reason to want to go along with that.

"However, out of that conversation came this cockeyed scheme to extort hush money from the Hermitage Group. And while it's possible that it was Albert's idea, I have the feeling it was at least partly yours. At least in the beginning, Albert didn't have any ax to grind with the Group. It wasn't personal. He was following what he thought would be the story of a lifetime. Maybe a story big enough to get him a book deal, or even syndication, except that at some point, either he was told, or else he figured out on his own that the *Times* wasn't going to print his story. You didn't care about that, though. You just saw the situation as a golden opportunity to hang on to a very nice lifestyle, one that was just about to go up in smoke.

"It might have worked with nobody getting hurt, too, except somehow Roger Seacrist, or maybe Carver Dickinson found out Albert was digging into Charlie Lambert's life. That made Roger decide to put a tail on Albert to see what he was up to. Then, when Albert realized he was being shadowed, he hired me to create a diversion so Roger's guys would follow me instead. I got Dave Quail involved, and now we've got three people dead and you with the money."

I sighed. "What was the problem, Audra? Wasn't a million-five in cash enough for you? Was having it all so important that you had to kill Albert?"

She sat down on the edge of the bed and folded her hands in her lap.

"You still don't understand, do you? Do you seriously believe I haven't thought this through? Nobody is going to arrest me, or prosecute me, or convict me of anything. You can go to the police, and they might believe your story, but they won't be able to do anything. They might want to charge me, but even if they do, the district attorney's office will decline to prosecute. Because if they open an investigation, the whole story about where the money in Roger's campaign fund came from will become public knowledge. That means come November, win or lose, he'll be impeached and removed from whatever office he happens to be holding at the moment. So rather than prosecute, they'll claim they have insufficient evidence, or that they can't use what they have because it was illegally obtained by some private investigator who has no official standing. And in any event, by now, if he hasn't already burned it, Roger Seacrist has buried that notebook so deep nobody will ever find it, because if what's in it were to come out, it would ruin his political career forever."

I thought about that, and much as I hated to admit it, I knew she was right, but only partly so. Nobody in law enforcement was going to touch her, at least not until after the election. But after that, she would be fair game. No matter how far she ran, or whether she changed her name, or settled in a country with no extradition treaty with the U.S., somebody would come looking for her.

I said, "Roger is going to want his money back, Audra. You have to know that. You'll be safe for a while, but my guess is, six months, or a year, or ten years down the road, there's going to be a boating accident, or an unsolved home invasion with a fatality. Something will happen, and the *Times* will be running your obituary." I shrugged. "Your friends will all be heartbroken, but then, they'll move on. You know how it goes. And I'll be sad for you, too, but I will never forgive you for the mess you made or the lives you've destroyed."

"You'll get over it," she said. "It's like you just got finished telling me. You'll be sad for a while, and then you'll move on." She gave me the tiniest of smiles. "After all, everybody does."

She picked up her jacket and her purse and walked to the bedroom doorway. "There's a key downstairs. Try to remember to lock up the house on your way out. Everything that's still here belongs to somebody else now, and I'd hate for anything to happen to it." She smiled. "I'll send you a little something to make up for your trouble. You should get it in a day or two." And then she was gone.

I watched through the bedroom window as she lifted her suitcases into her car and drove slowly down the driveway. At the end of the driveway, she turned onto the street, heading off to wherever she was going next.

I hung around for a while after Audra left. I'm not sure why. There was nothing left for me to do. I supposed I could have called the district attorney's office, or Harry Roodhouse, and had them pick her up and charge her with murder and extortion. But then I thought about the conversation we'd just had, and I knew she was right. Nobody was going to come after her, and nobody was going to charge her with anything, at least not right away. Roger Seacrist had an election campaign to run, and as far as Red Cherry was concerned, he'd just bought himself a free pass from the district attorney and maybe even the next governor.

And after everything was said and done, maybe Audra really did deserve the money. From what she had told me, the twenty-five years she had spent with Charlie Lambert had been a wild ride that, in the end, had left her alone and humiliated and broke. I was pretty sure the death of Albert Glass would be chalked up, unofficially, of course, as a public service killing. The cops might go through the motions, and the *Times* might wring its figurative hands on its editorial page, but in the end, nothing would happen, and it would end up a cold case. After all, Albert was nothing more than a grifter and a killer himself who had gotten exactly what was coming to him.

It was time to go. The pain pills I had taken earlier were beginning to wear off, and I could feel a headache coming on as well. I found the house key where Audra had left it and locked the door on my way out, just as she asked. It was the last thing I ever did for her. And then Audra Lambert was just one more woman in the wind.

Acknowledgements

As was the case with my previous Level Best novels, *Lost Little Girl* and *The Gone Man*, my thanks must first go to Verena Rose, my primary editor, as well as Shawn Reilly Simmons, who, together, are the Dames of Detection, the heart and soul of Level Best Books. Without their support and encouragement, Nashville PI Jackson Gamble would still be just a collection of bits and bytes hidden away in my computer. I would like to recognize as well the many "Besties" I have met through Level Best, including William Ade, Linda Lovely, Gerald Elias, Libi Siporin, Lori Duffy Foster, Virginia Welker (Lo Monaco), Wendy Eckel, Skye Alexander, Kevin Kluesner, Mark Levenson, Kerry Peresta, Lori Robbins and Cathi Stoler. You are all terrific writers and honest critics, and I'm grateful for our association. I also appreciate the efforts of my "civilian" friends who, although they are not associated with Level Best, have nevertheless taken the time to read my books and offer their suggestions for improvement. These good friends include Barbara Barbre, David Kwinn, Barry Pfanstiel, Nona Nan Chapman, Bill Wade, Georgeanne Syler, Leslee Pollina and Tom Neumeyer. I'm also appreciative for the support and encouragement offered to me by the Southeast Missouri Writers Guild and the Heartland Writers Guild. Kudos also to my publicity team at Blue Rooster Company, Robert Price and Gaëlle Byrne Freer, for kicking me out of my comfort zone. I didn't always like it, but I did always understand why. Lastly, thanks as always to my wife, Carol, who tolerates my long hours buried in the basement knocking out what I hope are deathless words of prose.

About the Author

Greg Stout is the author of *Gideon's Ghost*, and *Connor's War*, both young adult novels set in small-town America in the mid-1960s, and the Shamus Award-winning *Lost Little Girl*, and *The Gone Man*, detective novels set in present-day Nashville, Tennessee. A complete listing of Greg Stout's published works, including 22 non-fiction titles, can be found at www.gregorystoutauthor.com. Greg resides with his wife and two cats, Wallace and Gromit, in Cape Girardeau, Missouri, where he is a member of the Heartland Writers Guild, the Southeast Missouri Writers Guild and is a member of the board of directors for the Missouri Writers Guild.

SOCIAL MEDIA HANDLES:
  https://www.facebook.com/greg.stout.560
  https://www.facebook.com/greg.stout/gregstout48
  https://twitter.com/GregStout16

AUTHOR WEBSITE:

www.gregorystoutauthor.com

Also by Gregory Stout

Gideon's Ghost, Beacon Publishing Group, 2019

Connor's War, Beacon Publishing Group, 2022

Lost Little Girl, Level Best books. 2021

The Gone Man, Level Best Books, 2022

22 non-fiction titles, 1995-2021

www.ingramcontent.com/pod-product-compliance
Lightning Source LLC
Chambersburg PA
CBHW050201120726
47903CB00002B/715